We'll Always
Have Parrots

# We'll Always Have Parrots

## Donna Andrews

THOMAS DUNNE BOOKS
ST. MARTIN'S MINOTAUR
NEW YORK

*And*

THOMAS DUNNE BOOKS.
An imprint of St. Martin's Press.

www.minotaurbooks.com

Library of Congress Cataloging-in-Publication Data

Andrews, Donna.
    We'll always have parrots : a Meg Langslow mystery / Donna Andrews.
        p.   cm.
    ISBN 0-312-27732-6
    1. Langslow, Meg (Fictitious character)—Fiction.   2. Television actors and actresses—Crimes against—Fiction.   3. Women detectives—Virginia—Fiction.   4. Fans (Persons)—Fiction.   5. Virginia—Fiction.   I. Title.

PS3551.N4165W45 2004
813'.54—dc22

                                                                                2003058566

First Edition: February 2004

10   9   8   7   6   5   4   3   2   1

Many thanks . . .

To Ruth Cavin, Dan Kotler, and the staff at St. Martin's; and to
Ellen Geiger, Anna Abreu, and the crew at Curtis Brown. I love the
fact that these days you don't even blink when I mention
my proposed book titles.

To the friends who read and comment on whatever I come up with,
usually on shorter-than-reasonable notice—Suzanne, Maria, Kathy,
Dave, Paul, and the QBs. And to Dina and Rosemary for
special help on this one.

To all the people who answered questions and shared anecdotes
about the monkeys, parrots, and tigers they have known, with
apologies for poking gentle fun at the creatures you love—and the
hope that the resulting book makes caring for exotic animals sound
as tough as it really is. Particular thanks to Ellen, Kevin, Shadow,
Meredith, Pat (whose brother-in-law jogs with the tigers), the
patient employees of several Washington-area pet stores, and
the equally patient staffs of the D.C. Humane Society
and the American Humane Association.

To the organizers and guests of the many fan conventions I've
attended—the only people in the universe who know that I'm not
making this stuff up, just changing the names. With affection, from
someone who would be out there wearing a costume herself if it
weren't for all these deadlines.

To the Teabuds, who are always ready with cyber chocolate and
virtual champagne in the good times and purple power
for the tough spots.

To my family, who patiently endure being mistaken for Meg's family
and rarely ever throw things at me anymore when I exclaim,
"Ooh—do you mind if I use that?"

And most of all, thanks to the readers who make this all possible.

We'll Always Have Parrots

# Chapter 1

I woke up when Michael began screaming in the bathroom.

I pried open one eye and saw that it was 5:45. A.M.

"Michael," I called.

He probably couldn't hear me, given the volume of noise he was producing.

"Damn the man," I muttered, pulling the pillow over my head.

The racket from the bathroom changed to a loud gurgle, and while the hotel's meager pillow might be adequate for sleeping—just barely—it couldn't muffle the sounds of a classically trained stage actor, diligently performing his morning vocal exercises. And gargling repeatedly with a variety of concoctions, to counteract the effects of a bad head cold.

I'd have bet that the alternating doses of salt water, dissolved baby aspirin, and Listerine did more to irritate his throat than soothe it. But I knew better than to say so. In the several years we'd been together, I'd learned that things went more smoothly if I didn't try to argue with Michael about the various strange superstitions and crank health notions he shared with his theater friends.

I shoved the pillow aside, leaned over, and groped on the floor by the side of the bed until I found the program book I'd dropped there last night.

"Welcome to the Jungles of Amblyopia!" proclaimed the headline. I paused to look at the group photo below. Michael looked dashing despite the corny costume—a black velvet wizard's robe, covered with phony magical symbols and allowed to fall open to show that he was shirtless beneath. Of course, maybe I was biased. Maybe to an unprejudiced eye Michael looked just as ill-at-ease as the rest of the cast of *Porfiria, Queen of the Jungle*—the low-budget TV show that had catapulted him to sudden cult fame.

And brought us to this rather run-down hotel in suburban Northern Virginia, where the Friends of Amblyopia—the show's fan club—had organized their first East Coast convention. For the next three days Michael and his co-stars would endure an endless round of panels, banquets, and autograph sessions.

He'd tried to weasel out of it by claiming a conflict with his other career—his real career—as a drama professor at a small but prestigious Virginia college. But unfortunately his contract required attending a certain number of publicity events for the show—and everyone had to be at this particular convention on direct orders from Tamerlaine Wynncliffe-Jones, the aging B-movie actress who played Queen Porfiria and, more to the point, owned the production company. Apparently attendance had been embarrassingly low the last time they'd held a convention with only the QB, as the cast and crew usually called her. To her face, people pretended that QB stood for "Queen Bee," but even she wasn't stupid enough to ignore the obvious, slightly longer alternative to the second word. Since she never objected to being called the QB, I suspected she secretly relished the substitution.

So it was really the QB's fault that Michael had awakened

me this early. I liked that thought. Much more satisfactory to blame her for the loss of my beauty sleep.

I was already resigned to losing my identity for the weekend. Instead of Meg Langslow, blacksmith, I'd be Meg, she's-with-Michael. Meg, can-we-add-one-more-to-the-dinner-reservation. Meg, who should disappear gracefully when the swooning fans show up.

"It would be different if we were married," Michael said the last time we'd done one of these events. Reasons for tying the knot popped into our conversations with increasing frequency these days.

"True," I said. "But as a reason to commit matrimony, I'd put that only slightly above filing a joint tax return, and way below your offer to elope even if both mothers threw tantrums at being deprived of the wedding of the millennium."

And even if being married would make it easier for the convention organizers to recall my existence, it wouldn't change the way Michael's more devoted female fans hated me. But at least if I got enough sleep to look my best, "If only she didn't exist!" wouldn't automatically be followed by "What in the world does he see in her?"

I rubbed my eyes and flipped through the program to the Friday schedule. Aha. Michael had a 9 A.M. "spotlight"—a solo appearance on the main stage. Obviously he was in pre-performance mode. He'd spend an hour or so doing vocal exercises and another hour fussing with his hair and clothes. Normally this would leave him an hour to sit around making himself nervous, but I suspected today he'd spend that hour self-medicating for the cold. Applying nose drops and contemplating their effect. Sampling various cough lozenges. Dabbing lotion on the red, raw patches that appear on the cheeks and around the nostrils after several days of diligent nose-blowing.

Poor Michael. I could hear him cough—or was it only another vocal exercise? I made a mental note to see that he spent as much time as possible breathing on the QB. After all, thanks to her insistence that he attend, dozens of fans would probably go home with Michael's cold.

Some of them already had it, apparently. I heard a muffled sneeze from the balcony. I got out of bed and peered out through a tiny crack in the curtains. Yes, the fans were still there. They had figured out who was in what room shortly after the celebrity guests arrived, and had learned that if they could get up enough nerve to cross the two-foot gap that separated the various balconies, they could roam at will up and down the outside of the hotel and camp on the stars' balconies. We were only on the second floor, which meant that so far the ones who fell hadn't badly injured themselves, and obviously neither hotel management nor the convention organizers would do anything. Despite my calls to both the previous evening, the crowd on our balcony had grown overnight. Presumably they'd disperse when the panels began and they had a legitimate chance to see their idols.

I wondered what they thought of Michael's vocal exercises. Surely they could hear them. I also wondered, uncharitably, whether anybody was camped on the QB's balcony, next to ours. I'd bet not, but since I didn't dare go out to peek, I'd never know. I took a perverse pride in the fact that our balcony was brim full of bodies. I almost felt sorry for them— the weather had turned damp and uncomfortably cool in the night, and since the hotel only had two stories, the balcony had no roof to shelter them from the steady drizzle. They huddled together, wet and bedraggled, like a crowd of refugees.

Of course, my sympathy wasn't profound enough that I felt obliged to play Lady Bountiful, and make coffee for them in the room's minuscule coffee machine. After all, no one had forced them to sleep on our balcony, and they'd dry off quickly enough when the August sun came out.

I brewed some coffee for the two of us instead, and sat in the room's easy chair, studying the program while I sipped and waited for the caffeine to take effect. It wasn't working rapidly. Even the arrival of room service with breakfast didn't rouse me from my torpor. By the time Michael finished his vocal exercises and began rummaging through his suitcases, I found myself drifting off. Maybe I should just slip back in bed for a few more winks until—

I heard another shriek. Why had Michael started his vocal exercises again?

I opened my eyes and glared at the bathroom door.

Then blinked in surprise. Michael stood in front of the dresser, looking toward the closed bathroom door with obvious alarm.

# Chapter 2

We heard another ghastly shriek from the bathroom.

"What the hell is that?" Michael asked.

"Beats me," I said. "I thought it was you, doing your exercises again."

"I don't sound like that," he said.

Another shriek.

"Do I?" he asked, sounding less confident.

"Exactly like that," I said. "So if you're not doing it—"

"I'll call the front desk," Michael said, picking up the phone. "They need to—"

"Fat lot of good they'll do," I said. I was already stalking toward the bathroom, weapon in hand. Sword in hand, to be precise. Ever since I'd expanded my professional blacksmithing repertory to include making weapons, I'd realized how useful it was having a sword around the house. I can think of few things more satisfying to hold than a well-balanced sword when I'm investigating suspicious noises in the night, greeting persistent door-to-door salesmen, or making a point with annoying and demanding relatives.

"I wish you'd stop doing that," Michael said, putting his hand over the mouthpiece of the phone.

"Don't worry; I won't hurt anyone," I muttered. "It's not even sharpened. What does the front desk say?"

"They haven't answered yet," Michael said, dropping the receiver. "Dammit, let me do that."

We reached the bathroom, and I held the sword ready while Michael kicked the door open.

"Who's there!" he shouted.

Our intruder yodeled in response.

Michael stepped closer.

"Oh, for heaven's sake," he said.

I could tell from his suddenly relaxed posture that whatever he'd seen posed no threat, so I peered into the bathroom.

A large gray parrot perched on the edge of the vanity.

"Where the hell did that thing come from?" Michael said.

As if in response, the parrot laughed maniacally and preened itself, revealing bright red tail feathers.

"Good question," I said. The bathroom didn't even have a window—only a ventilation grate, and Michael tested it to find it firmly bolted in place.

The parrot leaped off the vanity with a flutter of wings and walked over to the room service cart.

"We want a shrubbery," it announced. It looked up at the cart, then ducked its head under the tablecloth and disappeared.

"Bingo," Michael said. "It came with breakfast."

"I don't recall seeing fricassee of parrot on the menu," I said. "And it looks underdone to me."

"Nobody expects the Spanish Inquisition," the parrot said, poking its head out from under the cart.

"At least it's a reasonably amusing parrot," Michael said. "I mean, a parrot who can quote Monty Python—"

"—Is no more likely to be house trained than any other parrot," I said, picking up the phone. "I'm going to call— hello?"

"Hello? This is the reception desk," a woman's voice said, on the phone. "Is anyone there?"

"I'll see if I can catch him," Michael said.

"This is room 207," I said. "Room service brought us a parrot along with our meal."

"Only one parrot?" the woman said.

"Only the one parrot, yes," I said. "But we didn't order any parrots at all. Could you please have someone come up right away to remove it?"

"I'm afraid we're giving priority to people with multiple parrots," the woman said. "We'll put you on the waiting list, and I expect we'll get to your parrot sometime later today. Is there anything else I can do for you?"

I was so taken aback that I couldn't immediately speak. The woman at the reception desk took that for a no, wished me a good morning, and hung up.

"The nerve," I said, slamming the phone down.

"What did they say?" Michael asked.

He'd begun to chase the parrot around the room. The parrot was enjoying this, if the maniacal laugh was anything to go by. Michael wasn't. The parrot was either unwilling or unable to fly, but he could travel very fast on foot, his huge beak and hunched-forward posture making him look rather like Groucho Marx.

"They seemed to think I was joking," I said.

"It is a little unbelievable," Michael said.

"They could still be polite," I said. I rummaged through my tote bag until I found the digital camera. I was supposed to take pictures of the convention so my nephew Kevin, who ran Michael's official fan website, would have new material to post. Meg Langslow, girl reporter. I took several close-ups of the parrot, and several shots of Michael chasing it, which I suspected he wouldn't let Kevin post.

"There," I said. "I've got proof, in case they think we're kidding. I think I'll stop by the manager's office a little later. Recommend some remedial training in customer service for that desk clerk."

"Good idea," Michael said. He sounded a little breathless.

"Do you think you should tire yourself out so close to going on stage?" I asked. I had moved to the window to snap a few pictures of the fans huddled on our balcony.

"Probably not," he said, sitting down on the bed and shaking his head. "I don't think I can catch him, at least not without getting all sweaty just before I go on. How much time do I have, anyway?"

"Um . . . about fifteen minutes," I said, as I began to throw on my clothes. "Wasn't someone from the committee coming to escort you down?"

"They're supposed to," Michael said. "What if they forgot and the stupid alarm clock in this room is slow and I'm already late?"

"Or maybe it's fast and you're just very early. God, I hope we're early," I added, grabbing a comb. Humidity is not kind to my hair. Overnight, the long, dark mane of which I was usually so proud had turned into a giant tumbleweed.

"Maybe we should go on downstairs?" Michael murmured.

But we both knew better than to venture out unescorted. Apart from the problem of lurking fans, the hotel was a sprawling maze, with at least a dozen wings added at various times in different styles, though none of them were more than two stories. Apparently, management had recently begun to renumber all the rooms, but then abandoned the project in mid-stream, so in many cases there were two rooms with the same number, distinguishable only by whether the number plate was old brass or new plastic.

At least when Michael and I arrived at our room, it was empty. I'd already heard several tales of people who entered their rooms to find them already occupied by other guests.

None of the floor plans posted in the hallways approximated reality, and even the bellhops got lost from time to time. So although the meeting rooms where the convention would take place were only one floor and a few corridors away, we could easily spend an hour getting lost if we tried to find them ourselves. Better to wait for our escort than end up in the kitchens again.

Michael was tying his shoes, and looking a little wild-eyed. I'd seen him less rattled before going on stage to play the lead in *Richard III*. Must be the cold.

Someone knocked at the door.

"Who's there?" the parrot called, in a surprisingly pleasant baritone.

"It's your escort, Mr. Waterston," a voice said through the door. "We've come to take you down for your spotlight."

"I'll get it," I said. "You go into the bathroom, in case it's only a group of enterprising fans."

I slipped the camera into my pocket, opened the door, and peered out at a tall, thin teenaged boy and a tiny, plump woman.

The boy caught my attention first. From the corner of my eye, he looked like Michael—but only for a moment, and partly due to the bad light in the hallway. He wore a home-made reproduction of Michael's Porfiria costume. In his costume, Michael really looked the part of Mephisto, the Machiavellian sorcerer. The boy looked as if he'd stolen his mother's velvet dressing gown and decorated it hastily with clumps of glitter and too much glue. From what I'd heard, fans waited eagerly for the moments when Michael threw off his sorcerer's robe to leap into action, revealing the black leather pants, hip boots, and red sash beneath. I hoped the hotel's overactive air conditioning would prevent this ersatz Michael from flinging off anything—what little I could see of his chest, when the robe shifted, was as acne-covered as his face.

The woman was dressed as one of Porfiria's Amazon guard, which meant she wore a chain mail bra, a matching miniskirt, and a pair of black spike-heeled boots. Had she failed to notice that you had to be about six feet tall and rail-thin to carry off that look? I certainly wouldn't try. And she probably weighed about what I did, which wouldn't be bad if she were also five ten, like me, but she was closer to five feet even. Still, I had to envy her nerve.

To my right, I could see a similarly clad though larger delegation waiting at the door of the QB's room. Obviously they had made the mistake of waking her to ask if she wanted to attend Michael's talk. I could hear her shrieking through the door at them. Did it never occur to the woman that these people were responsible for the show's success? I smiled at my visitors and invited them in. Some people, at least, knew how to be gracious.

Luckily, despite their strange appearance, our visitors both wore convention volunteer badges, along with the slightly harried and anxious look we'd learned to associate with the volunteers. And for some reason, they stood under a large blue-and-white golf umbrella.

"Aren't you worried about bad luck, opening that thing indoors?" I asked.

"Yes, but we wanted to protect Michael," the woman said.

I could tell by the breathy way she said his name that the woman was a Michael fan. Possibly a slightly barmy one. Or was that redundant?

"Protect him from what?" I asked.

"The parrots," the boy said, gesturing toward the ceiling.

"Parrots?" I echoed. But following his gesture, I could already see that the entire hallway was filled with fluttering, chattering parrots.

# Chapter 3

"This is fabulous!" Michael exclaimed.

Not the word I'd have chosen. I'd have gone for interesting. Mother taught us that when we couldn't say anything nice, we could always call something interesting. The hotel lobby certainly qualified.

Yesterday afternoon, when we arrived, it had looked like what it was—the lobby of a slightly run-down hotel, not a credit to the budget chain that owned it, but not an eyesore, either.

Overnight, someone had transformed it. Probably a small army of someones. Clumps of tropical plants filled every available space—a few of them real, but most fake; everything from authentic-looking silk shrubs to cheap construction paper trees. Plastic and crepe paper vines crawled across the ceiling from one light fixture to another, and the occasional papier mâché snake hung down fetchingly. At least I hoped the snakes were papier mâché.

Through this riotous jungle strolled several hundred people in costume. We saw the occasional Klingon, Vulcan, hobbit, or Imperial Storm Trooper, but most of the milling, babbling crowd wore costumes loosely inspired by the wardrobe they saw each week on *Porfiria, Queen of the Jungle*. Of course, since the show's costume budget was as limited as the imagination of its designers, most of the cast wore hand-me-downs from other films or TV shows. If nothing else, the display had the charm of variety. I pulled my digital camera out and began snapping atmosphere shots for the website.

"It's Amblyopia!" Michael exclaimed, flinging his arms out and accidentally knocking aside the blue-and-white golf umbrella held by his minder. Since at six feet four inches he towered over her, she wasn't having much luck holding it over his head.

"Whose idea was it to turn all these parrots loose?" I asked.

"It wasn't anyone's idea," the gawky young wizard said. "When we went to bed, they were all in cages."

Yes, I could see cages, dotted among the fake foliage overhead. Cages whose doors now hung wide open.

"Well, I suppose you could say it was the monkeys' idea," the diminutive Amazon said, trying to disentangle the umbrella, which had gotten caught in a philodendron.

"Monkeys?" I echoed.

"We also have monkeys," she said, as if this were an additional feature rather than another problem. I'd heard much the same thing said about bugs in software—perhaps she had a day job at a computer company.

Just then, a ball of fur fell from a chandelier onto a baby stroller, snatched something from the hand of the child within, and scurried back up a trailing vine.

After a moment of shocked surprise, the child burst into wails, and his mother began complaining loudly to everyone within earshot. The monkey, hanging upside down by one foot and eating a stolen tangerine, watched impassively. I wondered if it was entirely an accident that the monkey dripped juice directly onto the child's head.

"That's a spider monkey," the Amazon said helpfully.

"We also have a few capuchins and marmosets," the ersatz Michael added, pointing to another corner of the lobby, where Amazon guards of assorted sizes and shapes were poking brooms and floor mops up into the overhanging vines. Nearby, a bellhop perched on a ladder, holding a half-peeled banana, in a vain attempt to lure one of the monkeys closer.

"Fascinating," Michael said, sounding less enthusiastic this time. Or maybe he was just holding his breath. You could tell by the smell that the monkeys and parrots had been around for a while.

"Apparently the monkey-proof cages weren't," the young man said.

"We need to get Michael on stage," the Amazon said.

They scurried along, clearing a path before Michael. I followed along, snapping photos and trying to be reasonably unobtrusive, since I was the last person the female fans wanted to see. I usually tried to find something else to do while Michael played Mephisto.

This weekend, when I wasn't wielding the digital camera, I planned to sell my swords and other ironwork in the dealers' room. Porfiria fans spent vast sums of money at these shindigs, on anything even vaguely related to the show. Surely, after they'd bought their fill of Porfiria action figures and autographed cast photos, a few would have money left to buy real, live swords. Worth a try, anyway, since the experiment would cost next to nothing. My only expense would be half the rental on the booth I'd share with another swordsmith.

I trailed along, watching the various costumed Amblyopians bow to each other and pose for pictures in front of the jungle foliage. I wondered if I had time to duck into the dealers' room to see my booth. Maybe now would be a good time to check with Alaric Steele, the other swordsmith. But then I saw a sight I'd hoped to avoid.

A semicircle of about twenty fans were snapping pictures of two people in particularly elaborate costumes. The tall, stately blond woman wore an Amblyopian court headdress, designed to let the home viewer tell immediately how important a female guest star was by the number of purple plumes flopping around on her head. This particular headdress had denuded two average-sized ostriches, and its wearer would need someone to carry the ten foot train of her purple brocade dress. Beside her stood a short, round figure clad in the black velvet robes that marked him as a magician, carrying the snake-trimmed staff of one who specializes in the healing arts, and wearing a purple feathered turban that didn't resemble anything I could recall seeing on the show, but did look rather striking while disguising his bald head.

I tried to disappear into the shrubbery, but the healing magician spotted me and bounded nimbly through the crowd to my hiding place.

"Meg! What do you think!" he said, twirling in front of me.

"Very nice, Dad," I said. "I see you and Mother were serious about coming to the convention."

# Chapter 4

"I wouldn't miss it for the world," Dad said, obligingly striking a pose for a passing camera. Of course not; when had any member of my family ever passed up an opportunity to wear a silly costume in public?

Mother, whose train prevented her from skipping through the crowd, turned and waved from across the room. I noticed that she'd gotten quite good at the sort of genteel wave favored by the British royal family, a barely perceptible twist of the wrist that one could keep up for the entire duration of a parade with minimal risk of repetitive motion injury. And she'd already acquired parrot protection in the form of a purple umbrella.

My ten-year-old nephew, Eric, appeared in front of us, dressed as an Amblyopian knight, though most of his oversized armor looked as if he'd borrowed it from one of his older brothers. At first glance, I thought he was dragging a bundle of spare ostrich plumes behind him, but on closer examination I recognized a small dog, his black-and-white fur almost totally obscured by a headpiece of purple feathers.

"I see you brought Spike," I remarked, without enthusiasm.

"Grandma says for you to keep him, Grandpa," Eric said, handing Dad the leash. "I'm going to go carry her dress."

Eric trotted back to resume his post, and he and Mother

swept off toward the ballroom. Eric obviously considered it a point of pride to hold the train as high as possible, and I was relieved to see that Mother, perhaps anticipating this, had accessorized her outfit with only the most elegant frilly purple lingerie.

"Come on, Meg," Dad said, seizing the leash. "You've got to see what I found."

Spike didn't seem to mind his change of handlers. He appeared totally absorbed in staring cross-eyed at the plumes over his head and intermittently growling at them. I couldn't tell if he was moving his feet, or Dad was simply towing him gently across the polished lobby floor.

I followed Dad, trying to keep him from actually thwacking anyone with his magician's staff, until we arrived at a small side room whose entrance had been decorated to simulate the opening of a small jungle cave. Dad darted inside, ducking low to clear the overhanging foliage, and I followed more slowly.

"Look what I found!" he exclaimed, waving his staff. "This is Salome!"

"That's nice, Dad," I said, following his gesture. "But I don't think Mother will let you keep her."

Salome was a full grown tiger.

"Fascinating," Dad murmured, staring into the cat's eyes.

"Don't put your hands near the cage," said a man nearby. Presumably Salome's keeper.

"No intention of it," I said, and I got a grip on the back of Dad's robe, in case Salome's unwavering stare was having an hypnotic effect.

Salome blinked, and shifted her gaze up to the ceiling, where several monkeys and a parrot perched on the light fixtures, watching her. The monkeys chattered, nervously. I don't suppose it occurred to the silly things that if they didn't like sharing the room with a tiger, they could leave—she couldn't. Salome's mouth curled back as if she were snarling, but no sound emerged.

I pulled out my camera with the hand that wasn't holding Dad back and snapped a few quick shots of Salome's snarl.

Spike suddenly stopped snapping at his plumes and noticed Salome. He burst into growls and barks.

Salome dropped her gaze to Spike. Was I only imagining the mild annoyance in her previously inscrutable amber eyes?

"Don't let him go," Salome's keeper warned. "Salome could kill him with one swipe of her paw, and gobble him up before I could get the cage open."

"Promises, promises," I said. I shushed Spike, and he subsided into muted growls.

"Stand back!" the keeper snapped.

"We are," I said, tugging Dad a little farther away.

"Wasn't me," the keeper said, and pointed at a gray parrot perching overhead.

"Stand back!" the parrot repeated, in an uncannily accurate imitation of the keeper's voice.

"Amazing!" Dad said, shifting his admiration to the parrot. "I would never have guessed that wasn't you."

"African Grey," the keeper said. "They're the most talented mimics. A cockatoo or an Amazon usually sounds more like your stereotyped 'Polly want a cracker.' An African Grey could fool your own mother into thinking it was you."

I suddenly realized what my own mother would think if Dad brought home a parrot, however talented.

"We should go," I said, plucking Dad's sleeve.

Just then the parrot trilled a scrap of Vivaldi in the chirping tones of a cell phone.

"It doesn't just do voices," Dad exclaimed, with delight.

"An African Grey can do just about any noise," the keeper said. "Electronic noises are easy—a lot like the shrieks they use in the wild to communicate with the rest of the flock. I just hope this one's never heard a car alarm. And I'd appreciate it if you could take the dog away before it learns to do him."

"Surely it couldn't learn anything that quickly," Dad said.

"A talented African Grey can repeat something after one hearing," the keeper said. "Doesn't become a permanent part of its repertoire without some kind of reinforcement. Usually repetition . . ."

He frowned down at Spike, who was still growling repetitively.

"Come on, Dad," I said. "We'll miss Michael's spotlight,"

"Oh, right," Dad said. "I'll come back later," he told the keeper.

Yes and for that matter I planned to come back later myself, and find out why the convention organizers had arranged to have a live tiger as part of the proceedings, and why the tiger's keeper had agreed to this demented idea.

But for now, we left, with Dad dragging Spike, who continued to growl until we succeeded in pulling him out the door. Then he finally shut up and began prancing along behind us with a jaunty air, as if his barking and not our change of location had caused the tiger to disappear.

The organizers had scheduled Michael's spotlight in the convention's main event room—the hotel ballroom, which contained a small stage and several hundred chairs, set up auditorium-style. Mother, of course, had snagged a chair on the aisle, to accommodate her train. Dad and Spike joined her, but I turned down the seat she had saved for me. I preferred standing in the back, where I could escape quickly at the end of the hour.

And where I could survey the crowd, about ninety percent of them in costume. Of course, I was looking at the backs of their heads but, still, I could see a great many purple ostrich plumes and pointed wizard's hats, along with an astonishing variety of headgear—hennins, wimples, plumed knight's helms, musketeer's hats, space suit helmets, and even the odd set of antlers or insect antennae. This meant that as the crowd settled in, debates raged up and down the rows over whether or not people should take off their hats for the benefit of the fans behind them. The fans toward the back of the room also protested the umbrellas and parasols that some people wanted to use as protection from the monkeys and parrots—large numbers of whom, sensing something important afoot, had followed the human crowds into the ballroom and were squabbling noisily overhead for the available space on the crystal chandeliers.

By 8:57, the ballroom was packed. I was close enough to hear the convention security staff—all of them female, and dressed as Amazon guards—turning away latecomers.

"I'm sorry. Due to the fire marshal's regulations, we can't allow any more people in," they kept repeating. "You can watch the closed circuit broadcast in the Rivendell Room."

Closed circuit broadcast? I glanced up and saw that the ballroom boasted a small balcony that doubled as a lighting booth. At the moment, it held not only the lighting techs but also a camera crew, composed of a Klingon in full battle dress and a flying monkey from *The Wizard of Oz*. The cameras panned across the audience, setting the scene for the fans exiled to the Rivendell Room.

The cameras reminded me to pull out my own little camera and put in a fresh memory card so I could get plenty of photos when Michael took the stage.

I spotted familiar faces, but refrained from waving, since I couldn't figure out why most of them looked familiar. Were they people I'd met, however briefly? Or after half a dozen of these fan gatherings, had I started to recognize the die-hards?

I was almost relieved to spot one face I definitely knew. Francis, Michael's agent, stood off to one side, wearing the anxious look that no longer worried me, now that I knew it was his habitual expression. A pity because, as I'd told Michael, on those rare occasions when Francis relaxed enough to smile, he was reasonably attractive in a lanky, aristocratic fashion.

"Is it the long horsy face or the threadbare tweeds?" Michael had countered.

Obviously this wasn't one of Francis's relaxed days. I saw him reach into his right jacket pocket and then glance around to see if anyone was watching before slipping something into his mouth.

I sighed and shook my head. Francis had relapsed. Not that it was any of my business, but still. If it was humanly possible to OD on TUMS, one of these days Francis would do it. Should I sic Dad on him?

The crowd began shushing each other when a six-woman contingent of the Amazon security guards marched in and arrayed themselves in front of the stage.

"What the hell is this?" muttered someone to my right.

# Chapter 5

I glanced over and saw a small, round-faced man in a business suit standing, like me, against the wall. He stared at the crowd with—no, fascination wasn't the word. Horror. In college, I'd briefly dated a man who kept a snake. Briefly, because he'd made the mistake of letting me watch him feed his pet. The expression on the small man's face mirrored what I'd seen when the mouse spotted the snake at the other end of the glass enclosure.

We weren't the only people in the room in civilian clothes, but the man's conservative business suit, combined with the expression on his face, made me wonder if he'd strayed into the wrong convention. Possibly the wrong universe. He wore a convention badge, but turned around, so I couldn't tell if it was a *Jungles of Amblyopia* badge like mine.

"It's the opening session of the Porfiria convention," I said.

"Yes, I see," he said, holding up what I now recognized as a convention program identical to the one I'd studied earlier. "But just what is a Porfiria convention? I know I probably should have asked that question much earlier, but it never occurred to me."

"It's a television show," I began. "Called—"

"I only watch CNN," he said, with a slightly haughty air. "And sometimes The History Channel."

Heaven preserve us from TV snobs, I thought. Aloud, I explained.

"That could be why you find this so . . . different. You're at a convention for fans of a TV show called *Porfiria, Queen of the Jungle*."

"Ah," he said, still sounding puzzled. "And what are they all supposed to do at this convention?"

"They attend panels and presentations by the actors," I said. "Also the scriptwriters and the costume designers and anyone else the organizers can round up. And they stand in line for the stars' autographs, and they buy and sell Porfiria merchandise. Have a Porfiria costume contest. Things like that. Typical con. Convention, that is," I added, realizing that for someone who'd never been to one, con might have other more sinister meanings.

"They really spend the whole weekend doing this?" he asked.

"And pay handsomely for the privilege."

"Insane," he muttered. "No offense meant," he added, looking at me.

"None taken," I said. "I'm not a Porfiria fan."

"Then why are you . . . ah . . ."

He gestured weakly at the surrounding crowd.

"My boyfriend's on the show," I said, pointing to the stage, where Michael had just stepped out, accompanied by the diminutive Amazon, who walked to the microphone and began unsuccessfully trying to make herself heard over the cheering.

"Before I introduce Michael—" she began, but the cheers drowned out her words. She had to try again several times before the crowd finally let her finish.

"I wanted to remind you about our very special guest!" she said.

A murmur of anticipation swept through the crowd.

"Thanks to the diligent detective work of our organizing committee," the Amazon continued, "for the first time ever at a Porfiria convention, we will be presenting . . . Ichabod Dilley!"

For a few moments, the auditorium remained silent. I could see people looking at each other with puzzled expressions, and shrugging their shoulders.

"What's an Ichabod Dilley?" someone said, from the back of the room, and scattered titters followed.

Then Michael stepped forward and began applauding vigorously. I followed suit, as did the Amazon, and after a moment, so did the rest of the crowd. Still applauding, Michael took a step toward the tiny Amazon, bent down, and said something into her ear. She nodded.

"Yes," she said, when the clapping diminished. "Ichabod Dilley, the author and artist who created the original *Porfiria, Queen of the Jungle* comic books!"

The applause that followed this clarification was genuine, if considerably less passionate than that which had greeted Michael's arrival.

"Comic books?" said the civilian beside me.

"Yes," I said, as the applause died down and Michael stepped to the microphone. "The TV show is based on a series of comic books from the seventies—written and drawn by a guy named Ichabod Dilley. Apparently someone hunted down the old guy and invited him to the convention."

"Oh, my God," he said.

As Michael began, I saw the little man slip along the back wall and disappear through the exit door.

Well, to each his own. I was going to stay for Michael's talk, even though I'd heard it all before. There were only so many questions Porfiria fans ever asked, and only so many ways to answer them. I'd heard the same tales of his salad days in the soap operas, the same funny anecdotes about hi-jinks and bloopers on the set, dozens of times. Especially the story of how his old friend and fellow soap opera star, Walker Morris, who had been with the show since season one, had gotten him the part of Mephisto.

"They needed someone to play a dashing, debonaire, dev-ilishly handsome, but thoroughly corrupt and conniving wiz-ard," he would say. "Of course Walker thought of me immediately!"

It always got a laugh, even though some of the crowd had heard it several times before.

But if Michael was disappointed at hearing the same old questions and tired of delivering the same punch lines, you couldn't tell from his manner. That was part of his charm, I thought, with a sigh. Not only did he appear to be having the time of his life—he probably *was*. And he sounded better. The adrenaline boost he got from stepping in front of an audience had done the trick for his throat and nose, at least for now.

Of course he'd credit the gargling and the nose drops.

As ten o'clock approached, the Amazon came back to the microphone and reminded the audience that Michael would be signing autographs for the next two hours in the Innsmouth Room.

Two hours! Wonderful. His fans would get two hours of the cheerful, smiling public Michael. I'd get to hear about his writer's cramp. I turned and headed for the door, hoping to beat the crowd who would disperse as soon as Michael dis-appeared.

"And don't forget!" the Amazon chirped. "At noon, Blazing Sabers will be giving a stage combat demonstration, and at one o'clock, you can meet Ichabod Dilley, the creator of *Porfiria, Queen of the Jungle*! The man responsible for creating the wonderful fictional world we all know and love!"

"Balderdash!" exclaimed a voice behind me.

I glanced back to see a tall, gangly, fifty-something man, walking behind me toward the exit. His face looked vaguely familiar, though oddly naked. Probably because he was polishing rather than wearing his glasses, thick lenses set in thick, dark, retro-style plastic frames. When he replaced the glasses, recognition gelled—it was the show's chief scriptwriter.

"Hello, Nate," I said. "I see they let you away from the keyboard for the weekend."

"Hey, Meg," he said. "No, I brought the laptop along. Herself wanted to work on scripts for next season."

I was astonished—not by his dedication to the job, but by the fact that he deigned to recognize me. Nate was a consummate snob with an unerringly acute sense of the show's pecking order. The first time I'd visited the show's set, Michael had been encouraged to find Nate actually talking to me. He'd interpreted it—accurately, it turned out—as a clue that they might want him back. If Nate now actually called me by name, that meant Michael's position on the show was solid. Not a bad thing, since we could never afford the house we hoped to buy unless Michael continued plotting and conniving as Mephisto for at least another season.

"That's too bad," I said, as we escaped into the hallway.

"It's not enough that I have to be at her beck and call, twenty-four seven," he grumbled, falling into step beside me, "or that she has to mangle everything I write. But to sit there and hear some nitwit calling that stupid comic book writer the one responsible for creating the show! I'm the one responsible for the show! Every word of it!"

Except for the ones the QB mangled, I thought, and it seemed to me that the actors had more than a little to do with making it into a show instead of just a script. But I didn't think he'd like hearing that.

"He did do the original comic book series," I said instead.

"And who knocked that piece of junk into a working pilot?" Nate exclaimed. "Who keeps that heap of cardboard characters and clichés lurching along week after week?"

"You, of course," I said.

"Damn right," he said. "Do you know how hard it is to write an episode that lets Her Self-Centeredness think she's the star while still giving the fans enough of what they want to see? Which is not her tired old mug, believe me."

I made sympathetic noises. The first time I'd heard him raging about the QB I'd been flattered and a little worried that he'd be so indiscreet with a relative outsider. Now that I knew Nate better, I realized he wasn't that disgruntled, just a recreational complainer. His griping never got him in trouble because everyone had stopped listening.

"Every time I need to introduce a new character, I go through ten, twelve different names before I get one that she thinks sounds like a real Amblyopian name. Real Amblyopian name! Who the hell knows what a real Amblyopian name is, anyway?"

"Maybe you should use the same method Ichabod Dilley did," I suggested. "Haven't you noticed that every one of the original comic book names came out of a medical dictionary?"

"A medical dictionary?" he echoed.

"Precisely," I said. "Porphyria's an obscure but serious blood disease. Maybe he thought no one would catch on if he misspelled it. Amblyopia's an eye condition. All the original names were medical terms. You know the Duke of Urushiol, Porfiria's arch-enemy? Urushiol's the active ingredient in poison ivy; the oil that gets on your skin and causes the rash."

He stared at me, for a moment. Then he smiled.

"So all I have to do is get a medical dictionary, and flip through it for some obscure diseases, and I've got my genuine Amblyopian names," he said.

"You can tell whoever complains that you went to the original source material," I said.

"Oh, I like it," he said. "Is there a bookstore around here?"

"Probably," I said. "But even better—see that man in the purple turban? Ask him."

I pointed to where Dad stalked through the corridor in his wizard's gear, trying in vain to look dashing and sinister.

"Ask one of the fans?" Nate said, recoiling.

"He's not a fan—he's only pretending to be," I said. "That's my father—and he's a medical doctor. He probably knows more obscure diseases than Ichabod Dilley ever heard of. I'm sure he'd love to help."

"Fabulous," Nate said, and darted off in pursuit of Dad.

After several wrong turns, I found the dealers' room. A long line of fans waited outside the main entrance, so I sneaked around to a side door one of the convention organizers had shown me the previous night, when I'd come down to scout the lay of the land. Only dealers and convention staff were supposed to know that this door was unlocked. I slipped in and glanced around to get my bearings when—

"En garde, Madame!"

I looked down to find the point of a sword at my throat.

# Chapter 6

"Chris, that's not funny," I said.

The sword point drifted away from my throat as the burly man holding it collapsed in a fit of laughter.

"Meg, if you could have seen your face," he said, lowering the sword and offering me his arm. "Did you really think someone was trying to hurt you?"

"It's a fan convention, Chris, remember?" I said, ignoring his attempts at chivalry. "Half the women in the hotel wish I didn't exist, and odds are at least one of them is crazy enough to do something about it."

"Never fear!" he said, with a flourish. "I will defend you with all the skill at my command!"

"Never mind defending me," I said. "If you don't get your sword peace-bonded, security's going to take it away from you, and I just might help them."

"All right, all right," Chris said. "I'll put it back on your table in a minute."

"Chris," I said, and then stopped, and counted to ten. Chris knew the rules about weapons at a fan convention. Attendees could wear weapons as part of their costumes, but convention security would confiscate any weapon not peace-bonded—secured in its sheath, scabbard, or holster with an electric orange plastic binding that the guards could spot from across the ballroom. Chris's own weapon was neatly secured, so he'd picked up one of the swords I was selling—I recognized it now.

"Chris, the point is to sell my swords, not let security baby-sit them till the end of the convention," I said.

"Mercy!" he said, falling on his knees. "I come to beg you to lend your sword to my cause. Seriously," he added, in his normal voice. "I need a favor from someone who's reasonably good with a sword."

"What kind of a favor?" I asked, trying not to let the flattery sway me. Chris Blair was the show's blademaster, in charge of drilling the cast in fencing and stage combat and choreographing all the fights. I'd been learning as much as possible about sword fighting since I'd started making weapons, and fancied I was making progress, but to have Chris call me reasonably good was heady stuff.

"Can you fill in for Andrea? We're giving a stage combat demonstration at noon, and Andrea can't make it."

"Will you spell me for when I need to get away from the booth?"

"No problem," he said.

"It's a deal," I said. "What's up with Andrea?"

"Long story," he said, which, knowing Chris, meant that regardless of how long or short the story might be, it was none of my business. Not a good sign. In addition to being a member of his demonstration troupe, Andrea had been Chris's girlfriend for the last year or so. If Andrea had been sick or had a schedule conflict, Chris would have said so. I hoped there wasn't trouble between the two of them, but I knew better than to push it any further.

"Come on, then," he said. "We need to rehearse."

"Just let me touch base with Alaric Steele," I said. "Have you seen him?"

"Alaric Steele?" Chris said. "Why do you need to check with him?"

"We're splitting the booth, remember?" I said.

"Damn, and here I thought maybe you were getting ready to dump actor-boy and find a man who knows how to handle a weapon," Chris said.

"I thought you said Michael was the best swordsman on the show," I countered.

"He's not bad for an actor," Chris said, shrugging. "But if you get tired of watching him fight off all his groupies—"

"I'll come and watch you fight off yours," I said.

"Yeah, right," Chris said. But I knew from tales of past conventions that Chris had more than his share of female attention, even though his appearances on camera were limited to long-shots as a stunt double for Michael's old friend Walker, who couldn't be trusted not to injure himself with a pencil, much less a sword. I wondered, briefly, if the fans had anything to do with Andrea's absence.

"I'll make sure Alaric's okay with holding down the booth for a while and join you," I said.

"The Ruritanian Room, as soon as possible, then," Chris said, with a deep bow. Then he flung his black cloak dramatically over his shoulder and strode off, drawing admiring glances from all he passed. I shook my head. Loyalty to Michael didn't prevent me from noticing that Chris looked better than ever in the Van Dyke beard he'd grown. Especially when he was wearing his black hair long and flowing over his Amblyopian guard uniform—which, conveniently for the costume shop, looked remarkably like a French musketeer's uniform. I had to admit that if I didn't have Michael, Chris would be just the sort of temptation I'd have a hard time resisting.

Though the dramatically named Alaric Steele could give him competition. At least he could the last time I'd seen him, twelve years ago. And when I reached the booth, I saw he'd held up well. I noticed a few streaks of gray in the long brown ponytail, and his face was a bit more weathered—he was probably well into his forties by now. But he was still blessed with the kind of lean, angular body, high cheekbones, and deep-set, brooding eyes that would keep him in the Attractive Older Man category for another twenty years.

Hell, I thought, when he smiled briefly in greeting. Forget the older bit. Just plain attractive.

"You bring an outfit?" he asked, looking at my t-shirt and jeans.

"Is that required?" I asked, glancing around the dealers' room. Most of the people behind counters wore costumes, although they favored generic fantasy/Renaissance Faire gear over costumes specific to Porfiria's universe.

"Pumps up sales, or so the ones who've done this before tell me," Steele said. He had donned a well-worn leather jerkin over a loose-fitting white shirt with the sleeves rolled up. On him, it didn't look like a costume. It looked lived in. Not dirty, just familiar and comfortable.

"Your first time at a bash like this, then?" I asked.

He nodded.

"I've done a lot of Ren Faires," he said. "But this . . ."

He looked a little taken aback by the whole thing. Not encouraging. When I'd seen Steele's name on the vendor list—an established blacksmith I knew slightly—I'd assumed that the fan convention would be a reasonably profitable venue. It would have been nice if he'd mentioned that he'd never been to a fan convention before and had no idea if they were worth doing. Ah, well.

"I'm going to change in a bit," I said. "But right now, Chris Blair needs me to fill in at his noon performance—do you mind? I'll put in my share of booth time, don't worry, but I think he needs me to rehearse right now."

"No problem," Steele said. "Should help with business if people see you on stage. I'll catch you later."

I left him chasing a curious monkey away from some sharpened swords, struggled through the crowd to the exit, and then asked a passing bellhop for directions to the Ruritanian Room. Which to the best of his knowledge was in another wing of the hotel, so I decided to drop by our room on the way and get my costume.

Yes, I'd brought a costume, just in case. But not an Amblyopian costume. Just the all-purpose wench costume I used for Renaissance Faires.

I was startled to see a small knot of people huddled in the hallway outside our room. All wearing blue convention volunteer ribbons, which made me feel a little better. But still, disconcerting.

"Is something wrong?" I asked.

"Sorry," one of them said. "We were just getting up our nerve to invite Ms. Wynncliffe-Jones down for the VIP reception."

"It's your turn," another one said. They all looked at a tall, middle-aged woman sensibly dressed, I noted with approval, in the robes of an Amblyopian high priestess. Then I momentarily wondered what had happened to my frame of reference when I considered a lavender velvet robe trimmed with pink fur sensible, merely because it didn't expose several acres of flesh.

At any rate, the faux priestess planted herself in front of the QB's room. They'd put the QB in the last room in the corridor, with us beside her and the other celebrity guests nearby. This was supposed to give us greater privacy, but I'd already figured out that being at the end of a cul-de-sac made it hard to elude eager fans. Unless we wanted to flee through the emergency exit, we had no choice but to wade through the crowds that gathered along the one exit route.

The priestess took a deep breath, squared her shoulders, and knocked on the door.

"Miss Wynncliffe-Jones?" she called. "We're here to escort you to the VIP reception."

"Go away!" the QB shouted, through the door. "I need my rest! Go away! Leave me alone!"

The priestess's face fell, and she returned with a defeated look on her face.

"I suppose we'll have to apologize to the fans," she said.

I was tempted to suggest the ostensible star's absence wouldn't upset all that many fans. Not as many as if Michael or Walker missed one of their appearances. But I decided that in addition to being unkind, that would be a stupid thing to say to people who might eventually talk to the QB, so I wished them luck and went into our room.

The room service cart had disappeared, and the parrot with it. No doubt when housekeeping came they'd take care of the feathers and droppings.

I peeked out on the balcony. Most of the fans were gone, but the few remaining had made themselves quite at home. One had plugged a toaster oven into the balcony's electrical outlet to make grilled cheese sandwiches. Smelling them reminded me that I hadn't eaten yet. Maybe I should pick up something in the lobby on my way to the rehearsal, I thought, as I scrambled into the skirt and bodice of my costume and threw various accessories into the leather haversack that served as the Renaissance-period equivalent of a purse.

And maybe I should find Dad and borrow Spike to guard our balcony from squatters.

The phone's red message light was blinking so I called the message number.

"Michael?" I heard. Francis, his agent. "Listen, when you get a chance, we need to talk about that meeting with Miss Wynncliffe-Jones. I'm in room 108; call me."

Francis had been meeting with the QB? Or did he mean Michael's brief talk with her yesterday? Or maybe it was a future meeting. Perhaps the two of them were going to meet with her later in the weekend.

I'd find out soon enough. I scribbled a note for Michael, in case he came back to the room before I saw him.

Out in the hallway I found the pink-and-lavender priestess having hysterics just outside our door. Quiet hysterics, apparently in deference to the QB's sensibilities, but she was crying, wringing her hands, and generally working up as much of a fuss as possible without raising her voice above a stage whisper. The Amazon guards were fluttering around nearby.

"What the hell's wrong now?" I asked.

# Chapter 7

"She's ruining our convention," the priestess said, through sobs and hiccups.

"Nonsense," I said, in the brisk tone I've found effective with hysterical people.

"What will we do if she never comes out?" the priestess asked. "What's a Porfiria convention without at least one appearance by Porfiria?"

A vast improvement, if you asked me.

"Don't worry," I said aloud. "You've got your special guest: the first convention ever to feature an appearance by Ichabod Dilley!"

"If he appears," she said, her tears starting again. "He checked into the hotel, but he hasn't gotten in touch with us yet, and he's not in his room. What if we can't find him in time for his panel?"

"I'm sure he'll show," I said. "What does he look like? I'll keep an eye out for him. In fact, why not organize a task force to look for him?"

"We could if we knew what he looks like," she said, sniffling. "But we've never even met him. One of our committee found him through the Internet, and he sent us an e-mail agreeing to come. He didn't even send a photo for the program."

"Then let's all keep an eye out for someone who looks like an Ichabod Dilley," I said. "I'm sure a name like that leaves a mark on its owner."

With that, I left. As I turned the corner, I could see one of the junior Amazons steeling her nerves to knock on the QB's door again. Good; as a drama queen, the priestess left much to be desired. She could use a little more exposure to the techniques of an expert like the QB.

I only got lost twice on my way to the Ruritanian Room. Apart from the predictable difficulties of trying to fence in a room filled with curious monkeys, the rehearsal went well. I wondered if Chris had picked me because I was the best woman fencer available or only because I was the tallest. Harry, the troupe's other male cast member, was only five two, and half the sight gags in the skit drew on the eight-inch discrepancy in our height. But I did well enough that Chris talked me into rehearsing a second, more difficult show scheduled for Saturday night.

When we'd finished our rehearsal, Chris reminded us to meet him in the green room at eleven forty-five.

"Where's that?" I asked.

"It's not actually green," Chris said. "That's an old theater term for the room where the performers hang out while waiting to go on, and they keep snacks there and—"

"Chris, I live with an actor, remember?" I said. "I know what a green room is. I meant, what does the hotel call what we call the green room?"

Chris looked blank.

"The Baskerville Room," Harry said. "Ask around enough and someone can show you where it is."

Chris nodded and wandered off, looking anxious and distracted. We watched as he pulled out the cell phone for about the twentieth time.

"Wish Andrea would answer her damned phone," Harry grumbled.

"They have a quarrel?" I asked.

"A stupid quarrel," Harry said. "Like it's Chris's fault the QB fired Andrea."

"Oops," I said.

"Yeah." Harry shook his head. "Only a lousy bit part as an Amazon guard, but Andrea hoped it would lead to better roles. But the QB wants bigger guards."

"Bigger? Andrea's my height."

"Yeah, she's tall enough, but not burly enough," Harry said. "She wants guards who make her look petite and demure. I guess Andrea thinks Chris should quit his job in protest or something. But he can't—the QB owns him."

"Owns him?"

"Owns his contract," Harry said. "Same thing. If he quits, she can keep him from working as a blademaster anywhere else for the term of the contract. So even if he wanted to quit, he can't. Not if he wants to eat."

"He can't break the contract?" I asked.

"He could try," Harry said. "Might work, but it would probably take as long as just waiting out the contract, and do you have any idea how much a good contract lawyer charges?"

We shook our heads in sympathy for Chris and went our separate ways. I headed for the dealers' room to pull my weight for a while before the show.

On my way through the lobby, I ran across three musicians in scarlet jesters' costumes, singing familiar songs with the words changed to Amblyopian references. I stopped to listen to their version of the theme song from the *Beverly Hillbillies*, which began, "Come listen to my story 'bout a wizard named Mephisto." Unfortunately, before I could learn what they'd found to rhyme with Mephisto, the monkeys overhead drowned them out.

"Damn those things," I muttered.

"What have you got against monkeys?" asked a nearby tree.

"Nothing," I said, scanning the foliage for a face. It felt rude, addressing something without a face. "I just don't think they belong in a hotel lobby."

"I suppose you're the one who called the health department," the tree said, heaving itself up to reveal a pair of dirty white running shoes among its roots.

"No, it wasn't me," I said.

But the tree ignored me.

"Spoilsport," it muttered, and lurched slowly down the hall toward the conference rooms, waving its branches as it went.

Health department? I surveyed the lobby and spotted a middle-aged man whose brown business suit stood out in this costumed crowd. Unlike the civilian I'd talked to in the ballroom, he didn't seem particularly disturbed by the costumes, but evidently the monkeys and parrots alarmed him.

"Either they go or we'll close you down," he said, waving his hand at the ceiling, where a group of monkeys played tag while the nearby parrots practiced hooting and chattering like the monkeys. "I'll be back in three hours."

With that, he turned and marched out.

His audience stared after him—a man in a hotel uniform and the short Amazon who'd escorted Michael and me earlier.

"I'll round up a crew if you will," the Amazon said.

"It's your people who caused this," the hotel staffer replied.

"And it's your restaurant and hotel the health department

will close if we can't recapture them all in time."

I nodded with satisfaction. A monkeyless, parrotless hotel sounded excellent to me. Maybe when the health department man returned, I'd introduce him to Salome.

I left the musicians singing "Amblyopia, Here I Come!" and headed for the dealers' room, though I got lost several times on the way.

I wandered into a room where several earnest-looking young people under the direction of a bearded professorial type were discussing the use of Jungian archetypes in the first season Porfiria scripts—as if Nate had any idea what a Jungian archetype was. A list of upcoming panels posted outside the room featured a comparison between the *Iliad* and season two of the show, and a debate on whether or not Porfiria was a feminist. A room to avoid unless I needed to hide from someone.

Next door, in a room marked "Fan Lounge," fifty or so people sat in the dark watching a Porfiria episode on a medium-sized TV. Not an episode I remembered, which probably meant it was from season one. The sign outside confirmed that they were showing all the episodes, in order, throughout the weekend, interspersed with the blooper tape.

A slightly better place to hide. I wouldn't mind watching the blooper tape, a collection of outtakes from the show. The clips of cheesy scenery falling down or cheap props coming apart in the actors' hands got old rather quickly, but I loved watching how Michael could ad lib something funny when he or another actor blew a line. Also, the number of outtakes made necessary by Walker tripping, falling, or hitting himself with swords and other props still held a morbid fascination. How had the man survived three seasons of near-fatal klutziness?

On my third try, I found the side entrance to the dealers' room. Things were so slow I wondered if the customers had as much trouble finding their way here as I had.

I spotted a familiar face. Michael stared back at me from a hundred mugs, t-shirts, posters, 8×10 glossy photos, and dolls. Officially, action figures, but they looked like dolls to me. Some only six inches tall and made entirely of molded plastic; others twelve inches tall with real fabric robes. Not a bad likeness of Michael, either, but I found it disconcerting to see my boyfriend turned into a Ken doll.

But not as disconcerting as the remarkable number of Michael clones gracing the convention. So far I'd seen teenaged Michaels and senior citizen Michaels; authentically tall and lean Michaels, and even more short and pudgy Michaels. I rather liked the Asian and African-American Michaels, along with the Michael who tooled around in an electric wheelchair. But the cumulative effect of seeing ersatz Michaels everywhere got on my nerves.

I would be glad to escape this madhouse, I was thinking, as I reached the booth and found Steele studying the convention program. And frowning. Was something wrong?

# Chapter 8

"Found any panels you want to attend?" I asked.

"Hell, no," he growled. "I don't watch the damned show; I'm just selling swords."

But a smile undermined the gruff tone, and seeing it, I found myself wishing we were selling jewelry, or clothes—something that would let us use Steele's ability to attract women to the booth.

"I wouldn't watch it myself if Michael weren't on it," I said aloud.

"Your old man? Which one is he?" Steele asked, holding out the cover photo. "This one?"

"No," I said, glancing at his finger. "That's Walker Morris. He plays the Duke of Urushiol, Queen Porfiria's archrival. That's Michael, to his right, in the black robe."

"Hmmm," Steele said. "What's he play?"

"The wizard Mephisto."

"Mephisto?" he said. "I don't remember anyone by that name. 'Course it's been a year or two since I've seen it."

"I thought you didn't watch," I said, laughing.

"I don't," he said. "Not regularly. But yeah, I've seen a few episodes. When it first came out. Weird, seeing something you vaguely remember reading as a kid turned into a TV show. But after a week or two, I could see what garbage it was. No offense meant," he added, apparently remembering too late my tenuous connection with the show.

"No offense taken," I said. "It's not as if Michael has anything to do with the scripts."

"Yeah, the scriptwriter's the one who should be drawn and quartered."

"Don't blame Nate," I said. "He's on a pretty tight rein. Some of his original scripts aren't bad. Unfortunately, by the time they shoot, the QB mangles the script into the usual swill."

"The QB?"

"Tamerlaine Wynncliffe-Jones," I said. "The actress who plays Queen Porfiria. Also known as, um, the Queen Bee."

"Yeah, right," he said. "Tamerlaine Wynncliffe-Jones? Bet that's not her real name."

"You never know," I said. "Parents have done stranger things."

"And I bet that's not her original face," he said, shaking his head. "Thirty years ago, maybe even twenty, she was a looker; you can still see that much. But now—it's a bad joke. So what is this Mephisto character your guy plays?"

"He's a mercenary wizard introduced in the second season," I said. "Originally a one-episode guest shot, but he got such a good reaction from the fans that they brought him back for two more episodes that season, and he's in about half of them this past season."

That seemed to satisfy Steele's curiosity.

I spent a reasonable amount of time at the booth before running out again for the combat demonstration. Steele was good at security. Even while talking to one customer, he kept the whole counter covered with his peripheral vision, and I could see he suspected the same shifty-looking people who raised my hackles.

Definitely a talented swordsmith. Perhaps more than any other form of iron work, weapons and armor call for a perfect balance of form and function. Steele's swords had the spare and deadly elegance I was working so hard to perfect myself.

Not much of a salesman, though. Not that I was such a whiz, but even I was better at it than Steele.

I hoped to catch Michael before going on stage—I wasn't sure whether I wanted to brag or warn him—but they kept him in the autograph line until the very last minute. I didn't even know if he was in the ballroom when Chris, Harry, and I went on stage.

Chris acknowledged the audience's applause with a low bow, sweeping the floor with the white plume in his hat. Then he launched into an explanation of the difference between fencing, stage combat, and real combat—an explanation that might have sounded dry, if not for the practical demonstrations. Harry and I took turns sneaking up and attacking him, while Chris, waving his sword around to make a point or demonstrate a technique, parried each of our attacks, as if by accident.

"In stage combat, you always want your blade exactly where your partner expects it to be," he said, while parrying in a deceptively nonchalant manner. "Of course, in real combat, your goal is just the opposite—you never want your blade where your opponent expects it."

He continued with several practical demonstrations, having Harry and me execute a sequence of thrusts and parries at full speed, and then in slow motion, so the audience could see the techniques. For a grand finale, Harry and I ran through our side of a three-way battle, looking rather silly as we lunged and leaped about, slicing the air. But when we repeated the sequence with Chris defending against our combined forces, it brought down the house, and we took several bows. I felt like an imposter. Only their skill kept me from being skewered several times during the performance. And we'd managed to make my nearly pinning my own foot to the floor look like just another part of the act. From the way Chris beamed at me, I deduced that I'd made fewer mistakes than he'd expected. I'd decide later whether to feel relieved or insulted.

"I'll answer questions from the audience for the rest of the hour," Chris announced, sitting down on the edge of the stage with the microphone in his hand.

I was tempted to hang around. I loved listening to Chris talk about swords and combat. For that matter, I'd have liked to hang around and hear what the mysterious Ichabod Dilley had to say. But I'd already abandoned poor Steele for most of the morning. So I snapped some pictures of Chris and headed back to the dealers' room.

In the hallway, I saw small posses of Amazon guards and hotel staff, armed with ladders, nets, and heaps of fresh fruit, beginning the parrot and monkey roundup, accompanied by the scarlet jesters' soulful rendition of "Git Along, Little Monkeys." Probably my imagination, but the atmosphere already smelled fresher.

"Sorry," I said, as I joined Steele in the booth. "Were things too crazy?"

He shook his head.

"Biggest problem has been keeping the vermin from filching the merchandise."

"Vermin?" I said, looking around to see if anyone had heard. Not very tactful, referring to the convention goers that way. Or did he mean real vermin, I thought, peering down at my feet.

"Up there," Steele said, pointing to the ceiling. Though the roundup had begun outside, the dealers' room still had its contingent of escaped monkeys. Clusters of them hovered eagerly over our booth and those of two nearby jewelry makers. At least I assumed they were eager. Perhaps I'd feel differently if I were another monkey, but I couldn't see that their expressions ever changed. I found it slightly unnerving to look up and see half a dozen solemn, impassive faces staring down as if in silent judgment of our strange human antics. The parrots, by contrast, always looked cheerful, eager, and friendly, even while biting you. Over time, no doubt, we could all learn parrot and monkey body language, but fortunately, thanks to the health department, they probably wouldn't be around that long—although several other booths had already rigged makeshift canopies to protect their wares, an idea we might want to copy.

"Sorry I wasn't here to help," I said, turning back to Steele.

"They scatter if you wave a blade at them," Steele said, with a shrug. "And apart from that, it's been dead. Things get slow whenever there's an interesting panel on."

"Glad our panel counted as interesting."

"I wouldn't have minded seeing it," he said, smiling as he ran his eyes up and down my costume. He wasn't bothering to hide his appreciation, but he wasn't being obnoxious about it, so I smiled back and turned to help the customer who'd just stepped in front of the booth.

We got enough traffic to keep from being bored. Not many people buying yet, but then people often took a while to work themselves up to the kind of major outlay required for a handmade sword or a piece of armor.

At one point, I saw the small man in the business suit wandering around as if shell-shocked. He stopped in front of our booth.

"Now you're wearing a costume, too," he said, in an accusing tone.

"Sorry," I said. "It helps with sales."

He looked at our merchandise.

"Swords," he said. "Of course."

"You don't seem to be having a good time," I said.

"Am I supposed to?" he asked.

Light dawned.

"You're Ichabod Dilley, aren't you?"

# Chapter 9

The little man turned pale, and Steele looked startled.

"He can't be Ichabod Dilley," Steele said.

"Why not?" I asked.

"For one thing, isn't he a little too young?"

"Maybe he wrote the comics as a teenager," I said.

"In the womb, maybe," Steele said. "Didn't they come out in the late sixties or something?"

"Early seventies, actually," I said.

"Wrote what?" the little man asked. He did look a little young, perhaps, but then he had the kind of bland, round face whose age I find hard to pin down.

"And now that he has gone on to a respectable corporate career, he isn't sure he wants to be reminded of his wild and crazy youth," I continued. "You are him, aren't you?" I went on, turning back to the little man.

"I am named Ichabod Dilley," he said. "But I'm not *that* Ichabod Dilley."

"How can there possibly be two?" I asked.

"It's a family name," Dilley said. "I'll have you know that there was an Ichabod Dilley who fought in the Revolution."

"What do they call you, anyway?" Steele asked. "Icky?"

"I prefer Ichabod," the little man said, sounding sulky.

He'd probably been called Icky more than once in his life.

"If you're not the Ichabod Dilley who wrote the comic books, what are you doing here?" I asked.

"They invited me," he said.

"And you didn't find that odd? That a bunch of people you'd never heard of before invited you to be the special guest at a convention?"

"I speak at conventions all the time," he said.

"What kind of conventions?"

"Any convention that hires me," he said, drawing himself up very straight. "That's what I do. I'm a motivational speaker."

I managed to keep a straight face. Steele didn't.

"Oh, that's going to go over real big with this crowd," he said, through snorts of laughter.

"Have you ever spoken to a group like this?" I asked.

"No, mostly I've done conventions of accountants and actuaries," he said. "They're a little more . . . um . . ."

"Buttoned up?" Steele suggested.

"You could say that," Dilley said, glancing at two scantily clad Amazons strolling past the booth. "I did a convention of funeral directors, once."

"I bet they were a load of laughs," Steele said.

"Actually, they were, after the meetings," Dilley said. "They really cut loose and get crazy at conventions. I don't think I got to bed before midnight the whole weekend."

If staying up till midnight was his idea of cutting loose and getting crazy, Amblyopia had some surprises in store for him. I'd already received two invitations to con parties that didn't start till midnight.

Steele frowned, and I worried that he'd make another insulting remark about Dilley's name, so I glanced up at the wall clock and pretended to be alarmed.

"Look at the time!" I exclaimed. "You'd better get over to the ballroom. It's almost time for your panel."

"Oh, right," Dilley said, staring raptly at a woman walking toward the booth. Her barbarian warrior costume consisted of a few scraps of strategically positioned fur and a lot of leather straps holding her weapons.

She saw Dilley staring at her and smiled at him. He drew back as if she were a snake.

"This is crazy," he muttered, and scurried away.

The barbarian woman glanced at our booth, favored Steele with a smile considerably warmer than the one she'd given Dilley, and undulated on.

"Interesting costume," I said, into the ensuing silence.

One o'clock came, and shortly afterward, the dealers' room grew crowded. Very crowded. Not a ringing endorsement of Ichabod Dilley's motivational speech.

Sure enough, I overheard nearby fans talking about it.

"Good time to come to the dealers' room and visit my former money," one said.

"So what's going on in the ballroom now?" another asked.

"Nothing worth seeing," said the first.

"Some crackpot yammering on about daring to be yourself," said a woman dressed as one of Porfiria's ladies-in-waiting.

"As if we need that kind of advice," scoffed a pudgy Michael clone.

Poor Icky.

The crowd thinned out toward the end of the hour, so I deduced the fans expected something interesting in the ballroom at two. I was about to suggest to Steele that one of us make a food run when Michael appeared and beckoned to me.

"Sorry," he said. "Things have been crazy. I thought we could have lunch, but they've drafted me to coax the QB out of her room and give her moral support when she does her panel at two."

"She's still playing hermit?"

"Apparently. Can you come along and help us with her?"

"Me?"

I wasn't sure the QB even knew who I was. She'd been known to glare at me when I showed up at cast parties on Michael's arm, but normally she ignored me.

"We think she's feeling overwhelmed," Michael said. "We're rounding up people she knows."

Shaking my head, I followed him.

They had already gathered Michael's costar and buddy, Walker; Nate, the scriptwriter; blademaster Chris; and a perky young blond woman named Typhani who'd been working as the QB's personal assistant for an impressive six weeks. Previous personal assistants had flounced off in a huff or run off in tears by the end of the first week.

"Okay," Michael told the diminutive Amazon. "Let's go get her."

At first, I didn't think it would work.

"Go away! Leave me alone!" the QB kept shouting. But Michael kept coaxing, and periodically he'd say something like,

"Everyone's just waiting to see you!"

And the rest of us would ad lib encouraging comments.

Gradually, the protests grew less vehement. And finally, after one particularly impassioned plea from Michael, success.

She opened the door.

# Chapter 10

Even from where I stood, I could smell the blast of peppermint from her breath. Either she'd just knocked back a killer dose of mouthwash or she'd taken up flavored vodka. She gazed slowly around the circle of people outside her door, though it didn't feel as if she was looking at us. More like scanning us with some instrument other than her eyes. I could imagine a reptile performing the same emotionless survey. *It's not edible; it's not dangerous; I can't mate with it; it might as well not exist; I'll ignore it.*

Fine by me. I'd seen what happened to people when the QB stopped ignoring them.

I saw a faint spark of interest in her eyes when she spotted Michael.

"Come in," she said, beckoning to him. The rest of us followed. She didn't shriek, so I deduced she was in a good mood.

An artificially induced good mood, though. Her balance was worse than usual, and her smile had a certain wobbly quality.

I was surprised, and I could tell Michael was, too. From his tales of life on the set, her drinking was a menace, but only after the cameras stopped rolling. She might show up for work with a monumental hangover, but she'd be sober. I suppose we'd expected her to maintain the same discipline at the convention. After all, it was work.

"Oh, my God," the Amazon murmured. "She's—"

"A real trouper," Typhani said, in a loud firm voice. "I'm sure even though she's been feeling a little unwell, she'll do fine once we get her on stage."

It was that getting her on stage part that worried me. She chatted brightly with Michael, oblivious to the passing minutes.

Or perhaps less oblivious than determined to sabotage the schedule. Or unwilling to leave the comfort of a familiar environment.

Not my idea of comfort, but it looked a lot like her trailer on the set, from the brief glimpses I'd had of it. She'd made herself at home.

Bits of clothing covered most of the room's horizontal surfaces. At least a dozen pairs of shoes lay scattered about. An empty box of truffles sat on the bedside table, and from the number of fluted brown-paper candy cups strewn on the floor, it wasn't the first box. The contents of her purse carpeted the top of the dresser—she had an amazing number of credit cards.

Hard to believe she'd checked in the night before. I'd need a week to create that much chaos.

"Oh, they won't want to hear me," she was saying. "Not after the novelty of listening to Ichabod Dilley. What did he say, anyway?"

Her voice had an edge. Maybe she resented sharing the spotlight with Dilley. Maybe she was afraid he'd denounce the clever deal she'd made, thirty years ago, when she'd bought the film rights to Porfiria for what now seemed a ridiculously small sum.

Or maybe she was just afraid he'd mention how long ago that deal had taken place.

I wondered if someone should tell her that it wasn't the real Ichabod Dilley after all. At least, not the Ichabod Dilley who'd written the comic books. Would it calm her down to hear this, or further enrage her?

No one else answered, so I spoke up.

"I don't think any of us know what he said. Hardly anyone went."

She looked at me, as if seeing me for the first time, and I remembered why I usually held my tongue around her.

"Really?" she said. She smiled, and then, when I didn't say anything else, her glance flicked away as if I no longer existed.

I realized I'd been holding my breath.

"Look at the time!" Michael exclaimed. "We should be going!"

Michael continued to distract the QB while Typhani stuffed her employer into the glittering jacket of her costume, and combed her suspiciously jet-black hair into some kind of order. Then Michael offered his arm in a gesture whose apparent chivalry disguised its practical purpose. The QB clung to him as he half-supported and half-steered her out the door and propelled her down the corridor. The tiny Amazon trotted beside them, occasionally tugging Michael in the right direction when he made a wrong turn, as all of us did when navigating the hotel corridors. Of course, Michael had an excuse—he was chattering a mile a minute about what a lovely convention it had been so far and how enthusiastic the fans were.

To my surprise, they were enthusiastic. They greeted the QB's arrival noisily—had they been bribed, perhaps? As I stood in the wings, I could see them listening with rapt attention. Amazing. Perhaps my own dislike blinded me to the fans' genuine affection for her.

I was silently berating myself when Typhani came up and shoved a legal pad and a pen into my hands.

"Help us think up the trivia questions," she hissed into my ear.

"Trivia questions?" I stage-whispered back.

"The fan who can answer the most trivia questions about Miss Wynncliffe-Jones's talk gets a personally autographed picture," she said. "Of Michael."

Ah. That explained the rapt attention. I was right; they were bribed. I dutifully began scribbling notes.

"And she's supposed to be Porfiria?"

I looked up to see Alaric Steele standing at my elbow.

"That's her," I said. "Is the booth—?"

"Chris, the blademaster guy, offered to watch it," Steele said. "What is that getup she's wearing?"

"It's what she wears when she performs a sacrifice to the goddess Apnea.

"The goddess of snoring."

I watched his face as he studied the outfit. The costume shop had intended the gown's stiff brocade and voluminous folds to disguise the QB's girth while the high gold lamé collar camouflaged her chins. The headdress was supposed to make her face seem less round, though to my mind it only completed her resemblance to the top ornament on a Christmas tree.

"I understand that in the original comic books, Porfiria performed her sacrifices wearing a loincloth and a couple of tasseled pasties," I added. "Not that I've ever read them."

"Yeah, that sounds more like something from a comic book," Steele said, with a fleeting smile. "I might even have read some of them—I'm old enough, remember?"

"Problem is, so is Her Highness."

"And then some," he said. "And I don't think Her Highness is the right form of address."

"Her Majesty, maybe?"

"More like Her Tipsiness."

"Is it that obvious?" I said, wincing.

He shrugged.

"Are all the panels like this?" he asked. "Bunch of silly actors talking about the show?"

I decided, in the interest of harmony, not to remind him of my connection with one of the silly actors. I nodded.

"I'd better get back," he said. "Chris only agreed to watch the booth for a few minutes so I could get a gander at Her Elusiveness."

"I should go back and help you," I said.

"I can hold things down if you want to hang around with your boyfriend."

"Unfortunately, he'll be escorting Her Decrepitness for the next hour," I said. "So while I appreciate the offer, I might as well come back and make myself useful."

I handed the trivia questions I'd come up with so far to Typhani and followed Steele to the dealers' room.

Business wasn't as slow as it had been during Michael's appearance, but neither was it booming. Good. They probably didn't need the overflow room, but at least the QB would see a crowd large enough to keep her happy.

I was writing up a sales receipt for a couple of daggers when I heard a voice at my elbow.

"Did you see my speech?"

"Hi, Ichabod," I said. "No, sorry; I was here. Thank you," I added, to my customer. "Wear and/or use them in good health."

"Oh, that's too bad," Dilley said, sounding hurt. "I was hoping you had. Maybe you can catch me tomorrow, then."

"I'll try," I said.

"I don't think this crowd is receptive to motivational talks," he said.

"Oh, dear," I said. "So it didn't go well?"

"I've seen better audiences," he said. "But never mind. By tomorrow, I hope to have something to say about the other Ichabod Dilley."

"That should be interesting," I said.

"The weird thing is that I am probably the most appropriate person to represent the other Ichabod Dilley," he went on. "I didn't know it before, but he's my uncle."

"I'm surprised you didn't realize immediately that they were talking about your uncle."

"Maybe I would have, if my parents had ever told me I *had* an uncle," Dilley said. "Up until this weekend, I always thought my dad was an only child, and now I find out I'm named after his black sheep younger brother who died before I was born."

"Oh, he's dead," I said, feeling slightly disappointed.

"For thirty years," Dilley said.

"He must have been young," I said.

"Yeah, about twenty or so. Drugs," he added, solemnly.

"Drugs?"

"Yes," he said nodding. "I just finished talking to my parents. Dad wouldn't say anything; just kept yelling that his drugged-out brother was dead and buried, and he didn't want to talk about it. But after he hung up, Mom told me a little. She says the real last straw was when Dad had to pay off all these huge debts my uncle ran up. They almost had to sell the farm."

"Yeah, that could leave bad feeling," I said. "Although I

doubt if your uncle did it deliberately. At least the dying part."

"I'm hoping I can get her to tell me some more this evening. I need background for my talk tomorrow. And I'm sure there's some interesting stuff to tell. It seems my uncle Ichabod dropped out of college and went to San Francisco and got involved in drugs and pornography."

"Drugs *and* pornography?"

"It wasn't that uncommon, thirty years ago," Dilley said, sounding a little defensive.

"Drugs, maybe," I said. "But pornography?"

"Yeah, these underground comics," Dilley said, "really raunchy stuff, apparently. My parents were amazed to hear that anything he'd done had been made into a TV show."

"Consider the times," I said. "Thirty years ago, TV kept married couples in separate beds, and now, look what you see."

"True," Dilley said. "Maybe his work was only offensive to the backward, parochial sensibilities of the time. Perhaps today, instead of offensive, we'd find it bold, forward thinking, and socially relevant."

"That's the spirit," I said. "You can rescue your uncle from the slanders that have besmirched his reputation all these years."

"Yes," he said. "Only—"

"What's the problem?"

"What if it is pornography?" he said. "I've never seen his work."

"That's easily fixed," I said. "See that woman at the Dreamscape Booksellers counter?"

"The one wearing antlers?"

"Yes. That's Cordelia—she sells used and rare books. Go see if she's got some of your uncle's stuff for sale."

He started forward, then turned around, looking doubtful. "Now what?" I asked.

"She's a real book dealer," he said. "Won't she be insulted if I ask her about comic books?"

"She may be miffed if she doesn't have any to sell, but she won't be insulted," I said. "Call them graphic novels, if you're worried; it's a classier term."

He nodded and waded into the crowd.

# Chapter 11

I watched, with amusement, the conversation between Cordelia and Ichabod Dilley the younger. As I predicted, she wasn't insulted or even surprised at his question. She pointed to a couple of items in a locked glass case. He glanced down, and I saw him start. He'd seen the price tags, no doubt. Prolonged discussion followed. I wondered if Dilley was trying to bargain down the price—fat chance—or merely pleading with Cordelia to let him read her precious yellowing comics.

"What's up with Junior?" Steele, who'd been busy with a customer, asked me.

"Apparently he's decided to make up for his parents' neglect of his uncle by championing the late Ichabod Dilley's work. Although I think it's mostly because his parents paid off Dilley's debts when he died."

"They what?" Steele asked.

"Paid his debts. Large ones. Of course, before he can champion his uncle's work, he needs to know something about it," I added. "I steered him to someone who can sell him a copy."

"Hope he's well heeled," Steele said. "I bet they're charging a lot for those old rags."

"I hear the original first issue goes for over five hundred dollars now," I said. "Probably more than the real Ichabod Dilley got for it back in 1969."

"Probably more than he got for all twelve issues," Steele said.

"More than the QB paid him for the film rights, anyway," I said.

"How would you know that?" Steele said.

"She brags about it," I said. "Not in public, of course; but sometimes when she gets plastered, she gets careless."

At three, the crowd in the dealers' room thinned when Walker, the show's other leading heartthrob, took the stage for his appearance, while the QB held court in the autograph room.

Steele was talking to a slick-looking character who claimed to be the producer of an upcoming sword and sorcery flick that needed a vast quantity of custom armor and weaponry. If Steele asked me, I'd say make sure you get the money first, but so far he hadn't, and I didn't really know him well enough to offer unsolicited advice.

And Steele kept glancing at me as if he didn't want to say too much in my presence, so I took the opportunity to dash out for a much-needed bathroom break.

I was waiting for the hot air machine to finish chapping my hands when the door burst open and Typhani ran in sobbing.

"What's wrong?" I asked. I confess I was hoping she'd assure me that she'd only broken a fingernail. Or perhaps plead to be left alone and lock herself in a stall. Instead, she flung herself on me.

It took several minutes before she calmed down enough to talk. I stood there, awkwardly patting her on the back and wondering if I was a bad person for worrying about the mascara stains on my costume.

"Oh, she's—she's—she's impossible," Typhani wailed, finally managing to speak.

"The QB? Yeah, impossible works," I said. "Unbearable's good, too, and obnoxious. I'd even go as far as unspeakable, if you like."

"And mean!" Typhani muttered, with surprising venom. "Mean as . . . as . . . oh, I don't know."

Apparently vocabulary wasn't Typhani's strong suit.

"Too mean to live," she said, finally. "That's what my mother used to say. Too mean to live."

"What has she done now?" I asked.

Instead of answering, Typhani doubled over abruptly—was she having some kind of a seizure? No, she had put her head nearly on the bathroom floor and was staring past my feet, at the floor beneath the stalls.

"No feet," she said, bobbing up again. "Okay, I shouldn't really be telling you this, but it's about the hate mail she's been getting. She got another one today and—"

From one of the stalls, we heard the tinkling sound of liquid falling into a toilet. Followed by the sound of flushing.

"Someone's spying on us!"

She shrank into the corner farthest from the stalls and stared at them with a panic-stricken face.

"I'll take care of it," I said. I walked over to where I could see the doors to the stalls. All were ajar. Perhaps the eavesdropper was standing on the seat, hoping we wouldn't notice.

I strode over to the first stall and slammed the door open. Nothing. I did the same for the second, third, and fourth stalls. All empty.

She was in the handicapped stall at the end.

I took a deep breath and slammed open that door, too.

Empty.

Then, from near the ceiling, I heard the sound of liquid tinkling into a toilet. I glanced up to see a gray parrot sitting on an exposed pipe. As I watched, the parrot fluttered its wings and made the sound of a toilet flushing.

I sighed.

"Who is it?"

"It's only a miserable parrot," I said. "It's safe to talk."

"What if it overhears us and repeats what I say?"

Interesting point. If Salome's keeper was right, the parrot might imitate something shortly after we said it, but probably wouldn't wander around the hotel repeating it for the rest of the convention. But what if the wrong person walked into the bathroom too soon? Better safe than sorry.

"Can we talk somewhere else?" I suggested.

"No, it's okay," Typhani said. She was blotting her eyes with a damp paper towel. "I'm all right now, honestly."

She left.

So the QB was getting hate mail. If that surprised poor Typhani, she had a lot to learn.

I was making sure all the bits of my costume were back in order when my mother stormed into the rest room.

"There you are," she said, when she saw me, and I relapsed briefly into that dreaded childhood feeling of knowing I had displeased my parents, but not yet knowing how.

"What's wrong, Mother?" I asked.

"That woman," Mother said. "I could strangle her with plea-sure."

I winced. Over half the people in the hotel were female, but I had a feeling I knew exactly which woman she meant.

"You have to do something," Mother went on. "Your father is comforting Eric, but you have to do something about this."

"Eric?" I said, torn between anger and irritation. "What has she done to Eric?"

As if in answer, Mother handed me a convention program.

From the various stains and fingerprints, I deduced that it was Eric's, and that my parents had fed him pizza for lunch. From flipping through the pages, I further deduced that Eric had adopted the common convention-goer's goal of getting autographs from everyone pictured. He'd made a good start—I saw Nate's signature, Chris's, Walker's, even Dilley's, beside the giant question mark they'd used to substitute for his missing photo. When I got to the W's, I saw that Michael had signed, and after him, someone named Maggie West. The space beside Tamerlaine Wynncliffe-Jones was blank. Okay, this explained why Eric had gotten within striking distance of the QB, but not what she'd done to him.

"I don't get it," I said. "I know it's a pain, standing in line, but her line probably isn't as long as Walker's or Michael's. If he goes now—"

"He stood in line," Mother said. "And he asked her very nicely for her autograph. And that . . . witch threw the program back in his face and shouted at him!"

"Strangling's too good for her," I said. Actually, I thought Mother was overreacting a little. Not that I'd ever tell her.

"The child will probably be traumatized for life," Mother said.

Or perhaps the experience might teach him the folly of idolizing people on silly TV shows.

"What do you want me to do?" I asked.

Mother hesitated.

"I was about to say get her to apologize, but on second thought, I don't want her in the same room with Eric," she said. "But someone should tell her exactly what we think of her. I would, but I'm not sure they'd let me anywhere near her again."

What had Mother done to make herself persona non grata

in the autograph room? I decided I'd rather not know, though chances were I'd hear all about it before the end of the convention. And did she realize what she was asking me to do? Tell Michael's boss exactly what my family and I thought of her?

Then again, why not? Odds were the QB couldn't afford to fire Michael right now. It might be a good thing if she did, for that matter. Right now, at the peak of his popularity with the series, he'd probably find it relatively easy to find other roles. Meatier, more dignified roles that did not require him to prance around in tight leather pants.

And if not, well, eventually we'd find a house we could afford without the acting income.

"But first, get her damned autograph on the program," Mother said.

"Do you have any idea why she wouldn't sign it?" I asked.

"She kept shouting that she didn't want her signature on the same page as that imposter's," Mother said.

Imposter? I glanced at the page. I only saw signatures from Michael—that looked genuine—and Maggie West. Who, from reading her one-paragraph biography, had played the Duchess of Urushiol, Walker's on-screen mother, for the first half of season one. I'd only started watching when Michael joined the show, but she looked familiar. Then again, she was an actress; I'd probably seen her in lots of things, if she'd been in the business as long as the QB had. Of course, that didn't mean whoever signed the program was the real thing. Maybe the convention had invited the wrong Maggie West, too.

"I'll straighten it out," I said.

# Chapter 12

Straighten it out. Good idea. But how?

Play it by ear, I advised myself. So as I strode toward the Innsmouth Room, where the autograph sessions were held, I let my anger at the QB build up. Not only for what she'd done to Eric, but for everything she'd done to anyone. Everyone. All weekend. Ever since I'd met her. Her whole life.

I had a good head of steam by the time I reached the autograph room. Outside, I saw convention volunteers turning people away. Blast. I knew that my present mood would severely impair my ability to charm my way past security.

But no, actually they were recruiting people. Drafting passers-by to stand in line for autographs. And distributing 8×10 black-and-white photos to the draftees.

Okay, so breaking into line wouldn't cause a riot.

I moved along the side of the room. Michael wasn't there. Probably just as well. But Nate, the scriptwriter, and Walker were. Nate was hovering attentively over the QB. Walker was waiting to take his turn.

"Hey, Walker," I said, slipping into place beside him. "Any chance you could sneak me to the head of the line? I want to get an autograph for someone who can't make it."

"You sure you want to?" he said, surprised. "She's in a lousy mood."

"That makes two of us," I said. "Just do it."

He hesitated, no doubt suspecting that I hadn't suddenly become an avid fan. I nudged him into motion, and then walked beside him to her table. Amazon security ignored us, as I'd anticipated.

"Meg, how are you?" Nate said.

Walker retreated. Out of the corner of my eye, I saw him heading for the other side of the room.

"Wanted to get Miss Wynncliffe-Jones to sign a program for one of my friends."

"I'm sure she'd be happy to," Nate said.

He held out his hand for the program, but I didn't surrender it to him. Or to the QB when the person she was talking to moved away and she reached out mechanically to take it.

Maybe it was stupid, but I held the program out of reach until she finally looked up.

"Oh, hello. . . ." she said.

"Meg," I said. "You've seen me often enough to know my name by now. At least before the cocktail hour."

A faint crease appeared in her forehead. Anger? Alarm? I didn't care which. Maybe just irritation at the monkey who'd used a trailing vine to drop down nearly level with our heads, and kept looking back and forth between us, rapt by our encounter.

"What do you want?" the QB asked. Not openly hostile. Just cold.

"Sign this," I said, slapping the program down on the table in front of her. "I don't know why you wouldn't sign it for my nephew just now, and I don't care. If you have some problem with Maggie West being at the convention, take it out on the organizers, not on a child."

She was looking at me intently now, as if seeing me for the

first time. And she was taking a deep breath and drawing herself up for a tirade. I ought to know the signs—I'd seen her do the same stunt on every other episode of the show and countless times in person when hapless people crossed her. The monkey hissed, as if warning that danger approached.

"Stow it," I said. "If you start shouting at me, I'll shout louder, and you may not like some of the things I'll say, but I'm sure everyone else will be fascinated."

I wasn't sure exactly what I would have shouted if she'd called my bluff, but it's easy to blackmail the guilty. To my relief, she glanced over at the fans in line, and then bent her head and signed.

"You don't want me as an enemy," she said, handing the program back.

"No, I don't want anything to do with you at all," I agreed. "I'd be just as happy not to see you for the rest of the convention. Though you'll see me, if you mistreat another child the way you did my nephew."

I checked to make sure she'd really signed, and not just written something rude in Eric's program. No, there it was; Tamerlaine Wynncliffe-Jones. More legible than usual.

"You'll regret this," she said.

"What are you going to do?" I said. "Fire Michael? Go ahead, if you want to see your stupid show go down the tubes."

She jerked as if I'd struck her, and I smiled, and I'm not sure what would have happened next if the monkey hadn't startled us both by beginning to shriek loudly, baring its teeth in what was obviously a gesture of aggression.

Though when you come right down to it, so was my insincere smile. Points to the monkey for honesty, I thought, as I turned on my heels and walked out.

Behind me, I could hear someone trying to shoo the monkey away, and then the QB's voice.

"I'm tired now, Nate. I'm afraid I'll have to cut this short."

None of the people in line seemed upset that the QB was leaving before signing their programs. In fact, some looked relieved.

Mission accomplished, I decided to detour through the green room for a snack.

I found Michael there, sitting in a corner with Francis, his agent. Michael looked stern. Francis looked unhappy. Good. Michael needed to put some backbone into Francis. Or better yet, get a new agent. A good agent. He'd had a very good agent, back in his struggling, soap opera days, but unfortunately about the time Michael left acting for academia, she'd given up agenting to open a trendy restaurant. So when Walker recommended Michael for the part on Porfiria, Michael had started working with Walker's agent, Francis. Who had been a disaster.

Michael smiled when he saw me, and beckoned me over to their table.

"I mean it," he was saying, as I came within earshot. "You're the one who got me into this. If you can't fix it, I'll find someone who can."

"I'll try," Francis said, standing up hastily when he saw me. "I really will."

Michael was shaking his head as I took Francis's chair. I could see Francis leaving the room—almost running, with his hand in the tweed pocket whose edge was starting to show a faint, chalky residue of crumbled TUMS.

"So," Michael said. "What have you been up to?"

"No good," I said. "I've been ticking off Her Ladyship."

"Good," he said. "She needs ticking off."

"Will you still say that if I get you fired?" I said.

"I'd love it if you got me fired," he said. "It's more than Francis can do."

"Michael!" I exclaimed. "You don't actually want to be fired, do you?"

"I'd rather get fired by the QB than by the college," Michael said.

"Is there any danger of that?"

"The department was testy about how much time I spent away from campus this year," Michael said. "And the QB told me last night that she wants me in a lot more episodes next season. There's no way I can do that and keep up with my teaching, but the way the contract's written, I can't get out of it without a lot of expensive legal hassles. If Francis can't negotiate a compromise—Francis, or the replacement I'm actively looking for as of today . . ."

Michael shook his head, and took a long sip from the cup of hot tea he was drinking.

Just like Blademaster Chris's contract, I realized. Breaking it would take time, and money. Maybe too much time and money. I sighed, remembering all the seemingly necessary things that had eaten up so much of his acting income. Travel expenses, replacing his ancient car, preparations for the house . . .

"I'm pleased to see you're not dazzled by the cult stardom thing," I said aloud.

"Ten years ago, I would have been," he said. "Walker still is. But today—hell, it's been a lot of fun. But it's a bubble; I don't want to jeopardize a tenure-track position for a bubble. So what did you do to tick Her Ladyship off, anyway?"

I told him about Eric's program.

"Why is she so upset by this Maggie West person?" I asked. "Who the hell is Maggie West, anyway?"

In answer, Michael pointed across the green room.

Yes, it was the same face I'd seen in the program. Attractive rather than conventionally pretty. I guessed she was in her early fifties, like the QB, but there the resemblance ended. She hadn't had multiple facelifts, like the QB, and she wasn't wearing much makeup. I could see crows feet around her eyes, and laugh lines around her mouth, and the unruly mane of reddish hair had more than a few gray streaks.

When I looked at the QB, I found myself depressed at the inevitable damage time and gravity does to us all. Looking at Maggie West, I had the reassuring feeling that life wasn't over at any particular age; that maybe in some indefinable ways it got better.

She was listening to Walker—evidently he was telling her a joke. A few seconds later, she burst into laughter. It was a good sound, an exuberant, from-the-gut laugh that made people across the room look up and smile even though they hadn't heard the joke.

Half the men in the room had gravitated to her table, and most of the rest looked as if they wanted to.

"She and the QB aren't friends?" I said.

Michael laughed.

"If Maggie and the QB are both on-screen, who do you think the audience watches?" he said, with a laugh. "I only heard about it secondhand, from Walker and the others who were there first season, but I understand things got pretty hot before the QB fired Maggie."

Just then, I saw Nate walk into the green room. The

writer's reaction to Maggie was atypical. He started, and then headed for her table.

I was curious, so I signaled Michael, and we strolled over so we could eavesdrop.

"Please, Maggie," Nate pleaded. "You know how she gets."

"You mean she's not looking forward to our reunion?" Maggie said, in a husky voice.

"She practically took off some kid's head because he tried to get her autograph on a program you'd already signed. And if she sees you and—Oh, God, not you, too!" Nate moaned, catching sight of me.

"Someone else who has the temerity to displease the Great and All-Powerful Porfiria," Maggie said. "Nate, my enemy's enemy is my friend; please introduce me to my new friend."

"Maggie West, Meg Langslow," Nate said. "Now will you both please leave before she gets here?"

"So what's your crime against Amblyopia?" Maggie asked.

"It was my nephew she savaged in the autograph line," I said.

"So you're the one who rubbed her nose in it," Maggie said, with another hearty laugh. "Walker just told me."

Even Nate smiled at Maggie's laugh, but only faintly.

"Maggie, please," he said.

"Oh, all right," Maggie said, standing up. "I'm supposed to be going onstage at four—do you know where I can find the Atlantis Ballroom, Meg Langslow? Last time I tried to find my way around this dump, I ended up in the laundry room."

"I've been to the ballroom, though that doesn't mean I can find it again," I said.

"We'll give it a try together, shall we?" Maggie said.

I glanced at my watch. Only three-thirty—maybe Maggie wasn't that eager to meet the QB, either.

"I should stay here and take my turn on the front lines," Michael said. "Can you meet me for an early supper—about four-thirty?"

"Four-thirty it is," I said. "Yes, Nate, we're going now."

Maggie and I left through one door just as the QB sailed in through the other.

# Chapter 13

"Actually, I'd love to stay and rile up the old cow," Maggie said, linking her arm through mine as we strolled down the hall with her official escorts trailing behind. "But I don't want to spoil the convention for these nice people. Not the first day, anyway. Maybe Sunday; these things usually get deadly by Sunday afternoon. So you're the reason tall-dark-and-handsome Mephisto is out of circulation."

A trio of fans came up to talk to her, and no sooner had she finished autographing their programs and moved on than another group appeared, and I realized that it probably would take Maggie a full thirty minutes to work her way through the crowd to the ballroom. Watching her in action, I had flashes of recognition. I had seen her in movies after all—as a madam with a heart of gold in an otherwise forgettable western, and as a wise and caring therapist in a tear-jerker that had starred Julia Roberts or possibly Sandra Bullock.

After I dropped Maggie off, I checked back in the dealers' room. Things were slow. As I approached the booth, Steele was shaking hands with the sword-and-sorcery producer. Had they been talking the whole time I was gone? Maybe the guy was serious about hiring Steele.

"Sorry it took me a while," I said.

"No problem," he said. "Your sword-crazy friend Chris

seems happy to spell me if I need to step out."

"Have you eaten yet?" I asked.

"No," he said.

"I can mind the booth while you do," I said.

He shook his head, and I saw his eyes following the producer, who stood nearby talking on his cell phone. I still didn't trust the producer. And more than ever, I suspected Steele didn't mind my absences because he was nervous that I'd snag the commission instead of him. I could have told him that from what I'd seen of film work, I didn't want the commission. But I didn't think he'd believe it. And for all I knew, I'd change my mind if the big shot dangled a large enough check.

"Or if you like, I can bring you something," I said. "There's a fantastic spread in the green room; I can raid that."

"Yeah, that would be great," he said.

"I'll be back as soon as I can," I said.

"No rush," he said absently. The supposed Hollywood big shot was hanging up.

The QB had departed, fortunately, and the green room was more crowded than before. Probably because they'd just laid out an additional wine and cheese spread.

I stepped aside to avoid being trampled in the mad rush to the new food, and found myself standing by a table where Walker was sitting.

"Hi, Meg," he said.

"How's it going, Walker?" I said.

"Don't ask," Walker said. "Have a beer. Sorry, I forgot; you don't like beer. Have some wine. Have any damn thing you like."

He sounded as if he'd been acting on his own advice already.

"Walker, don't you have to go on stage later?" I asked. "For the auction?"

"For what it's worth," he said. "My swan song."

"What are you talking about?"

"The Duke of Urushiol is dead," Walker intoned. "Long live the Queen. Long live Queen Porfiria, the biggest, meanest ballbuster in the jungle."

"What do you mean, dead?" I asked.

"Dead as in deceased," he said. "That's usually what they do when they don't want to renew your contract. Kill off your character. Throw you a big, hokey death scene as a sop, and by episode four of the new season, no one remembers you."

"It's not really that bad, is it?"

"Yeah, I suppose the die-hard fans will remember," Walker said. "I mean, they still love Maggie. Hell, they still remember Ichabod Dilley, and he's been dead twenty years."

"Thirty, actually," I said. "But I meant, is it definite that they're not renewing your contract?"

"Herself told me an hour ago," he said. "I should have seen it coming. Nate stopped calling me by name. He's been calling me 'Pal' for weeks."

"Oh, dear," I said. "Have you told Michael yet?"

"If Michael hasn't noticed he's the new royal favorite, he's an idiot," Walker said.

"Maybe the fans will organize a write-in campaign," I said.

"My one big chance and it's over," Walker said. "I should have done what Michael did, a long time ago. Kick this rat race, get a real job, and settle down with a nice girl. I want Michael's life."

He frowned, as if thinking deeply. I had a feeling I knew where his thoughts were heading, and I looked around for an excuse to leave.

"Of course, now Michael has my life *and* his life," Walker said thoughtfully. "That's not fair, is it?"

Luckily, Walker found this idea so absorbing that he forgot I was there. I slipped away.

I felt bad for Walker. But if he was out and Michael was in, I was the last person Walker needed around right now.

Okay, the second to last. I spotted Michael coming in. Which mean he'd delivered QB safely to her lair. I went over to steer him away from Walker.

"Mission accomplished?" I asked.

"Next time, I want the easy job," he said. "Walker can bring Herself down; I'll go wrestle the damned tiger. Let's eat."

I figured Steele wasn't in a hurry for me to interrupt his tête-à-tête. We filled plates from the buffet and found a table in the corner. I snagged the seat facing out, so I could glare away anyone who tried to interrupt us. Michael looked exhausted.

"All in all, it went better than expected," he said. He lifted a sandwich and eyed it, as if trying to decide if it was worth the energy of taking a bite.

"And it's over," I said.

"Except that I have to do it again in a couple of hours," he said, putting the sandwich down and leaning back against the chair. "If I'm still alive in a couple of hours."

He closed his eyes, and I realized that he really did look quite ill.

"Let someone else do it," I said.

He shook his head.

"I could try," he said. "But they'd end up calling me in eventually."

"Then take a nap," I said.

"I only have an hour before my next panel," he said. "And I'm too wired to sleep."

"And too tired to eat," I said.

He picked up the sandwich and took a bite.

"Try the nap thing again," I said. "An hour's better than nothing, and even if you don't sleep, lying down will help."

He nodded.

"Yeah," he said. "If you don't mind, maybe I should. Only— damn."

"What's wrong?" I asked, as he patted his pockets. "Lose something?"

"The card key," he said. "I gave it to someone to fetch my throat spray sometime during the autograph session."

"Someone?"

"One of the volunteers."

"Who didn't give it back?"

"No, he gave it back," Michael said, rubbing his forehead. "I just remember putting it down someplace because I wasn't wearing my coat, and apparently I never put it back in my pocket. Damn."

"Use mine," I said, fishing it out. "I'll get the volunteers to look for yours."

"Thanks," he said. "Or if they can't find it—"

"If they can't put their hands on it pretty quickly, I'll drop by the desk and have them cut another set," I said.

"Thanks," he said. He wrapped the sandwich in a napkin and stumbled off. I had half an impulse to follow, and make sure he got to the room safely, but instead, I hunted down Michael's two handlers. I sent one to guide Michael and made enough of a fuss to get the other highly motivated to find the missing card key. Then I loaded a plate for Steele and went back to the dealers' room.

Steele had finished talking with the producer. Panels had ended for the day, and the ballroom was occupied by something called the Amblyopian Thespian Competition. The title intrigued me, and I slipped out long enough to see what it was, but the event itself proved tame—a dozen groups of fans reenacting scenes from their favorite episodes in front of an audience consisting almost entirely of other contestants.

"Everyone's probably off getting dinner somewhere," I reported.

"I'm told things will get even slower during the charity auction," Steele said. "How soon will that be?"

"Nearly two hours," I said. "It starts at seven; I know because Michael's one of the auctioneers."

"Unless things pick up between now and then, you might as well go watch him when it starts," Steele said. "I can close up."

"Thanks," I said. "I may take you up on that."

If Steele continued to be this agreeable for the rest of the convention, I'd tackle him on the subject of sharing a booth at future craft shows and Renaissance Faires. I'd been going solo lately, but this weekend reminded me how nice it was to have someone reliable to watch the booth when I was gone.

# Chapter 14

Maybe it's different for a sales clerk on salary, but the self-employed craftsperson or vendor dreads a long stretch without customers, abject boredom relieved only by acute financial anxiety. For the next hour, I exorcised my guilt by minding the booth so Steele could get some fresh air, but with no traffic, any houseplant could have done as much. By six-fifteen, the vendors had voted to close at seven, and Steele shooed me out shortly afterward.

"I can close up," he said. "Go get a good seat."

The ballroom had filled up again, and the Amazon security guards tried to direct me to the Rivendell Room with the overflow crowd. I managed to hook up with Nate in the corridor outside and make my way backstage.

The last amateur thespians struggled through their skit, visibly suffering from acute stage fright. Silly of them—the deafening noise level in the auditorium proved that no one was paying the slightest attention to their performances. Not even the judges, who kept craning their heads to see if Michael and Walker had arrived.

The last skit finally ended. I fished the camera out of my pocket and got ready to shoot. The Amazon mistress of ceremonies introduced Michael and Walker. When they walked onstage, a roar went up from the crowd, and suddenly I felt terrified.

How could someone be the focus of this much adulation and not be affected by it? I watched Michael smile and wave to the crowd. What if all his talk of TV fame being a bubble was just because he was tired and sick? What if, at some point, he decided this was what he wanted?

I didn't mind the occasional trip to a convention, or a set where Michael was filming. But if he got used to this—came to like it more, perhaps couldn't get out of his contract . . . what would happen to him? And to us?

He didn't look like the same tired, depressed Michael I'd seen a few hours earlier. The nap had worked wonderfully. The nap and the energy boost he always got from going on stage.

And I'd been worried about Walker, too, since I'd last seen him in the green room tying one on. He seemed, if not sober, certainly not incapacitated. Remarkably cheerful for a man who had just lost the biggest role of his career. If there was any animosity between the two, they certainly didn't show it on stage.

The two of them, clowning and playing off each other, auctioned off a motley collection of Porfiria paraphernalia for obscene sums. Several hundred dollars for an original script, or a prop actually used on the show.

But wasn't the auction hour nearly over? And yet Michael and Walker seemed to be stretching each item out. As if killing time. I glanced at my watch. Seven fifty-five. The QB was supposed to judge the look-alike contest at eight, and I didn't see her backstage.

"Hey, Meg," Nate stage-whispered at my elbow. "Can you donate something to the auction? Or sell me something, and

I'll donate it? We can't get the QB out of her room again."

"Oh, God," I said. "Yeah, let me run to the booth and find something."

I had to get an Amazon security guard to escort me into the locked dealers' room. Steele had secured the cashbox and the valuable stock before leaving. I rummaged through the cheaper items I had on hand, picked out a couple of daggers, and was about to leave when I noticed a note telling me to look in my cashbox.

I opened the cashbox to find my card key, and another note that said:

*Nate dropped off your room key. What was Nate doing with your room key, anyway? Oh, wait, maybe it's his room key . . . wouldn't you rather have mine instead?*
*Chris.*

I wondered if this was the card Michael had lost that morning or the one I had lent him in the afternoon. And whether the other one would ever surface. No matter. I shoved it in my pocket and raced back to the auction. I handed over one dagger, keeping the other wrapped in my haversack in case they got desperate. And watched Michael and Walker coax bids out of the audience until a beaming fan triumphantly claimed the dagger for three times what he would have paid if he'd bought it from me that afternoon.

While Walker auctioned off a lunch with Maggie West, I saw Michael slip backstage and exchange a few words with Nate. Then he came over to me.

"What's up?" I asked.

"They're still trying to coax the boss lady out of her room," he said. "Will you go see if you can lure her out?"

"Me?" I exclaimed, throwing up my hands. "You forget, I'm not her favorite person."

"Tell her if she won't come out, you'll knock her down and drag her out," he said. "She knows you'd do it, too."

"I'd sic Mother on her, but I suppose you want her alive," I said. "Has anyone tried having hotel security open the door with a master key? For that matter, I bet housekeeping could do it."

"No idea," Michael said.

"I'll go and suggest it," I said. "And then see what I can do."

"Great," Michael said.

He returned to the stage, and I hurried to the wing where the QB's room was. For once, I didn't make a single wrong turn.

A crowd stood in the hallway, staring at her door and arguing with each other in stage whispers.

"She still playing prima donna?" I asked.

"She still won't come out, no," one Amazon said.

"Have you called hotel security?" I asked. "They could probably open the door with a master key card."

"They did," a wizard said, shrugging. "But she has the latch on from the inside."

I could see now that the door was open, but the security latch was on. I pushed the door as far as it would go . . . just enough to peek through, but all I could see was a small slice of beige wall.

"We'll just have to be more persuasive," another Amazon said. She stepped up to the door and knocked.

"Go away! I want to be left alone! I need my rest. Go away!"

The Amazons retreated a little way from the door and looked at each other, shaking their heads.

"This is ridiculous," I muttered. Time to execute plan B. I fished out my newly recovered card key and went into our room. Taking out the dagger, I opened the door to the balcony. If any fans were still camped out, I expected they'd leave when I flourished the dagger at them. But the balcony was empty. I put down the dagger and climbed up onto the railing. The fans had been doing it for over a day now. Surely I could make my way from our balcony to the QB's.

Maybe the fans helped each other, I thought, looking at the gap. What had I meant, only two feet? Two feet was enormous. And how had I failed to notice that while grass and bushes would cushion a fall from the far side of our balcony, the gap between our balcony and the QB's had a concrete sidewalk below it.

Don't be a wimp, I told myself. Clinging with both hands to anything within reach, I stretched my leg over and got my foot solidly on the other balcony.

This is too much, I thought, and was about to retreat, when I heard another knock.

"Go away!" the QB screeched. "I want to be left alone! Go away!"

Stupid cow, I thought. Anger brought back my courage, and I heaved myself over the gap and onto her balcony.

"Who cares?" the QB said, inside. "It's mine."

Who was she talking to?

The sliding glass door to the room was wide open. I peered in.

I didn't see anyone. Not even the QB.

"Miss Wynncliffe-Jones?"

"Go away! Go away!" she shrieked.

"Don't be silly," I said, marching in. "You were due downstairs ages ago. You're keeping everyone waiting and—oh, God!"

Lying between the dresser and the bed was a body. The QB's body. Her dead body, given the wide open yet unseeing eyes. We needed the police—

And I needed to make sure I didn't join her. She'd been talking to someone, only a few seconds ago.

I heard a slight noise in the bathroom. I wished I'd brought the dagger with me. I settled for grabbing an empty wine bottle that was sitting on a nearby table. Holding it above my head, I tiptoed over to the bathroom.

Which was stupid, I realized. I should go to the door, unlock it, and send those persistent idiots outside for the police.

I was about to do so when they knocked again.

"Go away!" shrieked the QB's voice from the bathroom.

I lowered the wine bottle and used the base of it to shove the door open.

A gray parrot. I should have known.

"Miss Wynncliffe-Jones?" someone outside the door shouted.

"Go away!" the parrot screeched, fluttering into the shower stall. "Go away! I want to be left alone!"

"Stupid bird," I muttered.

"Same to you and twice on Sunday!" the bird cackled.

Maybe the bird was right, I thought. I saw a small red stain on the door, where I'd touched it with the bottle. I looked at the bottle. Around the base, I could see a few hairs stuck in something damp. Jet black hairs, with gray roots just barely showing.

Great. I'd not only found the body; I'd managed to pick up the murder weapon. I set it down on the dresser again, resisting the temptation to compound my idiocy by wiping it clean of fingerprints.

Instead, I walked over, unhooked the security latch, and opened the door.

"Miss Wynncliffe-Jones, it's nearly—what are you doing in there?" The pink-clad priestess stood at the door, her hand raised to knock again.

A small bevy of costumed convention staff stood around her, their faces set in worried frowns.

"She's dead," I said. "Call the police."

"Dead?"

"Dead, as in murdered," I said. "Don't come in here, unless you want to become suspects like me. Call the police. Oh, and another thing," I added, glancing at my watch. "Send someone down to tell them to start the look-alike contest without her."

I closed the door to shut out their questions. I figured since I was already in the room, I should wait here for the police. I didn't fancy standing there, staring at the QB's body, so I returned to the bathroom.

"Go away! I want to be left alone! Go away!" the parrot shrieked.

How odd, I thought. The parrot's voice sounded eerily like the QB's. Her words, her voice, even her angry, imperious tone.

But the parrot's body language belied the confident tone of the words. It seemed terrified, fluttering wildly around the shower stall.

Was it terrified of me? Or still terrified by something that happened before I arrived? Would the bird be terrified if it had witnessed the murder? Possibly, I supposed. But I thought it more likely the bird wouldn't react this way unless the killer had tried to attack it, too.

I moved a little closer, to see if the bird was injured. I wouldn't have thought the bird could get more frantic but it did, and called out something else in the QB's voice.

"I can do anything. I *own* them; I can——"

And then the voice broke off into a sound that chilled me. A death rattle. Not that I'd ever heard a real, live person make that sound. Other than Dad, of course, who'd heard it plenty of times during his medical career, and had been known to demonstrate it at the dinner table for the edification of his children and grandchildren. So I knew this sounded like the real thing, and I wondered if the parrot had just repeated the QB's last words.

Figuring I shouldn't scare the only eyewitness, I left the bathroom and found a spot reasonably close to the door where I didn't have to look at the QB.

And then, the minute it crossed my mind that I didn't have to look at her, the temptation to look became irresistible. I craned my neck in a couple of different ways before giving up and stepping closer.

Not a pretty sight, I thought, feeling queasy. I couldn't decide if her face was angry or terrified.

No sign of a wound on the front of her head. Or the sides. Odd. If she'd been hit on the back of the head, why had she landed face up? Maybe I was wrong—I'd have to ask Dad—but I had the distinct impression that if you coshed someone on the back of the head, they keeled over face first. Had someone moved her?

I inched forward, trying to see if there was anything that could explain this apparent discrepancy. From my new angle, I could see her right hand—before, the bed had blocked my view.

She was holding something. A small scrap of paper.

To get a good look at it, I had to lean over so far that I was in serious danger of falling on top of the corpse. But I did get a look.

It was the torn corner of a drawing. From a Porfiria comic book, by the look of it. A roughly triangular piece, apparently torn from the lower right corner of a page, and containing most of a single frame.

Just then, I heard a commotion out in the hall. Probably the police, I realized. Which meant that I didn't really have time to study the scrap of comic before they barged in. Taking it out of her hand would be a stupid idea.

I reached into my pocket and found that I still had the tiny digital camera. I took half a dozen shots of the paper. And a few of the position of the body, and a few more of the surrounding clutter.

I had just barely stuffed the camera back in my pocket when the police walked in.

# Chapter 15

The tiny digital camera in my pocket felt heavier with every minute the Loudoun County police spent interviewing me. I don't know why the photos in the camera worried me so much. If they searched me and found them—well, it wasn't as if they didn't have plenty of reasons already to suspect me. I'd made no secret of how much I disliked the QB, publicly quarreled with her a few hours before the murder, and then capped it off by burgling her room to find the body. My fingerprints were all over the wine bottle they were testing to make sure it was the murder weapon. Surely the photos would add only a slight weight to the evidence against me.

And I wasn't withholding anything the police couldn't find themselves. From the sound of things, they were taking plenty of photos, not only of the QB's room, but of Michael's and my room as well, since the security latch meant that the killer had escaped the same way I'd entered. The cops commandeered Walker's and Maggie's nearby rooms to serve as their temporary base of operations. Presumably they'd move the guests of honor, en masse, to another wing for the rest of our stay. I had no problem with that. Another hotel would be even better.

I could tell they thought I was too bossy. Maybe it wasn't

the smartest thing to do, trying to tell the first cops on the scene how to handle things.

"It might be a good idea to send someone down to the ballroom to tell them the QB—Miss Wynncliffe-Jones—isn't appearing tonight," I'd said when the cops arrived.

"Yes, ma'am," the young officer said. I could tell he was being polite.

"You don't have to tell them why, of course," I said. "But unless you want a constant stream of people coming up to fetch her for the next several hours—"

"We'll take care of that, ma'am," he said, sounding slightly impatient. Great, they'd already pegged me as a troublemaker.

But by the time the homicide investigators arrived, twenty-two more people had joined the crowd sitting in the temporary waiting room. Detective Foley proved more open to my suggestion; and his taciturn partner, whose name I didn't catch, went off to take care of the notification.

I considered it slightly unfair that, being the first person Foley talked to, I had to do all the work of explaining why he was investigating a murder at a hotel filled with papier mâché palm trees and people in strange, unflattering costumes. Also more than slightly unfair that he made only the most perfunctory attempts to shoo away the parrot infesting his temporary interrogation room. I wouldn't have minded if it had been the Monty Python parrot, or even the hysterical parrot from the murder scene, but this parrot's repertoire consisted entirely of trite scraps of dialogue from commercials.

And I was so tired I'd started to nod off whenever Foley stopped to think.

"So, Ms. Langslow—" Foley said, jolting me back to consciousness.

"Do you suffer from heartburn?" the parrot chirped. "Try—awk!"

The detective, who had begun throwing wadded up sheets of hotel stationery at the parrot, scored a direct hit, and the parrot fluttered indignantly to another corner of the room.

"So," Foley said, looking back at me. "Can you think of anyone who'd want to kill Miss Wynncliffe-Jones?"

He leaned back in his chair in a way that suggested a grand finale to the interview. Of course, perhaps that was just an act, and he'd be watching me all the more carefully, now that he thought he'd thrown me off guard. Little did he know that I was wise to the tricks cops play when interrogating suspects, thanks to a mystery buff father who regularly bullied me into reading his favorites so he'd have someone to discuss them with.

So I didn't blurt anything out immediately; I frowned and gave the question serious consideration.

"No enemies?" Foley said, after a few seconds. "What was she, Mother Theresa?"

"No, more like *Mommie Dearest*," I said. "Don't worry, she has plenty of enemies for you to choose from. I was just trying to figure out where to start."

"Take your time," he said.

"Time is running out!" the parrot squawked. "This special offer ends at midnight tonight!"

My paper missile missed the parrot entirely, but then I did have the excuse of being distracted.

"Well, she's been beastly to the hotel staff, the convention organizers, and any fans unlucky enough to cross her path," I said. "But—wait, I have an idea."

I pulled my copy of the convention program out of my

purse, flipped it open to the alphabetical list of guest biographies, and handed it to him.

"One of these three people?" he said, glancing down at the page.

"Not just that page, the whole guest list," I said. "All twelve of them. Well, eleven; I suppose you can rule the QB out. They all had something to do with the TV show, so they all had reason to hate her. You even have pictures of most of them."

He flipped slowly through the bios with one hand while tossing and catching a freshly wadded ball of paper with the other. I wasn't sure if he was reading the program, or just double-checking the number of suspects. Or possibly lulling the parrot into complacency.

"Know where I could find any of them?" he asked.

"Let me see the program a sec," I said. When he handed it back, I flipped to the Friday schedule.

"At the contest," I said, checking my watch. "Most of them are judging or watching the look-alike contest. That was supposed to go on at eight, for an hour. They probably started late, so it might still be on. And after that, I suppose some of them will stay around for a performance by the Amblyopian Minstrels, whoever they are. The rest will either wander through the hotel from party to party till dawn or go to bed."

"That late?" Foley said, frowning.

"These people keep vampire hours," I said. "I don't know what they do at home, but when they're at a con, they stay awake till dawn. In fact, I suspect some of them don't sleep at all until they go home."

Foley didn't look as if he believed me. Well, he'd learn.

"Where is this contest?" he asked.

"Down in the ballroom. I can show you, if you like," I offered, and then wondered if that was a mistake. What if he assumed my eagerness to end the interview was a sign of guilt?

"Yeah, let's check out the ballroom," he said, pegging the parrot with another paper wad as he stood up. "Lead the way. Oh, and we're trying to keep Ms. Wynncliffe-Jones's death as quiet as possible until tomorrow. I'd appreciate it if you'd avoid discussing it with anyone."

Keep it quiet? Was he kidding? What were the odds that when he turned loose the thirty or so people sitting next door in the other commandeered room, none of them told anyone where they'd been for the last hour? I'd lay odds that the whole convention would know within minutes of their general release, and at least a few unofficial fan sites would have the news posted by morning. But he looked serious, and I actually liked the idea of telling curious questioners that the police had ordered me not to talk.

"No problem," I said.

"Particularly details that might not be widely known," Foley said.

"Like the parrot?" I said. "Or the piece of paper in her hand?"

"Yes," Foley said.

I nodded gravely at that and meekly listened to the expected instructions not to leave town without notifying him. Then I led the way to the ballroom.

The look-alike contest was wrapping up when we arrived. The winners and runners-up from several categories cluttered the stage—half a dozen assorted Michaels stood stage left with a small band of Maggies, while a clump of Walkers milled around on stage right with the impersonators of minor cast members. In the center, a dozen pseudo-Porfirias anxiously awaited the decision of the judges. Michael, Maggie, Walker, and Nate. I noticed that the contestants included three men in drag, and wondered whether the QB would have kicked them out if she had emerged for the contest. In her absence, not only did no one object to their presence, one of them walked away with a well-deserved third place ribbon.

As I expected, the four judges awarded first place to the youngest, prettiest Porfiria clone. But then, they still expected the original to second-guess their decision in the morning, no doubt with a killer hangover to sharpen her tongue. They had no way of knowing she was dead.

"We want to thank all of you for coming," Michael announced, while Walker and Maggie shook the final winner's hand and held up her trophy. "Contestants, please gather in the lobby for your group photos."

"And don't forget, the Amblyopian Minstrels will be playing as soon as the tech crew finishes the setup," Walker added.

A cheer went up at this announcement. Michael thanked the crowd and left the stage, heading my way.

"Much as I hate to disappoint Walker, I don't think I can stay up to hear his band," he said, yawning. "I'm all in."

"Oh, so that's who the Amblyopian Minstrels are," I said. "I wondered why they were so popular."

"Yeah, the fans love them, and they're actually not bad, but I can hear them another time. So, even you couldn't talk the miserable troll out of her lair."

I glanced around to see if the detective was within earshot, and took a deep breath.

"No, even I can't raise the dead," I said.

"Dead?" he said. "What do you mean, dead?"

"Someone killed her."

"Please tell me you're joking," he said, suddenly looking much more awake. "Are you sure?"

"I found the body," I said. "Yes, I'm sure she's dead, and not from natural causes. I've been talking to the police for the last hour. They're probably going to want to talk to you and everyone who knew her well enough . . . well enough to be useful."

"Well enough to be a suspect, you mean," he said. "So I suppose there's no use going back to the room."

"It's part of the crime scene, anyway," I said.

"She was killed in our room?"

"No, but she had her security latch on," I said.

"So whoever killed her got in by climbing over from our balcony," he said, nodding.

"In, maybe," I said. "Out, definitely."

"And my card key's been missing since this morning," he said. "And who knows whether Nate was careful with yours before he gave it back to you. At least I assume he gave it back to you."

"Actually, he left it lying around in my booth."

"Figures," Michael said, nodding. We stood watching as the police officers drew various people aside. Maggie, Nate, Chris—most of the Porfiria cast and crew.

"Of course, we shouldn't worry too much," I said. "There's no shortage of suspects."

"No, there isn't," Michael said. "Poor woman."

"Who, the QB?" I asked.

He nodded.

"That's the sad part," he said. "As far as I could see, she was a wretched human being. I'm sure there's someone, some-where, who will grieve over her death, but I can't think who.

A few people will be pleased, though most of them wouldn't admit it, even to themselves. And a lot of people will pretend to be shocked when they're really only dying of curiosity. And some people will be upset, but mostly because they're worried about how her death will affect them. Their careers, mostly. I'm partly in that category."

"Only partly?" I asked.

"I feel a little sad," he said. "But mainly because it's such a waste—of her talents. She wasn't a great actress, but she knew how to make the most of what she could do. And in her own strange way, she was a hell of an organizer. Maybe it's just the waste. As long as she was alive, there was always the chance she'd do an Ebenezer Scrooge and turn into a decent human being. And now . . ."

"It's a wrap," I said. "No more retakes."

He nodded.

"Not to change the subject, but is that the detective?" he asked. "That man who's frowning so sternly at us?"

# Chapter 16

"Yes, that's Detective Foley," I said. "He's probably peeved because he told me not to tell anybody about the QB's death."

"And here you are, telling me," he said, with a chuckle, as Foley headed our way.

"You're not just anybody," I said.

"I suppose you told your boyfriend," the detective said, stopping in front of us.

"He'd have found out in a minute anyway; he was about to go up to the room and go to bed," I said, wrapping a protective arm around Michael's waist. "He's got a bad cold, and he's been up since before six."

"I'll try to make it quick," the detective said. "If you'll come with me, Mr. Waterston."

"Have you got another room for us to stay in?" I asked, as they turned to leave.

"The front desk is working on it," the detective called over his shoulder. "Check with them in half an hour or so."

"Great," I muttered. I couldn't sleep if I wanted to, and I really wanted to. I could keep my mouth shut about the murder with no problem if I could go someplace and collapse, but instead I had to spend the next half hour roaming through a crowd that would give me no peace if they found out about the murder and my discovery of the body. And they would find out, despite the detective's orders. Human nature would see to that. Although, so far, the only convention goers who'd noticed the police seemed to think they were a group of fellow fans who'd come costumed as cops. There were stranger groups wandering about, including a posse of seven large white rabbits sporting red bow ties.

I considered calling my parents who, warned by my description of how wild the convention could get after dark, had taken rooms for themselves and Eric at another nearby hotel. But then I'd have to tell them about the murder, and the last thing the police needed was Dad underfoot trying to help.

I wandered back into the ballroom, where the crowd still milled around expectantly. Musketeers and armored knights rubbed elbows with court ladies, harem girls, and giant iridescent beetles. The costumes had gotten either more elaborate or more revealing, I noted, and everyone was wearing one. And quite a few of the crowd carried umbrellas or wore improvised newspaper hats to guard against the wildlife overhead.

"Excuse me," someone said, tapping me on the shoulder. "Is this your tentacle?"

I turned to see a Michael clone—reasonably authentic, apart from being fifteen or twenty years too young. And he did appear to be holding a large rubber tentacle, though I had no idea why he thought it might belong to me. Probably just looking for an excuse to chat me up.

"Sorry, I have as many tentacles as I need," I said. "What's going on, anyway?"

"The Minstrels," he said.

"Are they still going to play?" I asked. I thought I'd seen the police escorting Walker off with the rest of the suspects and witnesses.

"Of course they'll play," the Michael clone said. "The program's only running an hour late."

"Yeah, an hour is nothing," said the bespectacled gladiator standing next to him.

"At least we're finally on con time," the clone said. "I was afraid this morning that it was going to be one of those totally lame cons where everything goes by the program book."

"Yeah, totally lame," the gladiator echoed. "And mundane."

Sounded heavenly to me.

"But now look!" the clone exclaimed, flinging his arms wide as if to embrace the crowd. "Things are finally happening!"

You could have fooled me. The costumed crowd stood around, talking and staring at the stage, where a few amplifiers, microphones, and other bits of electronic paraphernalia had been deposited, looking more like a stylized representation of a band's equipment than a working setup. Every once in a while, a technician would slouch out from the makeshift wings and fiddle with something, or add another component, and then amble offstage without looking at the audience, as if the success of the performance depended on maintaining the pretense that he was so focused on his job that he didn't even notice their existence.

Not that many people watched with impatience. Everyone seemed to be having a grand time.

Everyone except one small figure huddled in a back corner, clutching a bottle of beer with both hands.

Ichabod Dilley looked anxious when I approached him, as if afraid I'd try to lure him out of the corner.

"Finished with the police, I see."

I hoped he could tell me how the police investigation was going—maybe give me an idea when Michael might be free. But he stared at me as if I were speaking gibberish. Then he drained the bottle, set it carefully on the floor, reached into a brown paper bag at his feet, and extracted another beer.

I counted more dead soldiers in a precise line by the baseboard. Only three so far, but Dilley was rapidly working on another.

"I want to leave," he announced, enunciating carefully.

"Okay," I said.

"They won't let me," he said. "The police."

"Sorry."

"There's a man over there wearing a fur-covered condom," he said.

"Tell me to get lost if you like," I said, "but just how do you know?"

"Because that's all he's wearing," Dilley said.

"Ah," I said. "No shoes?"

"I didn't look," he said. "Not at his feet, anyway. And not at anything else, either. Is that important, the shoes?"

"Just curious," I said.

"I've never been to a murder before," he said. "The closest I've ever come was the funeral directors."

After that, he retreated back into his shell. I wondered whether to take his dazed condition as a sign of innocence or guilt. I shrugged and moved on in search of something more likely to keep me awake, and someplace less crazy to wait.

Just then, I saw a monkey drop into the crowd, swipe an ice cream bar from the hand of a mermaid, race to the edge of the ballroom, and scramble up again.

The hotel had become largely free of wildlife over the course of the day, but one of the last contingents of free-range monkeys had taken refuge in the upper reaches of the ballroom. Most of the chandeliers had one or two monkeys swinging gently on them, and you could see how the monkeys traveled across the ceiling using wires, decorative molding and, of course, the ubiquitous fake vines. Other monkeys dangled comfortably beneath the bottom of the balcony, nibbling bits of food and grooming each other.

The balcony. I could hide there.

I located the balcony stairs.

The lighting and sound techs and the camera crew glanced up when I arrived, but I nodded to them in an offhand but businesslike way, walked to the railing, took out my camera, and snapped a few shots of the stage. Then I looked at my watch, frowned, looked down at the stage again, shrugged, and settled in a corner where I thought I'd be out of their way.

I had no idea what I'd say if they challenged my presence, but I'd seen enough of the convention organizers' operating style to suspect that if I looked as if I knew what I was doing, no one would question me.

At first I thought I could doze off, right there on the floor—the balcony was dark, apparently the better for the techs' work, and every part of my body voted for sleep. Except my brain, which wanted to filibuster. I felt guilty. After all, Michael had been up as long as I had, and was sick to boot, and he wasn't sleeping yet. He was off getting interrogated, poor thing.

I took out my camera and flipped through the pictures until I got to the ones I'd taken of the crime scene.

I skipped quickly over the ones of the body. I wasn't even sure why I'd taken them. Perhaps a fleeting notion that Dad would find them interesting and possibly useful. I imagined, for a moment, how proud and excited Dad would be if he looked at my photos and spotted some key clue that solved the crime. But that seemed a long shot, even for Dad. No reason for me to stare at them.

I studied the shots I'd taken of the room. At first, the room's wrecked condition had excited the police, who assumed the killer had trashed it while searching for something. I hated to disillusion them, but thought they should know that the room already looked as if a hurricane had hit it at two o'clock, when the QB was very much alive. Which didn't mean that someone hadn't tossed the room, of course, but I doubted if anyone could tell which piles of debris had already been there earlier and which the killer had created.

And I studied the frame from the comic I'd seen in the QB's hand—part of a Porfiria comic. But since I hadn't read the comics, I didn't know what the story was about. The little screen that let me preview pictures was less than two inches square. Hard to see any details. A figure that seemed to be Porfiria reclined on a Roman-style couch, holding a wine goblet and saying . . . something. Possibly "Send in the Vegan ambassador!" which meant nothing to me. Then I decided it actually said Vagan ambassador. That made sense. I could see Ichabod Dilley naming a country for the vagus nerve.

But it didn't tell me why the QB had died clutching this scrap of comic. Maybe if I could see the damned thing better.

I recalled from my nephew Kevin's instructions that the camera had a button to let me zoom in on part of the picture. If I could do that, I might see more details. Could be useful.

I wandered over to the edge of the balcony, where the light was better, and studied the various buttons on the camera, all of them rather cryptically marked. I had the sinking feeling that I could play with buttons a long time before I figured out how to zoom in.

And what if I found the delete function instead? In my present exhausted condition, I'd better not chance it. Kevin could walk me through the zoom feature tomorrow.

Better yet, I could e-mail him the photos tonight—he'd made sure I had detailed, written instructions on how to do that—and ask him if there was a way I could get some blow-ups. Maybe if I could find someone at the hotel with a printer and—

"Wild thing!" boomed a voice, accompanied by crashing guitar chords, from a refrigerator-sized speaker about a foot from my head.

# Chapter 17

I fumbled, and nearly dropped the camera onto the cheering crowds below. Apparently I'd failed to notice the arrival of the Amblyopian Minstrels. Walker strutted up and down the front of the stage, belting out the lyrics to the ancient Troggs hit, while his fellow minstrels blasted an accompaniment on guitar, bass, and drums.

They weren't bad, actually. Walker had a decent voice, and more than enough stage presence to carry off the act. The other musicians were pretty good. Actually, they were damned good, and I had the sneaking suspicion that they weren't old buddies of Walker's but the three best studio musicians he could afford to hire. Still, they seemed to enjoy themselves, and the crowd went wild.

The volume of sound made coherent thought difficult, but it did occur to me that if the police had turned Walker loose, maybe the other members of the cast and crew would follow. I scanned the crowd for Michael.

Of course, odds were he'd find a place backstage. And I really ought to cruise by the front desk and ask about our new room before going backstage to look for Michael.

Though I found myself staring, fascinated, at the stage. Walker had been so despondent earlier in the day, and now he was positively exuberant. Yeah, he was an actor, making a professional appearance, but he wasn't that good. His happiness looked genuine. Understandable.

But dammit, didn't he realize how bad it looked?

Would look, anyway, when the fans found out tomorrow about the QB's death. Assuming word had leaked out about his firing.

Or if the police saw him tonight. And they would see him, one way or the other. If they weren't watching live, odds were the con would videotape the concert, like everything else this weekend.

Were they? Yes. Apparently the cameras pretty much ran themselves. One pointed at the stage and the other at the dance floor, and the techs only glanced over now and then— more at the readout that showed how much tape remained than at the monitor.

Did Walker realize this? Probably not. Or if he did, he probably hadn't thought through the implications.

For that matter, Maggie, now dancing exuberantly in the middle of the floor, was going to look pretty happy on the videotapes—though I wasn't as worried about Maggie. She was up front about the QB being her enemy. If anyone taxed her with insensitivity for dancing away the night of the QB's murder, she could simply shrug and say, "I didn't like her, and I wasn't that broken up."

After all, she hadn't gone around all day weeping and wailing to everyone about all the horrible things the QB was doing and then, when the QB actually appeared, doing an abrupt about face and sucking up to her. Like Walker.

But still, even Maggie's exuberance might seem a little insensitive in the cold light of day.

And what if it's not just exuberance, a small voice inside

me kept asking. What if one of them really has a reason to celebrate?

Their problem, I told myself. I scanned the floor one more time. I didn't spot Michael, but Chris Blair was standing at the side of the stage, looking a lot less exuberant than Walker and Maggie. Just then he glanced up, saw me, and waved. I waved back, and continued scanning for Michael.

Not there. Actually, a good thing; I'd have time to check with the front desk about our new room.

But on my way down the stairs from the balcony, I ran into Chris.

"Are you okay?" he asked.

"Fine," I said. "Let's not stand here blocking the stairs."

Not that the stairs were a high traffic area, but I could tell from his unsteady posture that the beer he held wasn't his first. The sooner he got back on level ground the better. I didn't believe in the old superstition that deaths came in threes, but just in case I was wrong, I'd rather see two more aging starlets buy the farm than two more members of the Porfiria cast and crew.

"I can't believe it," he said, breathing hops into my face. "Is she really dead?"

"Did you think it was some kind of publicity stunt? Yes, she's dead. Didn't the cops interrogate you about it?"

"Yeah, but I figured maybe they were just trying to scare us, you know? You're sure? She couldn't have just been unconscious?"

"Chris, I saw her," I said. "I've seen dead people. I know what dead looks like. She was dead."

"Damn," he said. He stared into space, shaking his head slightly. Then he took another long pull on his beer.

"You seem pretty upset," I said.

"I am, kind of," Chris said. "Upset. Feeling a little guilty."

"Guilty?" I echoed.

"Yeah, guilty," he said. "Because I can't help feeling . . . well, not exactly happy. But definitely . . . relieved. I guess that sounds pretty terrible."

"Actually, it sounds fairly normal," I said. "At least where the QB was concerned. You're probably not the only one who doesn't feel heartbroken."

"Yeah," he said. "I bet she wasn't trashing anyone else's life as badly as mine, but I'm not the only one. Look at this."

He opened his mouth, pulled his lower lip down with one hand, and tapped a tooth with his index finger.

"You see?" he said, his words slightly garbled.

"See what?" I asked. Chris had nice, even, white teeth. I couldn't see anything in particular about the one he'd indicated.

"It's a crown," he said. He shifted his head slightly and paused for a moment, so I could get a better look before he took his hand away and gulped his beer.

"That's nice," I said. But I felt puzzled—had the QB knocked one of his teeth out? Seemed extreme, even for her.

"She's got me so stressed that I grind my teeth at night," he said. "I actually broke this one. I have to wear this mouth guard thing to bed if I want to have any left. She's trashing my career; she's trashing my love life; now she's even trashing my teeth."

"Well, not any more," I said.

"No, not any more," he echoed. "So I don't see how anyone could expect me to feel all grief-stricken."

"I don't think anyone does," I said. "Although it might be wise to postpone any actual celebration until after the cops catch the murderer. To avoid confusing them."

It took a second, but he laughed.

"I get it," he said. "That's good. That's what I like about you, Meg. You have this great sense of . . . sense of, um . . ."

"Sense of humor," I said, backing away slightly, thinking that if he breathed on me one more time, I'd absorb enough beer fumes to skew a breathalyzer test. "Thanks. Look, I have to—"

"No, not just a sense of humor," Chris said. "You have a sense of . . . life! The sense that life goes on. I mean, even at a time like this . . . especially at a time like this, with death all around us, you have to affirm life! And grab it with both hands."

"That's not life you're grabbing, Chris, it's me," I said, pulling away from his hands. "I'm not available for affirming. Go back to the ballroom; I'm sure you'll find any number of nice women who'd love to affirm with you."

"But Meg," he protested.

"Chris," I said, "I'm serious. Go away."

Something in my tone got through to him, and he stumbled away, still mumbling protests and casting hurt glances back at me.

# Chapter 18

I straightened the bits of my costume that Chris's roving hands had knocked askew, and then tried to remember where I'd been going when he intercepted me. Ah, right. To check with the front desk about the new room.

Or more likely, do battle with the front desk. The way they'd handled things so far this weekend didn't exactly inspire confidence. For example, the way they'd failed to do anything useful about the parrots and monkeys until the health department showed up. And speaking of the health department, they weren't going to be happy if they returned to check on the progress of the cleanup. The parrots and monkeys had returned to the lobby with a vengeance. While I waited my turn at the desk, I overheard a bellhop giving instructions to a coworker who seemed to be starting his first shift. Or at least his first shift since the hotel's transformation.

"Those are blue and gold macaws," he said, pointing to two birds perched near the entrance to the hotel's restaurant. "They talk a lot. Don't say anything around them you don't want the brass to hear; they already got Jerry in trouble."

The junior bellhop nodded solemnly.

"Red-vented parrot," the senior said, pointing to a red, blue, and green bird that seemed to be sleeping in a chandelier. "They're pretty quiet, thank God. And you see the one over by the elevators? Gray and white, except for the red tail feathers?"

The junior bellhop nodded again.

"African Grey. Biggest troublemakers of the lot, the African Greys. Watch that one a minute."

I watched, too, as several costumed fans strolled up to the bank of three elevators. I heard the ding of an arriving elevator. The fans also heard it and began looking from elevator to elevator, and then at each other, puzzled.

The African Grey dinged again. The fans never did figure out where the dinging came from—eventually the elevator did arrive, and they got in, complaining loudly about what a lousy hotel this was.

The junior bellhop was giggling. I could tell the senior bellhop wanted to, but he kept a stern face.

"Yeah, go ahead and laugh," he said. "Just wait until they pull the same thing on you."

At that point, they spotted some late arriving guests and hurried off to pounce on the luggage. I had to smile when I saw that the new arrivals were a just-married twenty-something couple, the bride still improbably wearing her wedding dress and the groom in his tuxedo.

Had they been in such a hurry for the wedding night that they'd forgotten to change into their going-away outfits? And clearly the hotel hadn't warned them about who'd be sharing their honeymoon hideaway, I realized, as I stood in line behind them.

"I thought you said this was a *nice* hotel," the bride hissed through clenched teeth.

The groom shrugged, and pretended to be totally unaware of the group of Amblyopian belly dancers rehearsing in the middle of the lobby, although the bride seemed more disconcerted by the people bedded down for the night under the fake foliage. Evidently the hotel had given up trying to control the convention. Apart from the night cleaning crew, deliberately vacuuming as close as possible to the sleepers' heads, no one was taking any steps to relocate the squatters.

Well, better the lobby than our balcony, assuming our new room even had a balcony.

Just as long as we had a room. The lobby wasn't an option. The cleaning crew departed, but the scarlet-clad musicians returned and appeared to be succeeding where the vacuums had failed. Though it was less the quality of their performance that evicted the squatters than the fact that they were trying to compose a sentimental eulogy to the QB, set to the tune of Barry Manilow's "Mandy."

The newlyweds finally made it through registration and disappeared down a corridor, earning the bellhops' visible scorn by dragging their own matching wheeled suitcases behind them. My turn at the desk. Though the clerk initially seemed intent on ignoring my request that he find a new room for one of the convention's guests of honor, my eloquence charmed the steadily growing crowd of monkeys who suspended themselves from the ceiling as close behind me as they could manage, and who added a chorus of hoots, grunts, and shrieks to the end of every sentence I uttered.

"I'd like to speak to the manager," I said, finally.

"She's not here," the desk clerk said.

"What about the assistant manager?"

"They were both fired yesterday," the desk clerk said. "Their replacements are supposed to be here Monday. I'm acting manager, but if you want to wait and speak to the new manager . . ."

"No," I said, pounding my fist on the desk. "I want a room, now!"

The monkeys went wild at that. Several of them jumped down onto the registration desk and began pounding on it with their tiny furry fists. Inspired by their presence the desk clerk suddenly remembered an unoccupied room and managed, with trembling hands, to convince his computer that Michael and I should have it. I breathed more easily when he finally handed over a pair of card keys.

As I headed off to liberate our luggage from police custody, I passed the bridal party returning to the lobby. This time the husband was dragging both suitcases.

" 'Oh, no!' " the bride was saying, in a voice clearly intended to mimic her groom. " 'They're not heavy; we can carry them ourselves.' "

"I'm sure it'll be down that corridor," her husband replied.

She stopped in the lobby, hands on hips, looking round and nodding, as if the scene before her summed up some long-festering doubt about the wisdom of the day's proceedings.

"I'll get directions," her husband said, and began picking his way through the squatters. "Pardon me. Oh, sorry, sir; I didn't mean to step on your light saber."

His wife suddenly spotted something that made her jaw drop. Since I had paused to eavesdrop anyway, I sidled to a new vantage point where I could see what she was staring at.

A convention poster, with giant photos of Michael, Walker, and the QB arched across the top.

I frowned, and then realized, with a combination of relief and indignation, that she was gaping at Walker's photo, not Michael's. Well, to each her own. As I watched, she picked up her skirt at both sides and began sprinting down the corridor toward the ballroom.

"Jen?"

I turned to see the husband, still trailing the suitcases, looking around with a tired, puzzled expression on his face.

I shrugged, and continued on to our former room. Or the neighborhood of our former room, anyway. The POLICE LINE—DO NOT CROSS tape blocked the door. I stuck my head in one of the two nearby rooms that the police had commandeered for their operations center. The good-natured sergeant who seemed to be in charge told me that they'd packed our stuff and had it ready in the next room.

"Check it over," he said, waving to the connecting door. "Let me know if you see anything we've missed."

More useful to let me search our old room, I thought, but presumably that was against the rules.

While I was checking the luggage, as ordered, I heard voices in the other room: Detective Foley and his partner. Okay, I'm nosey. I stopped rummaging through the suitcases, kept very still, and strained to hear.

"—but I'm still in charge of this investigation," Foley was saying, "and that's not the way I think it should be handled."

The partner, whose voice was less penetrating, said something I couldn't decipher.

"Then he's an ass," Foley said.

I could hear the partner's chuckle, but not what he said next.

"No, not at all," Foley said. "If we make an arrest and the suspect still has it, it'll be a nice little bit of circumstantial evidence. But odds are it's history already. Or will be, pretty damned quick, if word gets out that we're looking for it."

Looking for what? Foley had the sort of nice, booming voice that's every eavesdropper's delight, but his attention to detail left much to be desired.

The partner rumbled again. Voice and diction lessons for that one, I fumed.

"You can tell him that I'm very suspicious of watches that stop at the time of death, convenient deathbed confessions, killers' names scrawled in blood on the walls, and especially critical bits of evidence found clutched in the victim's hand," Foley said.

Ah. The comic book scrap.

"Anyway, we're out of here," Foley said. "I want to get an early start here tomorrow."

I could hear him as he walked down the hall, complaining about how long it would take him to get home, and how much longer to get back here on Saturday morning. When he was safely out of earshot, I stuck my head in the other room.

"If there's anything you missed, I'm too tired to notice," I said. "Any chance you could call down for a bellhop to help me move the stuff?"

He not only called the desk for me, but when they told him it would take a while—maybe the bellhops were still in parrot awareness training—he offered to have the luggage moved. I left one of our new room key cards with him and went off with the other to find Michael.

Back in the ballroom, the concert was still in full swing. Up on stage, Walker was doing his best Mick Jagger impression, strutting and leaping about with manic energy. Several dozen women clung to the edge of the stage; including, I noticed with a sigh, one slender figure in a bridal gown whose trailing hem was getting a little ragged.

Maggie was still dancing with the energy of a teenager in the center of the dance floor. The Amazon security guard recognized me and passed me into the backstage area, which drew hisses and venomous stares from the women clustered near the stage.

Thank goodness, the police had finally released Michael.

"There you are," he said, spotting me.

"Sorry," I said. "I only just finished bullying the front desk into handing over the keys to the promised new room."

"Great. Let's go. Not that way," he said, as I headed for the way I'd come in. "We'd never make it though the crowd. We can go the back way."

"Will the back way lead us past the front desk?" I asked, yawning. "It just dawned on me that I have no idea where the new room is."

"Don't worry. I've got it covered," Michael said. "Just tell me the room number."

Since when had Michael become good at finding his way around this maze? But I didn't have the energy to protest, so I just handed him the card key folder so he could see the room number.

Michael's back way led through a narrow, shabby corridor into the kitchen, where Michael and the few employees on graveyard shift greeted each other like old friends. Another utilitarian hall led to a room where two middle-aged maids stood in front of a pair of washing machines, arguing in machine-gun Spanish. Michael asked directions in his slower but capable Spanish and one of the maids ended up escorting us to our new room, fuming the whole way at how *estupidos* the front desk staff were for assigning us a room that was so *pequeño y asqueroso*. I didn't know what *pequeño y asqueroso* meant, but I suspected it referred to the room's minuscule size, its shabby furnishings, and perhaps the faint smell of cooked cabbage that seemed to cling to the walls. But I didn't want to ask.

"It doesn't have a balcony, and it's not a crime scene, and odds are we won't be awake long enough to care," Michael said, as if he'd read my mind.

While Michael brushed his teeth, I copied the photos from the camera onto my laptop. I wasted some time trying to find a program that would let me look at them in larger than thumbnail size, but evidently my nephew Kevin hadn't expected that I'd want to do anything with photos but send them to him. So that's what I did. I managed to attach the two photos of the torn comic to an e-mail, telling Kevin enough about them to pique his interest without getting so graphic that my sister would object if she looked over his shoulder, and asking him to figure out a way for me to get some printed blowups.

Michael was asleep before I logged off, and I didn't plan to be far behind him. Still, it was past 2:00 A.M. before I fell asleep. Thank goodness Michael didn't have any panels until 11:00 A.M. Saturday, I thought, as I drifted off. I had to be in the dealers' room at ten, but I needed much less prep time. So we could actually sleep in until nine. Which wasn't all that great, considering how late we'd stayed up. Still, it was better than Friday morning.

The phone woke us up a little before eight.

# Chapter 19

Michael pulled the pillow over his head. I growled, and reached for the phone.

"Meg? It's Kevin."

"Kevin?"

I must have sounded pretty out of it.

"Kevin? Your nephew? You've only known me for, like, fifteen years."

"And I've only been asleep for, like, five hours," I said. "Give me a break. What's up?"

"These photos you sent me? The ones of the comic?"

"Right," I said, sitting up.

"Is that really her hand? That Porfiria lady?"

"That's her,"

"You actually found the body, and she was holding this in her hand?"

"Yes."

"Coo—ul!" he exclaimed.

"I'm glad you like it," I said. "I like it, too. At least I think I will, when I can see it well enough. Preferably on paper."

"An actual dead hand," he said

"Kevin!"

"Okay, okay," he said quickly. "I don't suppose you can leave the hotel and go to a Kinko's? According to MapQuest there's one about a mile from you."

"I really need to mind my booth," I said.

"You can't just leave it for an hour or so?"

"If you could get the photos to me without my having to leave the hotel, I might be persuaded to send you a photo of her whole body."

"Wow! Is it gory?"

"Exceedingly," I lied. "Now isn't there some way you could—"

"Hang on," he said.

It took half an hour, and in the long run I might regret giving Kevin my Visa card number, but he arranged to download the photos to the Kinko's, have the staff there print them out, and then call a courier to bring the photos to the hotel. When I was sure he had it all arranged, I sent him two photos of the QB's body, after checking one last time that they weren't really all that gory.

"I wouldn't have had the slightest idea how to do all that when I was his age," I said to Michael, who decided halfway through my conversation with Kevin that he might as well get dressed.

"You'd have managed," he said.

"I'm sure I would, but this kid is only fifteen, and he already knows. Should I worry about that?"

Michael seemed to find the question hilarious. He also reassured me that I probably wasn't warping Kevin for life by sending him the murder photos.

"After all, the kid watches all the forensic shows on the Discovery Channel," he pointed out. "Not to mention listening to your father."

I'm not sure that last point made me feel better.

Despite the lack of sleep, Michael's cold seemed better. Not to mention his mood. I heard him whistling cheerfully as he went through his usual morning routine.

Whistling "Ding-Dong! The Witch is Dead!"

"You might want to watch your musical selections when you go back out in public," I said, as he came out of the bathroom.

"Well, it's not as if I started it," he said. "Or didn't you like the Amblyopian Minstrels' rock rendition last night?"

"I seem to have missed that," I said, shaking my head.

"They were doing it when I came in," he said.

"Must have been when I was interrogating Chris."

"Interrogating him? Or fending him off?" Michael asked.

"That, too," I agreed. Obviously Michael had seen Chris at convention parties before. And luckily he appeared to consider Chris harmless. "Please tell me Walker wasn't singing that song."

"With gusto," Michael said.

"I'm sure the cops will love hearing about that."

"By now, they've probably seen the video."

"I worry about Walker," I said. "The man has no sense of self-preservation."

"I don't know," Michael said. "He was pretty quick to make sure the cops knew that Francis had the same motive he did, and then some."

"Isn't that pretty low, selling out your own agent?"

Michael shrugged.

"Right now, I have a hard time feeling too much sympathy for Francis. And anyway, the cops were breathing pretty heavily down Walker's neck."

"Probably because his motive is so obvious."

"His motive's not that much stronger than a dozen other peoples' motives. I think what really made the police focus on him was the whole alibi thing."

"He doesn't have an alibi?"

"No one has an alibi," Michael said. "Not for the whole time between when she was last seen alive at about three-thirty and when you found her, whenever that was."

"Sometime just after nine," I said.

"But Walker claimed to have an alibi, and then couldn't prove it. I think that made the cops more suspicious than if he'd just come out and said he didn't have one."

"What was this unproved alibi?"

"He claims to have been off being . . . comforted by a sympathetic fan."

"Sounds plausible."

"And possibly true, but unless he can come up with her name, or her room number, or pick her out of the crowd, I don't think the police will buy it. And for that matter, even if he does find his blond angel of the afternoon, I'm not sure the police will believe an alibi from a besotted fan."

"I'll ask around and see if anyone knows who she is."

"Ask who?"

"Fans," I said. "I'm sure someone will know something."

"God, depressing as it is, that's not a bad idea," Michael said. "If he's lucky, she'll have spilled the beans to someone."

"If he's lucky, she won't actually have had a digital camera with her, or who knows what kind of embarrassing corroborating evidence he'll find on the web later today. Who else did the cops seem to be interested in?"

"Well, Walker and Chris, mostly," Michael said. "And Chris's girlfriend, Andrea, when they find her, unless she can prove that she had an alibi. Maggie, but not as much, because they seem to think two years is a long time for her to hold a grudge over getting fired."

"Maybe they're misjudging her staying power."

"You don't suspect Maggie?" he said.

"Yes," I said. "I'm afraid I do."

"But that's—"

"Ridiculous? Not at all," I said. "I like her. Hell, I admire her; I want to grow up to be just like her. But that doesn't mean she couldn't have killed the QB. I don't suspect her any more than a lot of other people, but I don't suspect her any less, either."

"I'm glad you're not the cops."

"Although, come to think about it, maybe I do suspect her a little more than some people. Hard to imagine Francis or Walker having the guts to kill anyone. But Maggie? If she decided it had to be done, she'd do it with a steady hand and not a single backward glance."

Michael looked pained, but he didn't argue.

"But yeah, the police are probably right," I continued. "If she'd wanted the QB dead out of revenge for getting fired, she'd have managed to bring it off a long time ago."

Then again, what if she had another motive for killing the QB? Something a lot more current than her own firing two years ago.

What if I found out, for example, that Maggie was very fond of someone the QB was threatening to hurt in the present—Nate, or Walker or any of the rest? Killing to defend someone else seemed a lot more in character for Maggie than killing out of revenge for being fired.

Or was I only projecting my own values on Maggie, because I liked her?

"So who else do they suspect?" I said aloud.

"Well, me," he said, shrugging. "But only a little. I think they're still having trouble imagining that anyone would actually want a smaller part. They let that Ichabod Dilley guy go pretty fast once they figured out he's here by mistake. Should I assume from your questions that you're trying to figure out who did it before the police do?"

"I'm sure the Loudoun County police are perfectly competent," I said. "I'm just trying to make sense of it. After all, I did see her body. And probably heard her last words."

"Last words? I thought she was already dead when you got there."

"Yeah, but one of the damned parrots was fluttering around in the room, shrieking out things in her voice."

"I know," Michael said. "Get out! I need my rest! Leave me alone!" he added, in a half-decent imitation of the QB's voice.

"Not just that," I said. "The parrot said something else even more important. At least I think it is, and I'm wondering if the police realize it."

"What did it say?"

I closed my eyes and concentrated.

"I'm pretty sure it was, 'I can do anything. I *own* them; I can—ggggggggggg.' "

"Gggggggggg?" Michael repeated.

"Sorry, I don't do that very well," I said. "It was a death rattle, as they call it in the crime books. There may be a scientific term for it; you could ask Dad."

"Death rattle will do," Michael said, with a slight shudder. "Call me squeamish, but I hope I never meet that particular parrot."

# Chapter 20

I was still wondering what had happened to the poor witness parrot when Michael spoke up again.

"I see what you mean, that what she said before the death rattle could be significant. She was probably arguing with the killer about something she wanted to do with the show. Something the killer disagreed with, and the QB said there was nothing he or she could do, she owned it. Meaning the show."

"Can't be the show," I said.

"Why not?"

"She said 'them,' not 'it,' " I said. "The show would be an 'it.' "

"You're sure? 'Them' not 'it?' "

"Positive."

"Damn," Michael said. "So it's not the show; she only owns the one show that I know of. What else does she own, but in multiples?"

"People," I said. "When I was talking to Harry, the other guy in the sword skits, about Chris's problems with the QB, he said 'She owns him.' Meaning his contract, of course. But that's how he said it. That she owned him."

"And that's how she'd say it, too," Michael said.

"Especially if she was talking about people she was messing with, like Chris and Andrea."

"Not just Chris and Andrea," Michael said, shaking his head. "Even me and Walker. Oh, she wouldn't come right out and say she owned me, at least not to my face, but you could tell that's what she thought. So maybe she was talking to someone else she was jerking around. But no, that doesn't work either. If she was talking to me or Chris or Walker, she'd say, 'I own you' not 'I own them.' "

"True," I said. "Even if she was talking to Chris about both him and Andrea, it would still be you, not them. And while I can imagine someone getting so fed up that they'd confront her about their own complaints, it's hard to imagine anyone tackling her on someone else's behalf."

"Unless it's someone who's paid to do it," Michael said, slowly. "What if Francis went to argue with her about both my contract and Walker's?"

"Was he supposed to do that?"

"Yes," Michael said. "Remember when I was talking to him yesterday? I finally laid it on the line. Told him if he couldn't work out a compromise on my contract, a schedule that wouldn't interfere with my responsibilities at the college, I'd fire him and find an agent who could."

"So he was going to confront her."

"Yes, on my behalf," Michael said. "And I expect Walker wanted him to talk to her, too."

"Maybe Walker wasn't such a weasel, pointing the finger at Francis," I said. "Maybe just a realist. He's known Francis a lot longer than you have. When was Francis supposed to meet her?"

"Last I heard, he didn't have an appointment," Michael said. "I suppose he might have just gone to her room to confront her."

"Would he?" I asked. "Confront her that way? He always seems so . . . um . . ."

"Wimpy?" Michael said, with a sardonic laugh. "Yeah, it's hard to imagine him getting up enough nerve to tell the QB she can't do something, but if he did, that's just how she'd react. That she owns us. Which, from a contract standpoint, thanks to Francis, she does."

"Did," I said. "Not anymore. Who owns you now? Or rather, who owns the show and gets to decide what happens with it? If Francis knew he'd have more luck negotiating with whomever took over after her death, he'd have a motive."

Michael shrugged. I could see by his anxious expression that he didn't like talking about this.

"Who wouldn't be easier to negotiate with?" he said. "But I have no idea who will take over for her in the negotiations. If there are any negotiations; maybe whoever killed her killed the show, too."

"Not necessarily," I said. "She may be the title character, but she's not exactly the star."

"True," he said. "The show could go on without her."

"Queen Porfiria could die and be replaced by her sister," I suggested. "Queen Eczema the First."

"That would work," he said, with a faint smile.

"They'd probably want to rethink firing Walker, too," I said. "I don't think anyone but the QB wanted him to go."

"The fans certainly wouldn't," Michael said. "Walker has a lot of fans."

"Not as many as you," I said.

"No, but almost. The fans would certainly rather have Walker stay. And Nate. If Walker leaves, he'll have to scrap a storyline he really likes. And the way Nate felt about QB, if he hasn't already written a death scene for her, he could do it in a heartbeat. He was always complaining about how she mangled his words."

"You're right," I said. "Michael, what if she wasn't talking about people, but the scripts. What if Nate told her she couldn't mangle his words this time—"

"And she told him that she could do anything she wanted because she owned them," Michael said. "Yeah, that sounds like her."

"Although I have a hard time imagining Nate getting that worked up about it," I said. "I mean, he loves complaining, but would he really kill over a script?"

"I think he cares more than he admits," Michael said. "But getting up the nerve to kill her? Hard to buy. Just like Francis. You'd have to go a long way to find anyone as meek as the two of them."

"No, you wouldn't even have to leave the convention," I said. "There's at least one more person here who might have a good reason to confront the QB if he could get up the nerve—Ichabod Dilley."

"I assume you mean Ichabod the younger, rather than Ichabod the dead and buried and presumably rather smelly by now." Michael said. "What quarrel would he have with her?"

"He's been researching his uncle's work, remember? Maybe he didn't like what he found out. Maybe he read the comics, saw one of the episodes they're constantly running in the fan lounge, and decided to tell her she can't do something or other because it's a blight on his uncle's legacy, or some such thing."

"And she tells him that she owns them, meaning the comic books," Michael said. "Yeah, that fits, too."

We pondered a while in silence.

"So which of our three mild-mannered Dr. Jekylls is actually the murderous Mr. Hyde?" Michael asked.

"Beats me," I said, rubbing my tired eyes. "There's always

the possibility that the parrot just paired those words and the death rattle at random."

"Which takes the suspect list back up to just about everyone," Michael said, with a sigh. "Should we share all this with the police?"

I shrugged. "I'm not sure they care," I said. "When I told Foley what the parrot said, he didn't sound too interested."

"Maybe he's just playing it cool," Michael said. "I wouldn't like to have to put a parrot on the witness stand."

"Yes, and I don't think Foley likes birds," I said. "He spends a lot of time looking over his shoulder for them."

"Don't we all?" Michael said, glancing up at the ceiling in a gesture that had become habitual for all of us.

"Yeah, but most of us are just annoyed, and trying to avoid bird droppings," I said. "He looks nervous."

"Maybe he's afraid you'll solve the murder and show him up," Michael said.

"No way," I said. "I know Dad will be disappointed, but I have no intention of solving the murder."

"So all this brainstorming is just for the fun of it," Michael said, suppressing a grin. "You're just trying to satisfy your curiosity."

"Something like that," I said.

Although that was a lie. I had good reason to want the killer caught quickly. I didn't think the police seriously suspected Michael. But they didn't have to suspect him to hurt his career—his real career, as a drama professor.

I could imagine how the murder would look to the Caerphilly College Board of Regents, whose mindset was something out of the fifties—the eighteen-fifties. They already found Michael's role on Porfiria vaguely distasteful. The longer the police investigation went on, and the more publicity it generated, the greater the probability that it would hurt his chances at tenure.

But I wouldn't mention this to Michael. If he hadn't thought of it, why worry him? And if he had, why add to his stress by letting him know I was worried?

So I'd keep it light when he was around, and while he paneled and signed autographs, I'd do anything I could to help the police wrap things up quickly.

Handing them the killer would be nice.

"I should run," I said aloud. "Unlike some people, whose panels don't begin until eleven, I have to be in the dealers' room at ten."

"Have fun," he said.

# Chapter 21

A good thing the convention hadn't scheduled any 9:00 A.M. panels today, I thought, as I picked my way through the lobby. The squatters had returned, and most of them were still fast asleep—including the tuxedo-clad groom, nestled down between the his-and-hers suitcases. I didn't see the bride anywhere.

And, of course, since I was in a hurry, I ran into Mother. She was standing in a clearing, gazing up at something.

Probably a monkey doing something amusing, I thought, joining her.

But no. She was staring at part of the lobby decoration. Someone with more ambition and energy than artistic skill had constructed, out of papier mâché, the façade of a ruined jungle temple—the sort of thing you'd see on the set of a Tarzan movie, or maybe one of the Indiana Jones sagas. It didn't look all that bad if you half closed your eyes and squinted.

"Amazing," Mother said, tapping her chin thoughtfully with a finger.

"Yes," I said. "Though it's hard to decide which is more puzzling: that anyone would actually spend the time to do that, or that having done so, they'd embarrass themselves by exhibiting it in public."

"Oh, I know the workmanship is inadequate," Mother said, waving her hand dismissively. "But the concept . . ."

She began slowly turning in a circle, looking around her. I picked up her train and shifted it as she turned, so she wouldn't get tangled up.

"Yes," she said. "You know, Meg, the problem with most decorators these days is that they think small."

I made a noncommittal noise. I didn't like the sound of this. Mother had toyed for years with the idea of becoming a decorator, and in the last few months I'd begun to fear that she would actually go ahead with the plan. The one benefit of her coming to the convention was that it would distract her for a few days from her decorating ambitions, and here she was, back on the same subject again.

"Yes," Mother said. "They think small. They change a lamp here, a pillow there, instead of coming up with a truly revolutionary concept. Decorating should not be about creating pretty little rooms. We should be creating environments! Stage settings for more dramatic lives!"

She flung out her arms with enthusiasm as she said this, startling several spider monkeys on the face of the temple into flight.

"I can see it now," she said, staring at the ruin.

So could I. I backed up, quietly, and slipped out of the clearing.

"Meg, when you and Michael finally move into that house—Meg? Meg, where did you go? Eric, come here and pick up my train; I need to find your Aunt Meg."

I sprinted through the lobby and down the corridor toward the various meeting rooms.

Unfortunately, Eric must have been close at hand. I saw

Mother emerge from the underbrush not far behind me.

"There she is," I heard her tell Eric. "Now hold Grandma's dress very tight and—"

"Oh, Lord," I muttered, and looked around for someplace to hide. I ran through a vine-covered opening, then turned and watched the entrance. After a few moments, when no one else entered, I breathed a sigh of relief.

"You can't stay here," a voice said.

I turned and found myself staring into the eyes of Salome the tiger.

After a few moments her keeper's voice broke the spell.

"We're not open yet," he said. "We're only open from eleven to two. The crowds make her overexcited if we're open too long."

As if to demonstrate, Salome curled back her mouth in a growl, but I didn't hear anything.

"She has a soft growl, doesn't she?" I said.

"She's not growling, she's flehming," the keeper said. "When they open their mouths like that, they're actually sucking in air and sampling it with this extra scent organ in the roof of their mouths. It helps them sense things."

"What kind of things?" I asked.

"Food, for one."

Salome flehmed me again.

"I liked it better when I thought she was growling," I said.

Salome dropped something she'd been chewing—the shredded remains of a leather baseball glove—padded over to his side of the cage and rubbed her head against the bars. The keeper stuck his hand through the bars began scratching her behind the ears.

He saw me watching and frowned.

"Don't try this," he warned. "You might think she's just like an ordinary housecat—"

"No, actually the four-inch claws and fangs are a dead give-away. I suppose you can do that because she knows you."

"Yes," he said, giving Salome one last scratch before withdrawing his hand. "And because I accept the fact that she might kill me, or do something like this again."

He pulled back the sleeve of his sweatshirt to reveal two red scars running parallel down his right arm, from wrist to elbow.

"Yikes," I said, stepping a little farther from the cage.

"She ate a Pomeranian once," he said, pulling the sleeve down again.

"You're not serious?" I said, frowning.

"She tried. She would have, if I hadn't distracted her."

"So you're just trying to scare me."

He shrugged, and walked over to the door to hang up a CLOSED sign. I noticed that he didn't have full use of that badly clawed arm. I edged farther away from Salome's cage. Maybe "scared" was good in this case.

"So what makes you want to own a tiger?" I asked.

"I don't own her."

"Sorry," I said. "I realize you can't own a wild animal, or even a domestic one in the same sense you can own a car or a house; that at best we're only temporary guardians of the earth and—"

"No, I mean *I* don't own her," he said. "I can't afford it. I work at the sanctuary. The Willner Sanctuary. They take in big cats and other exotic animals that have been mistreated or abandoned, and try to give them an appropriate environment."

"Sounds worthwhile. But what's she doing here? Even with

the jungle decorations, I'd hardly call this an appropriate environment."

"It takes a lot of money to run a place like that. Do you know how much meat a tiger eats every day?"

Salome chose that moment to yawn.

"I don't even want to guess," I said, watching Salome's teeth.

"Eight pounds, in her case," he said. "Not as much for the smaller cats, of course, like the servals and bobcats, but more, for some of the larger cats. And the sanctuary currently has thirty-seven big cats."

"Expensive."

"So we do educational and fund-raising events," he said, pointing to a jar in the corner.

I walked closer to the jar—it took me farther from Salome as well. The jar contained a scattering of coins and one lone dollar bill.

"Doesn't look as if it would pay for the gas to get here," I said.

"This doesn't seem to be a very generous crowd," he said. "A shopping mall appearance does better."

"So, if it's not working out, do you take her home early?" I asked.

"I only hope I get to take her home at all."

"Why wouldn't you?"

"Mrs. Willner is negotiating to sell her," he said. "The sanctuary's having a hard time making ends meet as it is. If she sells Salome, she has one less mouth to feed, and the proceeds can support the others."

"Sounds reasonable, I guess," I said. "Sort of a bloodless way to let one tiger feed the rest."

"If the buyer likes her, and the sale goes through, I'll have to escort her to her new home."

He stared mournfully into the cage. Salome stared back, looking equally depressed, though for all I knew she merely regretted that the bars prevented her from making him an hors d'oeuvre.

Maybe separation from Salome was exactly what this guy needed.

"So she's going to another sanctuary?" I said.

"No. To a private owner."

"Is that legal? I mean, can anyone just go out and buy a tiger?"

"In most states, perfectly legal," he said. "And it should be illegal to own an animal unless you're genuinely qualified to take care of it, and willing to take the responsibility."

"If you tried to enforce that, half the cats and dogs in the country would be homeless."

"Probably," he said. "Certainly most of the people who own big cats wouldn't be allowed to. And that would be just fine with me."

He fell silent, and I decided that if he and Salome faced separation, maybe I should give them a little time together. I pulled out my camera and took a picture of the two of them, and then I fished into my wallet, plunked a ten dollar bill into the jar, and tiptoed out.

Mother had disappeared by the time I emerged, but I ran into Dad.

"Meg! Just the person I was looking for!" he exclaimed. "I want to hear about the body."

"You generally do," I said. "Walk with me."

I told him the gist of what had happened while we waited

in line at the hotel coffee shop's carryout counter—our new room didn't have amenities like a coffee pot. And then he peppered me with questions as we threaded our way through the crowd to the dealers' room. He paid no attention, as usual, to who might overhear us. Of course, most of the people in the hotel already knew there had been a murder on the premises, but most of them still looked startled when they heard someone at their elbow asking questions like, "Had rigor mortis begun to set in?" and "Can you describe the head wound?"

The answers, incidentally, were "I have no idea; I didn't touch her" and "No, because she was lying face up."

"I wish I could have seen the body," he said, with a sigh.

"I took pictures," I said.

"Really?" Dad said. "How clever of you! Let me see."

But, of course, the tiny camera screen was just as unsuitable for his study of the body as for mine of the paper scrap.

"Kevin's having blowups made for me of a couple of the photos I took of the crime scene," I said. "Call him, and maybe he can add in some blowups of the body."

"Excellent idea," Dad said, "and I should probably see if I can talk to the medical examiner."

He didn't mention the medical examiner by name, so I deduced that it wasn't one of his old buddies.

"If you manage to talk to the M.E.," I said, "see what you can find out about the paper she was holding in her hand."

"What was it?" Dad asked.

I decided to evade that question. Not because I suspected Dad, but because I knew that his idea of keeping quiet would be to swear everyone he met to secrecy before blurting out everything he knew. And if too much information about the comic fragment got out, Detective Foley would know exactly who to blame.

"The police don't seem to think it's very important," I said, shrugging. "Could there be a medical reason for that?"

"Possibly," Dad said. "Of course, they would have to wait for the M.E.'s report to be sure, but a seasoned homicide detective would suspect if something had been staged—if someone placed the paper in her hand after death, for example. Do you think it's important?"

"No idea," I said. "Just curious."

"Morning," Alaric Steele said, falling into step beside us. "Rumor has it you had quite an adventure last night."

"Adventure's not the word I'd use," I said, "but if you heard I was the one unlucky enough to find the QB's body and spent the next hour getting interrogated, then you heard right."

"I'll let you know what I find out," Dad said, "meanwhile, I'll be following a line of inquiry of my own."

With that, he trotted off.

# Chapter 22

While Steele and I opened the booth, I wondered briefly what Dad's line of inquiry was, and whether it would unduly annoy Detective Foley. And then I decided I'd have enough to worry about, trying not to annoy Foley with my own line of inquiry, whatever it turned out to be.

And what I'd overheard Foley saying bothered me. It sounded as if Foley didn't plan to investigate the comic fragment seriously. I couldn't help thinking that the fragment was more significant than he realized.

Of course, maybe I couldn't help thinking that because it was the one genuine piece of evidence that I knew as much about as the cops. And it must be important if I found it, right?

I felt a renewed temptation to pull out the camera and study the photos, a temptation I resisted, partly because I knew there wasn't much more I could learn from the tiny little screen, and partly because the dealers' room had opened and customers were straggling in.

Steele didn't badger me with questions about finding the QB's body, which increased my appreciation of him enormously. Of course, he didn't need to ask questions, just keep his ears open for the next half hour or so while everyone I knew and not a few total strangers plied me with questions. But still, I appreciated the restraint. Almost as much as I appreciated being able to say,

"I'm sorry; the police have ordered me not to discuss that with anyone."

I was saying this for about the seventeenth time when Dad showed up again.

"Meg," he said, "any chance I could borrow that little tape recorder of yours? Unless you're going to use it in your sleuthing."

"I'm not sleuthing and the tape recorder is Michael's," I said. "He uses it to study lines. I don't even know if he brought it, but you could ask him."

"Great!" he said. "Where is he?"

I glanced at the clock and then pulled my program out of my purse.

"He'll be in the Ruritanian Room at eleven," I said. "If you hurry over there, you can probably catch him."

With half an hour to spare, but I didn't want Dad hanging around talking about rigor mortis and alarming the customers.

"Wonderful!" he said, turning to leave.

"And Dad," I said, "please don't go around telling people that I'm sleuthing."

"Oh, right," Dad said. "Keep it discreet. Check."

He nodded repeatedly, looked around to see who might be listening, put his finger to his lips, winked, and slipped away in a conspicuously furtive manner.

"Good grief," I muttered.

"You're some kind of detective?" Steele asked.

"Dad wishes," I said. "He's a big mystery buff. I wish I was the brilliant amateur sleuth he imagines me."

"So you could get the glory of solving Porfiria's murder," he said.

"The hell with the glory," I said. "I just want the cops to solve this as soon as possible. If I could help them, I would. All this notoriety isn't good for Michael's career."

"I should think an actor would welcome the publicity. Especially when he's cleared of any suspicion, as I assume he will be," Steele added, with a half bow.

"I'm not sure even an actor benefits from the publicity of being a suspect in a famous homicide," I said. "But I didn't mean the acting; I mean his career at the college. In the real world, Michael's an assistant professor of drama at Caerphilly College. The administration's already a little dubious about offering tenure to someone who runs around on TV every week in a pointy hat and a black velvet bathrobe. A star turn on *Court TV* might finish his academic career."

If this weekend's notoriety hadn't already, I thought, feeling a queasy sensation in my stomach. Or maybe I was just hungry.

"Are you hungry?" I asked. "I could raid the buffet in the green room."

"I had breakfast just now, thanks," he said. "But you go ahead. And if you need to lie down or something, feel free; you had a long night. It's not like we're swamped or anything."

No, and it wasn't because there were any particularly exciting panels, either. I poked my head in the main ballroom where a woman was presenting a slide show on Porfirian costumes to a sparse and apathetic crowd.

I checked my program. Yes, she was one of the twelve unlucky invited guests.

Then I realized that this wasn't my program—I'd given that to Detective Foley. It was Eric's.

He'd gotten signatures from seven out of the twelve invited

guests—including the QB's, which no one would be able to get from now on. I could use the program as an excuse to talk to the remaining five, several of whom I didn't actually know. Not that I needed an excuse but this would put them off their guard. And I knew I could find a chance to talk to the rest, no problem. And then—

Of course, before I started interrogating people, I would need some idea what to ask.

I shook my head, and continued toward the green room.

At least I'd solved the mystery of where all the fans had gone. Most of them were milling about in the hallway and the lobby, trading misinformation about the murder and gaping at the news crews that had appeared, overnight, to besiege the hotel. Salome's keeper loitered with the rest—the lure of staring at the media must be irresistible if he'd leave her so he could do it.

A blond reporter for one of the local network affiliates was talking earnestly at a camera in front of the main entrance and, out in the parking lot, a petite Asian woman was interviewing several costumed fans. The three red-clad musicians were singing a parody of "Car 54, Where Are You?" in the overly cheerful manner performers use when pretending not to mind the lack of an audience. Near the front desk, where the "Welcome to Amblyopia!" sign marked the entrance to the convention itself, another blond reporter was arguing with three Amazon security guards, while her cameraman stood nearby, holding his equipment at the ready. And, of course, several monkeys hovered overhead, watching intently. They seemed intrigued by any conflict or argument.

"This is a public place!" the reporter was saying.

"Not this weekend," the senior Amazon said. "If you don't have a ticket for the convention, you can't come in."

"Then I'll buy a ticket!" the reporter said.

"Sorry," the Amazon said, crossing her arms. "We're sold out."

"Sold out!" the reporter exclaimed.

The other two Amazons crossed their arms, too, as did the monkey perched on the shoulder of the taller one.

The reporter took a deep breath and was opening her mouth to protest when she suddenly began batting at her head and shrieking. Apparently one of the hovering monkeys had become fascinated with the wire leading to her head and made a grab for it, ripping the earpiece out of her ear and the lavaliere microphone from her lapel.

The reporter retreated from the lobby, shouting something rather incoherent about lawyers, rabies, and the First Amendment. One of the Amazons tried to retrieve the microphone and earpiece from the monkey, resulting in a lively game of tug of war, while the cameraman had begun filming some nut who'd shinnied up a pillar in the lobby and was doing something to one of the parrots.

I moved to where I could get a better angle and saw that it was Dad, teetering just below the lobby ceiling, his legs locked around the pillar. With one hand, he was waggling a piece of fruit, trying to catch the parrot's eye, while the other hand held Michael's cassette recorder as close to the parrot as possible.

"I don't even want to know," I said.

# Chapter 23

In the green room, I scanned the occupants covertly while filling a plate with bacon and hash browns. Yes, several suspects were available for questioning, if I could think of anything to ask.

I scored another autograph for Eric and eliminated one suspect immediately. The mild-mannered elderly actor who played Porfiria's chief counselor had only just come from the airport, and was all agog to hear about the QB's death. I was a little worried that I'd get stuck answering his questions, but the bearded professor I'd seen lecturing several times Friday interrupted his monologue about the similarities between the modern TV series and Chaucer and barged into our conversation. After also signing Eric's program, he began telling Porfiria's counselor all about the murder with endless details. Though not, I quickly noticed, much accuracy.

A convention volunteer standing nearby saw the expression on my face and ambled over.

"Pretty amazing, isn't it?" he murmured. "Just wind him up, give him a topic, and he can go on for hours."

"Amazing, yes," I said. "You'd think by now he'd have accidentally gotten one fact right, but so far he's batting zero."

"Well, what do you expect?" the volunteer said. "Last night we decided, for the good of the convention, to take him out for dinner and keep him away as long as possible. So we all drew straws and I was one of the ones who lost. We collected him at four, after his last panel, and we didn't manage to dump him off again until two in the morning. He missed the whole thing."

"So anything he knows about the murder is secondhand."

"And probably wrong," the volunteer grumbled. "Even if someone told him what really happened, there's no way he'd stop talking long enough to hear it. His mouth doesn't have an off switch, or even a pause button. God, what a night."

"Your valiant service to fandom shall not pass unnoticed," I said. "For that matter, the police might be mildly grateful that at least you've given one possible suspect a good alibi."

"We could be persuaded to frame him, if you'd like," the volunteer said. "We could suddenly recall that he made a very long trip to the bathroom, and came back covered with blood, complaining about a broken paper towel dispenser."

"Sounds suspicious," I said. I couldn't decide whether or not to laugh—I wasn't entirely sure he was joking.

"Just tell me what time the murder happened," he said, "That's all I need. And I'm sure the rest of the pita patrol would be happy to remember it the same way."

"Pita patrol?" I echoed. "Do I deduce that you took him to a Middle Eastern restaurant?"

"No, actually pita stands for pain in the . . . ah . . ."

"Gotcha," I said. "But if you're the pita patrol, what should we call the crew who were shepherding Miss Wynncliffe-Jones around?"

"Happily unemployed, now," he said, "and maybe prime suspects."

I noticed that Porfiria's counselor seemed to have gone into character—not surprising, since much of his on-screen time was spent maintaining an expression of rapt attention while Porfiria delivered harangues at least as tedious as the professor's. "I do chess problems in my head," he'd explained once, when I asked him how he put up with it.

"Maybe you should rescue the poor man before too long," I suggested to the volunteer.

"Yeah, I'll be dragging the professor off to a panel in about five minutes," the volunteer said.

I left him leaning against a wall watching his unwanted charge with a commendably neutral face, and strolled over to a table where Francis and Walker were sitting, both staring down at a sheaf of papers.

Francis, who startled easily at the best of times, nearly leaped out of his chair when he noticed me, and reflexively held out his hand to shield his document. Walker glanced up, waved his coffee cup to me in greeting, and then took a deep swallow, closed his eyes, and sighed with the ecstasy of the true caffeine addict. A transient ecstasy, though. Almost immediately he opened his eyes again and frowned at Francis.

"Have a seat, Meg." Walker said. "You probably want to hear about this, too. We've been studying my contract."

"You can't assume that Michael's contract is identical," Francis said, looking anxious.

"Yeah, right; like you'd actually bother to fight for any changes," Walker said. "Never mind, we all know this clause is pretty standard with her contracts. The upshot," he continued, turning to me, "in case Michael hasn't managed to pry it out of Francis yet, is that as far as Francis can tell, the clause in our contracts that lets her hang onto us for three more years, whether we like it or not, still applies, because our contracts are with her production company, not her."

"Only as long as the show is still being filmed," Francis said.

"If the network cancels the show, you're released."

"But we don't yet know if the network will cancel the show. Do you have any idea when we'll find out?"

"It could be as soon as Monday," Francis said.

"Or not for a couple of months," Walker added. "And even if the show goes on, we have no idea whether they'll keep me or not. Who gets to decide that? The network? Her heirs, whoever they are? Nobody seems to know. So I'm in limbo. Can't take another job, because there's no knowing whether they'll call me back to Porfiria."

"Wouldn't her firing you break the contract?" I asked.

"It would, if she'd actually done the paperwork," he said. "But she didn't; just told me she was planning to. And I have no proof. No witnesses. They could say I was making it up."

"They wouldn't say that," Francis said, in his most soothing tones. "More likely they would say that you were overreacting to something Miss Wynncliffe-Jones said in the heat of a creative discussion."

"Yeah, whatever," Walker said. "I'll still go crazy waiting to find out."

"It could be as soon as Monday," Francis repeated, with more patience than I would have managed at this point in the discussion.

"If I'm not in jail," Walker said. "This is great: the police want to arrest me because I was fired, and the production company still might claim I wasn't fired. Great. Even dead she's wrecking my life."

"She'd have made a hell of a contract lawyer," Francis said.

"And an even better contract killer," Walker added. "You knew her; you used to represent her. Why didn't you warn me?"

With that parting shot, he stormed off. His exit would have been more dramatic if I hadn't noticed that everyone with an eleven o'clock panel was leaving anyway, while some of the ten o'clock panelists had begun to filter into the green room.

I noticed Francis slipping something into his mouth. Another antacid tablet. Why would someone who handled stress this badly ever go into a career like agenting? He had steepled his hands in front of his face and appeared to be taking deep breaths while he chewed.

"Ridiculous," he said, with the overly precise articulation of someone who would really rather be screaming and breaking things. "It would be different if we actually had anything lined up that this would interfere with. Or if people were beating on our doors."

And then he glanced at me as if suddenly realizing that he had accidentally revealed embarrassing, confidential information about one client to the girlfriend of another. I didn't believe it was an accident, but I didn't really blame him.

"You represented the QB?" I asked.

"Years ago," Francis said, shuddering. "About twenty-five years, to be exact. She's gone through a lot of agents since then. And it wasn't precisely me, individually. I had gone to work for a rather large agency—I think they called me a 'document specialist,' but it was really just a glorified name for a file clerk. And then one day, one of the agents called me into his office and told me they were giving me a chance. Assigning me a client. It was all rather disconcerting."

"I can see how it would be, to have the QB as your first client."

"Well, at first it was having a client at all that disconcerted me," he said. "Apparently most of the thankless, low-paying jobs in this agency were taken by would-be agents. I was the only one in the lot who simply wanted a paycheck. Perhaps I should have spoken up then."

"You didn't want to be an agent?"

"I had no objection to it," he said. "The idea just never occurred to me. And, of course, I quickly learned that the reason they'd picked me was that they couldn't really afford to lose clients at that juncture, but no one else at the agency could stand to deal with her."

"And you could?"

"I didn't like it, if that's what you mean," he said. "But apparently I managed to keep her on board longer than anyone imagined possible. By the time she'd moved on, I'd become sort of an agency specialist in . . . um . . ."

"Difficult, high-maintenance clients," I suggested.

"In a word, yes. And after about ten years, another agency offered me better terms for doing essentially the same thing. And four years ago, I decided to go out on my own. I thought maybe I could finally pick and choose my clients. Unfortunately, about half of the clients I was representing at the time chose to go with me."

"Including Walker?"

"Yes, including Walker," Francis said.

I burst out laughing, and Francis looked deeply offended.

"I'm sorry," I said, "but I just realized that you've spent your whole career on pita patrol!"

And to my relief, after I explained the phrase, Francis wasn't insulted.

"Pita patrol," he said, as if savoring the word. "Yes, I like that. I usually refer to them as 'my little flock,' but pitas is more like it."

"Always nice to find a new way of looking at the world," I said. "It's divided into pitas and non-pitas."

"More like pitas and other people's clients," Francis said. "Except for one or two. Michael, for example, but I know perfectly well that I won't be keeping him much longer."

If he was trying to win my sympathy, it was working. I found I not only felt sorry for Francis, but I liked him more than I had before. And felt even more strongly that Michael needed a new agent.

"What was she like back then?" I asked. "The QB, back when you represented her."

"Younger," he said. "But then, weren't we all? I don't remember much about her, back then. I know that sounds implausible. After all, I worked with her for a year and a half. But all I remember from that whole time is a sort of ghastly feeling, like getting hit over the head repeatedly with a sledgehammer."

He sat staring into space for a few moments, as if trying to remember.

"Of course, she hasn't changed much," he said, finally.

"Then why did you let Walker sign with her?" I asked.

"Well, it's not as if we had a lot of other options, did we?" he said. "Not like Michael. If he did decide to put his academic career on hold, there's no end to what he could do."

Time to hit the trail, I thought, if Francis was going to keep dragging the conversation around to his uneasy relationship with Michael.

# Chapter 24

I glanced around, searching for an excuse to leave, and noticed that the show's costumer had come into the green room.

"I'll catch you later," I said. "I'm trying to get all the guests' autographs for my nephew, and I just spotted someone I'm missing."

Not to mention someone whose motives for murder I wanted to explore.

Karen, the costumer, happily signed Eric's program, and I didn't have any trouble dragging the conversation around to the topic of the day.

"Wasn't it exciting, being questioned by the police!" she exclaimed. "Of course, I'm lucky I had an alibi, aren't I? I mean, under the circumstances."

"What circumstances?" I asked. "Was she firing you, too?"

"Well, not that I know of," she said. "But it was only a matter of time, of course. I'm the show's thirteenth costume designer, you know. I bet that's some kind of a record. Anyway, it was such a relief to say that I'd gone straight from my four o'clock panel to dinner. A little early for me, normally; but I understand your mother wanted to get your nephew away from the convention for a while. Poor dear; he did have an awful experience, didn't he?"

"You had dinner with my mother?" I asked.

"Oh, yes; didn't she tell you?"

"I haven't talked to her much today," I said. "But that's good news. After her quarrel with the QB, I'm relieved to hear that Mother has an alibi."

"You don't really suspect your own mother?" Karen exclaimed.

"Of course not," I said. "But the police might feel differently. After all, they don't know her the way I do."

She nodded approvingly.

"I know perfectly well that Mother wouldn't kill anyone," I said. "At least not by bludgeoning. Too strenuous, messy, and generally inelegant. It'd be different if the QB had been poisoned in some clever way."

Karen's mouth fell open, and she stared at me for a few seconds. And then she burst into laughter.

"Oh, my! You had me going for a minute!" she said, through her giggles. "Your mother should have told me what a tease you can be."

If she thought I was kidding, I wouldn't argue.

"I hope you went someplace nice," I said.

"Well, actually we went to one of those noisy places where they have a whole room full of video games for the kids," she said. "But your nephew had fun, and your mother and I had such a nice talk. She told me all about your decorating plans for the new house. It sounds so . . . unusual!"

"Yes, any decorating scheme Mother comes up with usually is," I said. I wondered if she was still enthralled with a jungle theme, and whether or not her rendition of it would include live animals. "Don't noise it about—you know how Michael is about keeping his private life private."

Although, considering how rapidly costumers appeared to come and go on the show, I supposed she'd be lucky to know Michael's face.

"Right," she said, looking momentarily quite solemn. And then her face broke into a smile again. "I was so sorry your father couldn't join us."

Damn. Too much to hope for that both of them had been out of harm's way.

"But it was so nice of him to baby-sit your niece."

"Niece?" As far as I knew, Mother and Dad had only brought Eric along to the convention. Much as Mother adored her grandchildren, she preferred having them around one at a time, ideally with Dad and other adoring relatives available to take care of any actual work the little dears caused.

"Yes, little . . . Samantha? Or was it Sabrina?"

"Salome?" I suggested.

"Yes, of course! Such an unusual name; I do think it's so much better for children to have their own names, instead of a name every other child in their school has."

I made a mental note to speak to Salome's keeper. What the devil did he mean by putting someone he hardly knew in charge of Salome? Especially someone like Dad?

As the costumer nattered on about baby names, I found myself warming to this cheerful and apparently uncomplicated woman. She was probably the only person from the Porfiria cast and crew who hadn't yet said an unkind word about the QB. Despite, I suspected, considerable temptation. And I had the reassuring feeling that anything that came into her ears or surfaced in her memory would come straight out her mouth, unless it was too negative to repeat.

If I could just drag the conversation back to the show.

"Oh, was that Nate?" I said, pretending to spot him behind her.

"Was it?" she said, turning to look. "Well, he must have gone out again."

"Now he's been with the show a long time, hasn't he?" I asked.

"Since the first episode," she said. "Isn't that amazing? He's the only one, apart from Walker and Miss Wynncliffe-Jones herself."

"Makes you wonder what he's got on her," I said.

She blinked, and then decided to assume I was kidding.

"Oh, you," she said, giving my shoulder a gentle, playful shove. "No, if you ask me, he's sweet on her."

"Nate?" I exclaimed.

"Of course," she said. "He's been with her for ever so long—since they were much younger. Why else would he stick with her through all the . . . difficult times."

Yes, difficult would pretty much describe any times spent in the QB's company. But Nate and the QB? Why did I suddenly have the picture of an ordinary housecat yearning after Salome?

I pleaded the need to mind my booth, and headed back to the dealers' room, still pondering what the costumer had said. I took a long way round, though—deliberately—a way that took me past Salome's lair.

I ducked under the vines that screened the room's doorway—had they gotten thicker since yesterday? I was pretty sure they had, and I doubted the convention decorating committee had time to make the changes. Someone definitely wanted the room's doorway to be hard to find. I could think of only one person who would care.

Salome lifted her head and inspected me briefly before closing her eyes and returning to her nap. That was more reaction
than I got from her keeper.

"Didn't I just see you in the lobby?" I asked.

He looked up, puzzled. He was holding a coffee cup that
he hadn't had earlier.

"I went for breakfast," he said.

"Leaving Salome all alone apparently. Not that your choice
of cat sitters is exactly inspired—do you really think my father is the right person to look after Salome while you're off
doing whatever you were doing yesterday afternoon?"

"I have to eat, don't I?" he said, "and go to the bathroom
occasionally? Besides, I'm not really worrying about anyone
going near her with him around."

I glanced over and saw Spike. Someone had tied his leash
around a pillar, and he had pulled the leash taut, straining to
get closer to Salome's cage. He seemed oblivious to anyone
else in the room.

"Anyone goes near her, he barks his head off," the keeper
said. "Freakin' weird if you ask me, but not my problem."

Salome lifted her head again, and when he saw her move,
Spike began straining even harder and whining pathetically.

"And what happens if the knot slips, or he breaks the leash?"
I asked.

"Beats me," the keeper shrugged. "This wouldn't be a problem if you had had him fixed."

"He's been fixed," I said. "This is as good as it gets."

"She probably wouldn't eat him, anyway," he said. "Too
much fur. She hates getting fur stuck in her teeth, especially
for so little meat. So, I hear you found the old dragon's body.
Why didn't you tell me when you were here earlier?"

"Is it just me?" I said. "Am I too hung up on appearances?

Or doesn't anyone else think maybe it might be a good idea not to seem all that cheerful about Miss Wynncliffe-Jones's death? Just while the police are hanging around looking for a murderer and all."

The keeper shrugged.

"Way I see it, they're probably more apt to find it suspicious if you walk around moping as if you'd just lost your best friend," he said. "Nobody liked her; some of us are just as happy she's dead; and the rest aren't all that upset."

He might have a point, I thought. But I felt like playing devil's advocate.

"Oh, come on," I said. "Do you mean to say you don't think anyone will be upset by her death?"

"Well, Caroline Willner, my boss. She won't be pleased, but it's not as if you could call it upset. And I'm definitely not upset. At least now Salome is safe."

"Safe? How?" I asked.

"Well, it's not likely a dead person's going to buy her, is it?"

"The QB was the private owner buying Salome?"

"Yes," he said. "Can you imagine?"

I made a noncommittal noise and wondered if he realized he had just added himself to the suspect list. My suspect list, anyway.

"The woman had no understanding of what's involved in keeping a big cat," he went on. "No real interest in Salome. She just wanted to keep her in a cage in her garden to impress her guests. You can't do that with an animal that's been socialized by humans. If you suddenly deprive them of any real contact with people, it traumatizes them. The mental anguish can make them psychotic and violent."

Way to the top of my suspect list. But I had to admit, as

Salome turned her inscrutable golden gaze in my direction, that if he turned out to be the murderer, I'd feel a lot more sympathy for him than I would for some of the others.

I had a hard time believing that anyone would have killed the QB because of creative differences over Porfiria scripts, comic books, or even the whole TV show. Not that I doubted that it might have happened, but if it did, I'd never really understand the murderer. Financial motives I could understand a little more easily—misguided people often killed for gain, or in a desperate attempt to prevent a loss. But if Salome's keeper genuinely believed that she would be mistreated in the QB's hands, and could find no other way to stop the sale— that I could understand. Maybe not condone, but understand.

I heard a voice from the doorway. Maggie West.

"I just want to look in here for a minute," she was saying, popping out from the tangle of vines.

"Miss West!" the keeper exclaimed.

"Hello, Brad," she said. "How's she doing today?"

"Just fine," he said.

"So you like tigers, too?" she said to me, smiling.

"From a respectful distance, yes," I said.

She laughed, and walked up to Salome's cage. Salome padded eagerly over to meet her and began rubbing her head against the bars. Spike barked a couple of times, and then returned to whining. Some watchdog.

"Oh, that's a pretty little girl," Maggie cooed.

"Little?" I echoed.

Maggie laughed.

"She's on the small side for an Amur, even for a female," she said. "What does she weigh, Brad? Maybe two hundred and fifteen pounds?"

"Only a little over two hundred," he said.

"There, you see?" Maggie said. "I've got two big boys at home who are easily three times that."

"You have two tigers?" I said, looking at Brad to see how he felt about this revelation.

"Eleven, actually," she said. She reached in and began scratching Salome's head.

"Miss West runs an animal sanctuary," Brad explained, "Jungle West."

"Miss West!"

An Amazon guard was peering into the room, apparently unwilling to enter.

"Yes, I'm coming," Maggie said.

Brad, the keeper, watched with adoring eyes as Maggie ducked under the trailing vines and left the room.

He didn't seem to notice when I followed her example— after first checking the knots holding Spike's leash and reassuring myself that he was in no danger of getting loose.

# Chapter 25

As I passed through the lobby, I saw people clustered around the closed door of the hotel restaurant. Shouldn't it be open for lunch by now?

I pushed closer, and saw a sign taped to the door: CLOSED UNTIL FURTHER NOTICE. Below that, in bright red letters, someone had added, "BY ORDER OF THE HEALTH DEPARTMENT."

The fans were already responding to the health department's action, in a variety of ways. Several rude remarks in felt-tip pen already graced the margins of the sign. A few people were organizing parrot- and monkey-catching squads. A few more were organizing fast-food runs. And most were milling around, grumbling.

"I was getting to like the animals," I heard one fan say.

"Yeah, only I was thinking we should have more of a variety next year," another replied.

"And bigger ones," a third suggested. A murmur of general approval followed. I made another entry to my growing mental list of reasons to avoid next year's Porfiria convention. Assuming there even was a next year's convention.

I headed for the dealers' room. Not that I expected much to happen there. The only vendor doing much business was the enterprising owner of the Undiscovered Treasures booth, who'd bought a case of cheap, brightly colored umbrellas and was selling them as "parrot-sols."

I'd begun to regret taking the booth. Of course, when I'd signed up for it, I hadn't expected having a murder to distract me and, more important, my potential customers. Maybe business would pick up later in the day, but for the moment, when the convention-goers weren't in panels, they were out in the lobby and the halls, watching the reporters outside, trading rumors, and getting underfoot whenever the police tried to do anything. Judging by the crowds that followed him, Detective Foley was fast becoming one of the most popular guests at the convention, though he wasn't going to stay popular if he kept refusing to autograph programs.

I found Harry from Blazing Sabers loitering near the booth, talking to Steele.

"Chris said to remind you that we're doing another demonstration tonight," Harry said. "Doesn't look like we'll get much rehearsal time, so we'll just do the same bit as yesterday."

"Do they really think anyone wants to see it twice?"

"Why not?" he said, shrugging. "Twice is nothing; this crowd'll watch the same Porfiria episode twenty times and come back for more."

"Yeah, that's true," I said. "Hey, sign my nephew's program, will you?"

"Sure," he said, taking the pen I handed him and flipping neatly to the center spread. "I love these things; only time I ever get asked for my autograph. Of course, from what I hear, fans have started asking the police for their autographs now, so I guess I shouldn't get too stuck up."

With that, he turned to stroll off.

"Harry," I called. "Are you busy?"

"Nah," he said. "Chris and I were going to work out some new routines, but he's still off driving the porcelain bus."

"He's that hung over?" I said. "Please tell me not to feel guilty that I didn't confiscate his beer last night."

"He's a big boy," Harry said. "Besides, it wasn't the beers, numerous though they were; it was the tequila shooters later on."

"Later on? How late did the bar stay open?"

"Only till one, but the parties went on long after that," Harry said. "In fact, I think there's still one going on down in 232 if you get bored."

"I'll pass," I said. "Look, do me a favor, will you?"

"Sure," he said.

I grabbed a Magic Marker and a sheet of paper, scrawled a sign that read "Get the edge in your next argument . . . swords, daggers, and other implements of destruction—booth 13," and pinned it to the back of Harry's costume.

"And while you're wandering around, how about carrying this?" I suggested, handing him a knife. An unsharpened one, of course, and safely peace-bonded so the security guards wouldn't confiscate it.

He wandered off, chuckling. I stood behind the counter.

Steele had tipped his folding chair back against the mound of empty boxes stored behind our booth, pulled his battered period hat over his eyes, and appeared to be dozing.

"Think that'll do any good?" he asked, from under the brim.

"Who knows?" I said. "Worth trying. Business is a little slow."

"Slow? Try immobile," he said, his voice still emerging slightly muffled from under the hat.

I envied his calm. I kept tapping my feet and drumming

my fingers on the table. I decided not to look at the clock until I was sure fifteen minutes had passed.

Oops. Try four minutes.

Not that I was waiting for anything in particular. But it annoyed me, being stuck at the booth with nothing to do.

In fact, it was driving me crazy. I envied Steele his apparent tranquility.

And I couldn't resist interrupting it.

"So where did you learn blacksmithing, anyway?" I asked.

"In a commune," Steele said.

"A real commune? What was it like?"

"Not my scene," he said, shrugging. "Stuck around till I got the basics of blacksmithing down, then I split."

I waited for more. Anyone who asked me how I got into blacksmithing risked a half hour monologue.

"So you liked blacksmithing?" I asked, finally.

"Seemed useful," he said. "Better than all the odd jobs I'd been knocking about with up till then."

Obviously Steele and I were not kindred spirits. I went back to drumming my fingers.

Luckily, before my nervous percussion drove Steele crazy, a visitor finally stopped by the booth. Not a customer, of course—Steele disappeared back under this hat. But then, I needed to talk to this visitor.

"Feeling any better, Chris?" I asked. He seemed to be holding his head a little carefully.

"I see you've been talking to Harry," he said.

"Look, Chris, I'm trying to get a program signed for my nephew—the one who had such a bad experience with the QB yesterday."

"Sure," he said, reaching for the program and flipping it

open, almost by instinct. He'd obviously signed a few of them this weekend. He had his pen poised above the space before he noticed it was already signed.

"Hey, one per customer," he said, laughing, and handing it back to me. "I already did this one. In fact, I think I remember your nephew. Tow-headed kid with a mean little dog, right?"

"That's him," I said. "Chris—tactless question of the century, I know, but I'll ask it anyway—any chance of getting Andrea to sign? Did she even come?"

He shook his head.

"Back in California," he said. "I found out that much from the police. They, uh, checked up on her. Won't tell me where she is, though."

"For all they know, you could be an abusive boyfriend trying to hunt her down," I pointed out.

"Instead of just a philandering one, you mean?"

I shrugged.

"Look, I'm sorry," he said. "Last night was out of line. I know that now."

"And you didn't know it last night? Maybe Andrea's got the right idea."

"Yeah, probably," he said. "Hey, at least she's got an alibi, thank God. And she's not stuck with a future jailbird."

"You think it's that bad?"

He shrugged.

"The one thing I've got going for me right now is Walker," he said. "They like me for it, but they love Walker. Stupid as that is."

"You don't think it could have been Walker?"

"No way," Chris said.

"Why not? Not that I necessarily disagree with you, but I'd like to hear your reasoning."

"Oh, it's not that I don't think he could kill someone," Chris said. "If he was mad enough, and scared enough, I can see him losing all sense of reality and doing something he'd be very sorry for, five minutes later. But I don't see him daring to kill the QB, even if she was firing him, and from what I've heard of how it happened, there's no way he could have done it."

"Why not?" I said. "No guts?"

"No head for heights," Chris said, "and absolutely zero sense of balance or coordination. I'm his stunt double, remember? And not just for sword fights. Anything where he goes more than three feet off the ground, or anywhere near an edge, they bring me in. Rumor has it you did the balcony climb when you found her, right?"

I nodded.

"Not a lot of fun, was it?" Chris said. "No way Walker would even try that. The man won't even climb a stepladder to change a light bulb."

"Did you tell the police about this?"

"Yeah, of course I did. I'm not trying to withhold evidence that would help the poor guy. I know I didn't do it, but I don't think he did, either."

"Do you think they believed you?"

"Probably not. He's lawyering up, anyway. Don't you love that phrase? Lawyering up."

"I'm fonder of the phrase, 'no longer a suspect,' " I said. "Who do you think did it, anyway?"

"No one with the show, if you ask me."

"Why not?"

"Because it's just a show," he said, sounding rather surprised. "Just a job. Yeah, we all gripe about how she treated us, and if she fires us, we're upset for a while. But it's only a job."

"Spoken with the sublime self-confidence of someone who can probably walk into half-a-dozen better paid jobs the minute Porfiria's canceled," I said.

"Yeah, but even so—the crew can get work, no problem," Chris said. "The actors—maybe some of them won't ever work again, but none of them believe it. They all think the next audition will get them *the* part. That's where Andrea is now. Off in California auditioning. You want to know who I think they should be looking at? Them."

"Those two people in the Amblyopian ranger costumes? Why?" I asked, following the direction of his pointing finger.

"No, I mean the fans generally. All of them. They're the ones who get obsessive about this. They don't like the way a character is developing or how an episode ends, and the next thing you know, there's a dumpster full of petitions in the mail room; the network's mail server is down from the overload; protest sites all over the web. It's a job to us, but for them it's reality. So when the police finally figure out who killed her, it won't be someone who got fired or was paid too little or treated badly on the set. It'll be someone who doesn't think Porfiria should have declared war on Urushiol, or double-crossed Mephisto, or slapped her maid Alopecia in season two."

"That's crazy," I said.

"And killing people is sane?"

I couldn't exactly argue with him.

"Just do me a favor, okay?" he went on. "When you and Michael move into that fancy house in the country with the jungle room and the Moroccan tent room and whatever else your mother has planned, get a damned good security system, okay? 'Cause I'd hate to wake up one morning and read in the paper that you got stabbed by some wacko who thinks she's the chosen bride of Mephisto, and you're messing with her man."

And with that rather melodramatic closing line, he tapped his watch, picked up his musketeer hat, and strode out in the direction of the ballroom.

Okay, he had a good point. Several good points, in fact. I made a mental note to talk to Michael about installing a security system, and another mental note to have a serious discussion with Mother about her decorating schemes.

And then I sat back to ponder his take on who killed the QB.

A fan? Maybe. His reasoning sounded logical to me. But somehow, it didn't feel right.

I was trying to figure out why when a voice interrupted my reveries.

"Have you seen Nate?"

# Chapter 26

I looked up to see Typhani standing in front of the booth.

"No, sorry," I said. "Anything important?"

"Damn," she said. "It's just that I'm trying to be as helpful to Nate as possible. I mean, it would be really cool if he could get me another job in television, you know?"

"So you liked working for the QB," I said.

"Not really," she said. "I'd have quit after the first week, except I knew she'd give me a lousy reference, and bad-mouth me to everyone in the industry, and I really want to work in television. So I stayed—what could I do? Anyway, it's a pain not to have another job lined up and all, but it's not like this one was much of a loss."

For some reason, Typhani's cool reaction to the QB's death bothered me more than most people's. Or maybe hers was just the last straw.

"God, is there anyone not happy that she's dead?" I said. "It doesn't have to be someone who was actually fond of her, you understand. Just someone more hurt than helped by her death."

Typhani was frowning. Good grief, she was taking me literally.

"I can't think of anyone offhand," she said. "But I can ask

around if you really need to talk to someone like that. Only I don't understand what you want them for."

"She's gotten you used to trying to do six impossible things before breakfast, hasn't she?" I said. "No, that was just a rhetorical question."

"That means she was just blowing off steam," Steele translated. "She doesn't really want an answer."

"Okay," Typhani said, and from the look on her face, I could tell I'd just been filed in the category of people to be avoided because they asked boring questions, like what were you going to do with the rest of your life.

"I'll go find Nate," she said, and hurried off.

"Sorry," I said. "She gets on my nerves."

"Look on the bright side," he said. "I bet she got on her late employer's nerves, too."

Even in my temporary, feeling-sorry-for-the-QB mood, I had to smile at that.

But I also remembered how, when I'd found her crying in the bathroom, Typhani had said the QB was too mean to live. I agreed. Hardly enough to make her a suspect though.

A little later, I spotted a suit jacket approaching through the fur, feathers, and chain mail.

"Morning, Ichabod," I said.

"Good morning," he said. He grabbed the edge of our booth table like a swimmer reaching a life raft. He looked awful. Not hung over, like Chris. And not dazed and shell-shocked as he'd been yesterday. More like profoundly despondent.

"Is something wrong?" I asked.

"I learned some very strange and disturbing things last night," he said. "I'm not sure how I can possibly face the fans at my panel today."

"Don't worry about it," I said. "Those con parties always get pretty wild. Chances are, most people won't remember whatever it is you think you did, and even if they do, it's a very tolerant group."

In fact, if he'd gotten a little wild and crazy, it might improve his image.

"It's nothing I did," he said, looking horrified. "It's something I learned about my uncle."

"What's that?" I asked.

He frowned, and stared at me for a few moments, as if unsure whether to trust me. Then the need to unburden himself won out.

"Remember what I told you yesterday?" he said. "About my parents paying off my uncle's debts?"

I nodded.

"It's worse than I thought," he said. "After he died, some very unsavory people came to see my parents and claimed my uncle had borrowed a lot of money from them. Thousands and thousands of dollars."

"What for?" I asked.

"Drugs, obviously," he said. "What else could it be?"

"A lot of things," I said. "Maybe he gambled. Maybe he had some kind of medical expenses. Who knows? I have an aunt who practically went bankrupt buying stuff on eBay."

"They didn't have eBay in the seventies," Dilley said.

"No, but buying stuff you don't need and can't afford has been around for centuries," I said.

"Would anyone other than drug dealers send thugs to collect their money?" he asked.

"You've obviously never met any loan sharks," I said. "Don't automatically assume the worst about your uncle."

"I suppose you're right," he said. "But even so—what am I going to say to his fans?"

"The truth," I said. "Just not the whole truth. And put a positive spin on it."

"How?" he asked.

"Your uncle died impoverished and unknown, thanks to a world that failed to appreciate his genius," I improvised. "And only the love of a few far-seeing and dedicated fans like those attending this convention kept his work alive until the television show could bring it to a wider audience."

"Yes," he said, nodding. "I can work with that. Died impoverished and unknown. Yes."

He wandered off, muttering to himself. He looked much more cheerful. Perhaps I could count cheering him up as my good deed for the day.

And perhaps he'd solved the mystery of why his uncle had sold the rights to his work to the QB for such a low price. He'd been desperate for money.

But did that get me any closer to finding out who killed the QB? Not that I could tell.

I whiled away a little time trying to close a tough sale. Okay, it was for one of Steele's swords, but considering how much I'd left him to his own devices, maybe it was only fair.

Steele gave up as soon as a customer expressed the slightest reservations about a sword. Usually about the price tag. But while he was talking to another customer, a prosperous-looking fan in an Amblyopian ranger costume asked the price of one of Steele's swords and gulped at the answer. So I went into full sales mode. Described all the steps that went into making the blade and then the hilt. Showed him some of the finer points of construction that you wouldn't find on cheap, mass-produced swords. Opened up a couple of reference books to prove how historically accurate it was. And as a grand finale, I dragged out a similar sword that I'd gotten from an inexpensive mail order catalogue, let him see the two, side-by-side, and let him pick them both up.

"You see," I said, as he hefted the two appreciatively, "the hand-made one's at least a pound heavier, but the balance is so good it actually feels much lighter."

"You're absolutely right," he said, nodding.

Of course, you'd notice the extra pound quick enough, if you actually tried to fight with the thing for a few minutes, but I doubted if this particular ranger would ever take it off his wall.

I confess: I was showing off for Steele's benefit. Nice of him not to laugh when my would-be customer said he'd have to think about it, and slipped away, his body language clearly telling me that he wasn't coming back.

"Now I know why you had that piece of junk around," was all Steele said.

So much for my superior sales skills.

"Hey, Meg!"

I turned to see Eric standing in front of the booth.

"Hey, kiddo," I said. "Are you all by yourself?"

"No, Grandpa is over there talking to another parrot," he said. Dad had acquired a stepladder from somewhere, and was perched atop it, holding the tape recorder out toward a pair of blue and yellow birds.

"Great," I said. At least Eric didn't seem bored or unhappy. He was watching Dad's latest antics with the same bemused interest all the grandchildren felt before they got old enough to be embarrassed by them.

"Where's Grandma?"

"She went to a fabric store."

I winced. Mother didn't sew; she only went to fabric stores when she got the decorating bug.

"Oh, Eric," I said. "I got the rest of the signatures on your program. All except Andrea; she didn't come at all this weekend."

"Wow," Eric said. "You mean, you even got . . . *her* autograph?"

"Piece of cake," I said, flipping to the QB's picture. "Nobody's tougher than your Aunt Meg; you remember that."

"Cool," Eric said. "I was going to get her to sign the big photo at the beginning, but this is probably better. It all matches."

Big photo at the beginning?

"Can I see that for a second?" I asked.

Eric obediently handed back the program.

The guest biographies were arranged, three to a page, in a section toward the middle of the program book. Arranged alphabetically. The fourth page, where I'd had the QB sign, contained Michael Waterston, Maggie West, and Tamerlaine Wynncliffe-Jones. I flipped forward one page and saw that the middle spread included Walker Morris, Andrea and Harry from Blazing Sabers, the elderly character actor who played Porfiria's chief counselor, Karen the costumer, and the professor I'd seen holding forth on Jungian archetypes in Amblyopia: The guests whose last names fell between *F* and *T*.

Flipping forward again, I saw a full page portrait of the QB occupying the page opposite the first three guests: Nate Abrams, Chris Blair, and Ichabod Dilley. Eric had already gotten signatures from all three before tackling the QB.

"This was where you were asking her to sign?" I said. "When she said that funny thing to you?"

"That she wasn't going to sign on the same page as that imposter," Eric said, nodding. "I guess she meant Ichabod Dilley, since he was only the nephew of the real guy."

"That must be it," I said.

I handed the program back, and Eric trotted away holding it.

Yes, she probably did mean Ichabod Dilley. But how had she known he was an imposter? I'd probably found out before anyone at the convention, but that was still only a few minutes before one. When we'd gone to her room at two, she hadn't called him an imposter. She'd sounded worried about what he would say. And I doubted the subject had come up during her panel. When did she find out?

Maybe there was no particular mystery about it. Maybe someone had told her between the time she left her room and the time Eric went through the autograph line. Or maybe she already knew. Even if she didn't know him well enough to keep in touch after she bought the comic book rights from him, thirty years was time enough for her to have heard about his death somehow.

But if the QB already knew Dilley was dead, why hadn't she said something when she saw his name on the program?

And if she didn't know he was dead, how did she know Dilley the younger was an imposter, sight unseen?

And, in either case, why had she been so worried about what Ichabod Dilley, real or fake, had to say?

"Something wrong?" Steele asked, interrupting my reverie.

"Long story," I said, slightly distracted. I'd spotted Nate cutting through the dealers' room. He looked upset about something—news about the show perhaps?

"Mind if I run out for a minute?" I asked. "I need to ask Nate something."

"What? And leave me with all these customers?" Steele said. Since the only three customers in the room were browsing in the used book and video booth, I took that for permission.

I caught up with Nate just as he stepped out into the hall.

# Chapter 27

"Nate, what's up?" I asked. "You look like a man with a mission."

"Just getting some coffee before another panel," he said.

"Damn; I was hoping you'd had some news about the show."

"Not yet," he said. "And frankly, I don't think we'll get a decision until the police solve the murder. What if the network announces that the show will go on, and then the police arrest the wrong person?"

"By wrong person, I assume you mean someone connected with the show."

"Well, yes," he said. "I mean, I don't know what we'd do if that happened. And if the police don't find the killer soon, then I think the network will pass, even if the killer ultimately has nothing to do with the show."

We'd reached the green room by this time, and found Maggie, Walker, and Michael seated around a table, laughing uproariously. Detective Foley stood nearby holding a cup of coffee and looking puzzled.

"What now?" Nate muttered.

I strolled over to perch near Michael. Nate followed more warily.

"Have a seat, Meg," Maggie called, waving a spiral-bound booklet toward a chair. "You've got to hear this one."

"This one what?" Nate asked.

"She's a hoot when she does this," Michael murmured in my ear.

Maggie sat up very straight, assumed a solemn expression, and began reading out of the booklet.

" 'Your bath is ready my lord Duke,' the buxom servicing wench announced."

"Servicing wench?" Walker interrupted. "Shouldn't that be serving wench?"

"Shush," Maggie said. "The Duke of Urushiol dismissed the comely wench who had drawn his bath water and removed his clothes after she was safely out of the room."

"Wait a minute," Michael said. "How could she remove his clothes after she's out of the room?"

"She didn't," Walker said. "He did."

"No, Michael is right," Maggie said. "Grammatically speaking, she did, from afar. She has strange gifts, this buxom, comely servicing wench."

"Go on," Walker said. "Get to the part where the babe shows up."

"Oh, God," Nate said. "Please tell me you're not doing what I think you're doing."

"I'm not doing anything!" Walker said, with mock innocence. "See, my hands are on the table."

"I can't stay and listen to this!" Nate warned.

"The duke, hearing a noise behind him, startled," Maggie intoned.

"Startled who?" Michael asked. "Or should that be whom?"

"Yes, it should be whom," Maggie said. "And yes, startled is usually a transitive verb. Has anyone got a red pen?"

"Here," Michael said. "It's not red, but it makes nice little blots all over everything you write on."

"Serves you right for bringing a cheap pen to your autograph line," Walker said, shaking his head.

"I had a nice pen before someone stole it," Michael countered.

"I'm leaving," Nate said. "You know I can't listen to this."

Maggie made corrections on the page, and then resumed.

"Expecting to see the beautiful Sebacea——"

"Ooh, the comely mermaid queen!" Walker crowed.

"Doesn't do a thing for me; I'm a leg man," Michael said.

"The embarrassed duke looked around for something to salvage his modesty."

"Finding nothing large enough——" Walker said, with a swagger.

"Imagine his surprise," Maggie continued, "when he saw the sinister magician Mephisto standing in the doorway, eyeing him with a strange look of intenseness in his aquiline eyes."

"Ick!" Walker exclaimed. "Not of general interest."

"Aquiline eyes?" I said.

"I don't know," Michael said. "I'm dying to find out what the sinister magician's up to, aren't you, Meg?"

"I do not do slash," Walker said. "Maybe it's a character flaw, but I just can't deal with it."

"Would someone mind explaining all this?" Foley said.

Maggie and Michael collapsed in giggles. Even Walker looked mildly amused. Foley looked at me. Was I doomed to spend the entire weekend explaining TV fandom to the police?

"I'd be happy to explain if I knew what was going on," I said. "Why are you all sitting around reading fan fic?"

"I asked Ms. West to explain something one of my officers overheard in the hallway," Foley said, "and the next thing I know, I'm standing here listening to them read me bits of badly written erotica."

"He wanted to know what slash was," Maggie said, fighting laughter. "So we were showing him."

"I came in late," Walker said. "I thought you were doing ordinary fan fic."

Foley sighed, and looked at me.

"After the fans have watched every single episode of Porfiria about seventeen times, some of them write their own stories," I said, "set in the same universe, using the same characters."

"As they understand them," Michael said.

"That's what you call fan fiction," I said. "Or fan fic for short."

"Are they allowed to do that?" Foley said, frowning.

"Bingo!" Walker exclaimed.

"Technically, no," I said. "Technically, Miss Wynncliffe-Jones owns—well, owned, anyway—not just the show but the characters, setting—everything."

"I own them," Michael muttered, but so softly that I wasn't sure anyone else heard him.

"And if you want to use them in any way, shape, or form you need her permission or you're in violation of copyright or trademark, I forget which," I continued. "Say a toy manufacturer wants to do an action figure like this one of Walker," I said, picking up a six-inch plastic toy that Walker had apparently been playing with. "Before they can do it, they have to get Miss Wynncliffe-Jones's permission. Or her heirs' permission from now on. Nice likeness, by the way," I said, holding it out to Walker.

"Keep it," he said, folding my fingers around the doll. "I put myself entirely in your hands. Be gentle with me."

"Watch it," Michael said. "My aquiline eye is on you."

"And how rigorously is this enforced?" Foley asked,

"Speaking completely unofficially," I said, "since unlike anyone else at this table, I have no actual connection to the show—"

Maggie laughed at that, and Michael and Walker looked sheepish.

"As long as they aren't blatant about it, no one really cares, as far as I can see," I said. "If you come home from the movies and fantasize that you're hunting for the lost ark with Indiana Jones, or maybe playing one of the lead roles in *Body Heat*, who cares? It's harmless."

"And it sells tickets," Maggie said.

"And if you're a would-be writer, and you want to put your wish fulfillment down on paper, again—who cares? But at some point, if you start passing it out to other people and putting it up on web sites, and even selling it, the production company has to do something or risk losing their rights."

"It's a little hard to see how anything like that could steal the show's thunder," Foley said.

"No, but what if some other production company wants to do a Porfiria movie?" I said. "They'd have to pay through the nose for the rights—unless they can prove that the QB hadn't done anything to defend her ownership. So, petty as it sounds, by law, unless she wants to let some big crook take advantage of her, she has to slap around all the harmless little fans who are only having fun playing with characters they adore."

"But she doesn't want to slap them around," Maggie said. "For one thing, it creates ill will, and for another, who wants to pay a bunch of lawyers to do it?"

"So nobody's going to search every booth in the dealers' room to see if some of them might be selling fan fic," I said. "As long as they're discreet, they can do whatever they want."

"Except hand it to us," Michael said. "Technically, we're employees of the production company. We're not supposed to look at the stuff. Because as long as the company doesn't officially know it exists, it doesn't have to do anything."

"Besides, it creeps us out," Walker grumbled.

"Speak for yourself," Maggie said, with a grin. "When I find out some guy gets his jollies writing steamy fantasies about me—hell, at my age, I'm flattered."

"Well, you don't get the slash," Walker said.

"That's where I came in," Foley said. "Maggie, someone said you broke up a group peddling slash in the lobby. That was what I wanted to hear about."

"Slash is fan fic that takes two characters from the show who would absolutely not be involved," Walker said, "and puts them in a . . . romantic relationship."

"Usually two male characters," Maggie said, "and for 'romantic,' substitute 'erotic.' But apart from that, yeah."

"So this isn't anything horrific," Foley said. "For some reason, I got the idea it might be something like a snuff film. Or something drug related."

"Nothing like that," I said.

"Just fan fic written by gay fans," Foley said.

"No, usually by women," Maggie said. "God knows why; if I see an actor I like, I fantasize about seeing him with me, not with another guy. The name comes from the slash sign used to punctuate it. Mephisto-slash-Urushiol. For some reason, it bugs Walker."

"Duchess-slash-Porfiria," Walker countered.

"Point taken," Maggie said, with a laugh.

"So we're not talking about anything violent," Foley said.

"No, but it does bring up an interesting possible motive for murder," Walker said. "What if one of the fan fic people got a cease-and-desist letter from the QB's lawyers and took it way too personally?"

"I'll keep it in mind," Foley said, not sounding convinced. He swallowed the last of his coffee and tossed the cup in the general direction of the trash can as he turned to go.

"You know," I said. "Since Porfiria's based on a comic book, I suppose the show's lawyers also have to worry about fake comics, too."

Foley stopped when he heard that, and turned back.

"You see a lot of that?" he asked.

I shrugged.

"Do we see it? No," Maggie said. "We work very hard at not seeing it. But it happens."

"I suspect you can find a lot of it in the dealers' room," I said. "Most of it's probably pretty crude and amateurish, but some of it, I bet you'd think it was the real thing."

Foley glanced back at me and nodded. Then he turned on his heel, and this time, he made it out the door.

"What was that in aid of?" Michael said.

Okay, so maybe the cops weren't as short-sighted about the comic scrap as I'd assumed.

"I wish they could leave the poor fans alone," Maggie said. "Who are they really hurting?"

"It's a legal thing," Walker said, with a shrug.

"Oh, and as long as it's legal, it's perfectly fine, right?" Maggie said. "Remember that the next time you're complaining about your contract."

"You know what strikes me when I look at this stuff?" I said. "It's not that different from what Ichabod Dilley was doing when he first started writing and drawing the Porfiria stories."

"He made up his own world," Michael said.

"Out of bits and pieces of popular culture," I said. "Tell me you don't see bits of Conan and Tarzan and Tolkien characters in the Porfiria comics. And I bet the early underground comics were just as crudely produced as these are."

"Worse, from what I remember," Maggie said.

"And come to think of it, if Ichabod Dilley were still alive, I wonder if he'd have to get the QB's permission to do new Porfiria comics, too."

"Is this significant?" Michael asked. He didn't say more, apparently remembering that he was the only one here who knew anything about the scrap of comic I'd found in the QB's hand.

"I don't know," I said.

Just then, we noticed a couple of convention volunteers lurking in the doorway.

# Chapter 28

"Come on, boys," Maggie said. "It's time for lunch with the stars. Assuming they've found a restaurant that's open."

"Lunch with the stars?" I repeated.

"We each sit at a table with eleven people who have donated obscene amounts of money to charity for the privilege," Michael said. "Dinner, however, is another story. I would rather dine with the star of my own personal firmament, if you can get away from your booth for an hour."

"Flattery will get you anywhere, and Chris can fill in at the booth," I said. "He owes me. What time?"

"Probably around six," he said. "Early, anyway. I can come by when I'm free. We have to make it early, because the festivities start up again at seven. We're judging the open costume competition."

"And Chris and Harry and I are doing another stage combat demonstration," I said. "As if everyone at the convention didn't get to see me stab myself in the foot the first time around."

"Well, I didn't see it," he complained. "I was off signing, remember?"

"I take it back," I said. "For you, I'll gladly make a fool of myself again."

"That's the spirit," he said. "I've been doing that all day, and people keep applauding. Gotta run; try not to tick off

Foley so much that he arrests you before dinner."

"I have no intention of ticking him off at all," I called after him, as he headed for the door. "I'll be sitting in my booth."

"I thought you'd be sleuthing,"

"That, too."

As I turned to go, I realized that they'd left the dozen or so samples of fan fic on the table. I tidied them into my tote. Odds were they had nothing to do with the murder, but you never knew.

But as I walked back to the dealers' room, I found myself thinking about the fan fic. And about the scrap of paper I'd found in the QB's hand. Was it fan fic, or the real thing?

And was it perceptive, or just stupidly obsessive, to keep coming back to that scrap of paper? And to the perhaps irrational feeling that to understand it, I needed to know a lot more about what happened back in 1972? Maybe it was a good thing that I'd steered Foley to the fake Porfiria comics in the dealers' room. But it would be even better if he'd poke into the real ones. Into the past. Would it do any good to suggest it?

No harm, anyway.

When I got to the dealers' room, I found Foley himself standing just outside the door. He looked free, so I decided to tackle him.

"Have you got a moment?" I asked.

"Yes," he said, glancing at his watch as if to say, "But only a moment, so make it snappy."

"Look, this may sound stupid, but are you looking at what happened back in 1972?"

"For example?"

"For example, that around 1972, Miss Wynncliffe-Jones bought all the rights to the Porfiria comic books for a sum now widely considered larcenously low? That shortly afterward, Ichabod Dilley, the creator of the comics, died under suspicious circumstances? And that the piece of paper found in her hand appeared to be a portion of one of those comics? A piece of paper, of course, that I haven't told anybody about, apart from Michael."

"We appreciate your discretion," Foley said. "And we'd appreciate if you'd continue keeping quiet about the scrap of paper, although I don't think it's that strong a link to 1972. From what I hear, even the original comic books wouldn't be all that valuable if not for the TV fans."

He sounded—well, not exactly patient. More like he'd had plenty of practice in not sounding impatient.

"What about the fact that Francis used to be her agent back then?"

He looked a little less deliberately patient at that.

"I imagine he's had a lot of clients if he's been in the business that long."

"You're probably right," I said. "And he's probably seen a lot of them murdered, too; you know what a cutthroat place Hollywood is."

Foley's lips twitched slightly, but he didn't say anything.

"Was there anything else?" he asked.

"What about the rumor that the relationship between Nate Abrams and Miss Wynncliffe-Jones was more than professional?"

Okay, I was grasping at straws here. The more I thought about Karen the costumer's hint that Nate was—how had she put it?—sweet on the QB, the more I dismissed it as her overly romantic interpretation of events. And did Foley's remarkably blank expression mean that he found this interesting, or just that he was really tired of listening to me?

"I don't suppose you know anything to substantiate this rumor?" he asked.

"No, but if I hear anything, I'll let you know."

I expected him to ask who I'd heard the rumor from, or warn me about not interfering in a police investigation, but he simply nodded and walked off.

Damn. I didn't get the feeling he'd totally ignored me, but I knew I hadn't convinced him. Not surprising; all I had was my gut feeling that whatever happened in 1972 had something to do with the murder. Not much to go on.

But it was all I had. And just in case Foley's focus on present-day motives didn't work out, maybe someone should look into the past. Or start looking, anyway. By Sunday afternoon, the suspects would scatter over the continent. How far could I get in a day and a half?

At least I knew where to start. With the comic books.

"No way," Cordelia said, a few minutes later. "Do you know what those comics are worth?"

"I don't want you to give them to me," I said. "I just want to look at them. It's important."

"Why?"

Probably not a good idea to say I was trying to solve the QB's murder.

"There were only twelve Porfiria comic books ever published, right?" I asked.

"Right."

"So what would you say if I told you there might be another one?"

"You have a lead on the Lost Thirteenth Porfiria?" Cordelia said, in hushed tones.

Apparently I'd accidentally tapped into an existing rumor.

"Maybe," I said. "I need to study the twelve again first."

Again. As if I'd ever actually read any of them.

"If you get it, you'll let me handle the sale? This could be the biggest thing since . . . well, I don't remember anything like it. You will, right?"

"Absolutely."

Definitely an existing rumor—and not just any rumor, but one of mythic proportions in the comic book world.

It took me fifteen more minutes of wheedling, and in the end, I had to bribe her, but I finally talked Cordelia into letting me borrow all twelve issues of the original Porfiria. Chris willingly agreed to take my place at the booth. I left him and Steele perched at the two ends of the booth like matching gargoyles and stole away to my room to read the comics.

And was surprised to find Michael there, lying on the bed with a wet washcloth draped over his face.

"In the movies, they usually find something a little larger to put over the body," I said.

"Well, I'm not that far gone yet," he said, with a weak laugh. "Head's killing me, though. Congestion. Thank heaven I have a break."

"What happened to lunch with the stars?" I said.

"Postponed until tomorrow," he said, "assuming either the health department reopens the restaurant or they find an alternate site. Just as well. I'm exhausted."

"I could leave," I offered.

"No, stay," he said. "Your company will hasten my recovery, as long as you can manage not to tell me all the medical events currently happening in my lungs and sinuses. I really don't want to think about all that."

"Ah, you've been talking to Dad, then," I said. "I was wondering what he was up to."

"I just thought I'd ask what decongestants he recommends,"

Michael grumbled. "How was I supposed to know that he considers decongestants a dangerous interference with the drainage that is part of the body's natural healing process?"

"Because it's been at least a year since you had a cold," I said. "He goes off on these natural healing kicks every few years. I happen to have brought some of the decongestants he recommends when he's in his normal, better-living-through-chemicals mode. I suspected you might need them before the con was over."

"You're an angel," Michael said. "And if you wouldn't mind running some hot water over this compress . . ."

With his compress reheated and the promise of relief washed down by a cold Coke, Michael perked up sufficiently to notice what I was doing.

"I presume there's a murder-related reason for you to be sitting here reading comic books instead of minding your booth?" he asked, in a voice slightly muffled by the washcloth.

"Was that a slam at comic books?" I asked. "Although actually, I think 'graphic novels' probably are better words after all."

"Makes you feel less silly?"

" 'Comics' seems to imply a cartoonish style, and there's nothing cartoonish about Ichabod Dilley's drawings. Elegant's more like it. The man's brilliant. Or was brilliant, more's the pity."

"I could work up a good fit of jealousy over that remark if the poor wretch weren't dead," Michael said.

# Chapter 29

In between trips to the bathroom to reheat Michael's compress, I went through all twelve comics, page by page, comparing each frame with the shot in my camera. It took most of the hour. I could probably have done it in half the time, even with the compresses, if not for the plastic gloves I was wearing.

"What's with the gloves, anyway?" Michael asked.

"They're supposed to protect the paper from the oils on my skin," I said. "I suppose it makes sense; the paper's pretty brittle and yellow already."

"I didn't realize you collected comics."

"I don't," I said. "I borrowed them from Cordelia. She provided the gloves. And even though she isn't here to see, I have this sneaking feeling she'd find out if I don't follow orders. She probably has an inventory of every nick and tear on every page, and I'll never hear the end of it if I make any more."

Of course, after a while, I did get used to the gloves, but by that time, I had gotten caught up in the story.

"Caught up in Porfiria?" Michael echoed, when I told him as much. "Maybe you need the compress."

"No, seriously," I said. "It's not that they're necessarily better than the TV show, but they're certainly different."

"From a different era," Michael suggested.

"That's partly it," I said. "Definitely pre-PC. In the TV show, Porfiria's a very modern woman. Undisputed ruler of her country. Courtiers and counselors leap to do her bidding. Whenever things look darkest for Amblyopia, Porfiria frowns, looks thoughtful, and then comes up with a plan that saves the day."

"Or at least knows exactly who to send for to save the day," Michael said. " 'My lord wizard, I have need of your subtle and devious mind.' "

"Don't gloat. Yes, on TV she usually calls Mephisto, but he doesn't exist in the comics. The way Dilley wrote it, Porfiria was ruler in name only—her regents were supposed to run things until they found her a suitable husband; and since whoever married her would, under Amblyopian law, become king, the regents were in no hurry to arrange the wedding."

"Is that our problem?" Michael asked. "Evil regents?"

"I don't know about evil," I said. "Porfiria seems to enjoy her unmarried state. She spends most of her time lolling around scantily dressed, eating bonbons, taking endless bubble baths, and ogling whatever handsome young men wander into the frame."

"Sounds like the QB," Michael said.

"And in each issue, whenever things look grimmest, Porfiria arrives on the scene, bats her eyelashes, and uses her apparently irresistible charms to save the day—usually by seducing one or more of Amblyopia's direst foes."

"So there's something to the Kansas relatives' accusation of pornography, after all," Michael said, with a muffled chuckle. "I should have read those comics ages ago."

"I wouldn't bother taking off the washcloth," I said. "The relatives overreacted. Everything happens off-stage. Porfiria invites the Pellagran ambassador or the heir to the throne of

Niacin into her private garden for a conference, and the next few panels show her courtiers standing outside, watching garments sailing over the garden wall, hearing titters and bits of mildly risqué dialogue. But only mildly risqué; not pornographic or raunchy."

"That's odd," Michael said. "Doesn't fit my image of underground comics."

"Mine either."

"I mean, with the TV show, we've got the network standards and practices office to keep us from going too far," Michael said. "Much to Nate's dismay; he has a positive genius for writing accidental double entendres."

"Fine by me," I said. I might be in the minority, but I was just as happy that the QB's vision for the show hadn't included graphic love scenes. I could do without seeing Michael in bed with any of the show's parade of twenty-something starlets.

"But Dilley didn't have any censors watching over his shoulder, unless the early seventies were a great deal less freewheeling than people made them sound," Michael said.

"And yet there's nothing here that would upset the network," I said. "You see worse on sitcoms every day. I wonder why."

"Good taste?"

"Or maybe just a lack of firsthand material to work from," I said.

I flipped back a few pages.

"Yeah," I said, "My money's on inexperience. There's a certain adolescent quality to the drawings. The content, not the style. Exuberance and bashfulness in equal measure. A desire to shock the audience, but underneath, the lingering fear that the audience might not be shocked after all—might only laugh."

"That's surprising," Michael said.

"Why? After all, his nephew said he was only about twenty when he died. He might not have had all that much sexual experience."

"You'd think he'd have learned a few things, hanging around Haight Ashbury in the Summer of Love," Michael said.

"You can't prove it from the Porfiria comics. Maybe he was a late bloomer."

Michael abandoned his compress long enough to look over my shoulder and agree that, yes, the comics were singularly innocent, all things considered.

"I wonder why," he mused, disappearing again under the washcloth. "I think it's more apt to be lack of nerve, not lack of experience."

No way to tell, really, I thought. Not my generation or my gender. I just filed away my gut impression that the Ichabod Dilley who'd drawn these pictures hadn't left Kansas very far behind.

"A penny for them," Michael said, and I realized I must have fallen silent for rather a long time.

"Just wondering what Dilley might have done if he'd lived longer," I said. "The kid had talent; you can see that in every drawing, and he was getting better all the time. If the issues weren't numbered, I bet I could have figured out the order by seeing how his skill increased. Talent. And training. By the eleventh or twelfth issue, you'd need a few hundred words of description to say what he can show in one panel, in the arch of a courtier's eyebrow, or the way Porfiria casts a come-hither look over her shoulder. Most artists don't get that good without years of practice, including a lot of life-drawing classes. And this was only his progress over a year. Imagine what he could have done if he'd lived to keep getting better."

"And this relates to the murder . . . how?" Michael asked.

"Not at all," I said. "It's fascinating, but it's not getting me anywhere. I was hoping it might prove useful if I could figure out which issue the drawing had come from."

"And search everyone's rooms for a torn comic book?"

"No, it's too much to hope that the murderer would still be carrying it around. But I thought if the issue was important enough for the murderer to take it to that final, fatal confrontation, maybe the theme of the issue would give me a clue to the murderer."

"Which it hasn't, I gather."

"No, my scrap isn't from any of the twelve published issues. Maybe Cordelia isn't pulling my leg, and there really was a lost thirteenth issue."

"Is there supposed to be?"

I shrugged, and then realized he couldn't see me.

"Who knows?" I said aloud. "Maybe it's just the kind of rumor that always swirls around an artist who dies young."

"You could show the scrap to Cordelia," he suggested. "If she's an expert in Dilley . . ."

"I'm not sure I'd want to, even if I hadn't promised Foley to keep quiet about it," I said. "She'd probably laugh at me."

"Why?"

"I don't know," I said. "What if I'm being fooled by an obvious imitation?"

"Do you think it's an imitation?"

"No, but I can't prove it. Maybe I'll show her when Foley lifts the embargo. Oh, have you got a moment?"

"For you, any number of moments," he said, pulling off the washcloth. "Though if you were planning to ravish me while I'm in a weakened condition, I should point out that your timing stinks; I'm due back in the ballroom in ten minutes."

"I'll try to plan better next time. For now, just sign this photo, will you? Here's the inscription they want."

"We'll always have West Covina," Michael read aloud. "West Covina? Where is that? I assume it's a where; it sounds like a where."

"I have no idea where it is, but if I hadn't bribed Cordelia with the promise of a personalized photo for one of her best customers, who lives there, she would never have let me borrow the comics."

"Shameless, the way you exploit me," Michael said. "I will exact compensation after dinner."

While Michael signed, I slipped the last comic back in its acid-free archival-quality plastic cover, pulled off the gloves, and breathed a sigh of relief. I hadn't mangled any of them. And then I headed back to the dealers' room while Michael freshened up for his coming panel.

"So?" Cordelia asked, when I returned the comics. "Did you find anything?"

"I won't know until I check a few other things," I said. "Do you know anything about Dilley's life?"

"I know everything there is to know," she said. "Not that there's that much of it. He was only twenty-one when he died, you know."

"How did he die?" I asked.

"Mysteriously," she said.

"I was talking the method, not the mood," I said. "I heard it was drugs."

"Yes, but it wasn't straightforward. There were rumors that it wasn't an accident."

"Suicide?"

"Or murder. Rumor had it that he owed money to some pretty shady people who finally got tired of waiting for him to pay back. I talked to the private eye his family hired to go down to Mexico and find out what really happened. He never did figure out exactly what was up, but the way the Mexican cops acted, you knew someone had paid them off to cover up something."

"They actually hired a private eye?" I said. "I thought from what his nephew said that they'd disowned him."

"Only after they read the PI's report," she said, with a laugh. "He was this straight-arrow kid from this small Kansas town—president of his class, captain of the debating club, drama society, varsity athlete—the whole shebang. He goes out to Stanford on a scholarship and disappears into the counterculture by Thanksgiving. And they come out to rescue him from whatever they thought was the problem—a cult or a gold digger or something, and he tells them to get lost, 'cause he's not from Kansas any more. They keep calling, writing, and eventually he starts mailing them rude cartoons making fun of them, their town—everything. And then they hire this PI to go and try to talk to him, and apparently the kid freaked, ran off to Mexico, and by the time the PI got a line on him, Dilley was dead and buried. Drug overdose, according to the autopsy, but no one ever believed it was accidental. Maybe the people he owed caught up with him, or maybe he figured doing himself in would be less painful than whatever they had in mind. The PI never figured out which."

"Dramatic," I said.

"So you can imagine how dramatic it would be if you really did find the last comic he'd been working on," Cordelia said.

I wanted to say that I thought the artist's death was a lot more dramatic than any comic could ever be, but I just nodded and took my leave.

I was relieved to find I'd accidentally told Foley the truth

when I'd called the circumstances of Dilley's death mysterious. Or had I said suspicious? Same difference; either way, if
he checked, he'd find I was right.

On the way back to the booth, I stopped by a vendor who
sold fan fic and spent way more money than seemed reasonable
to buy two dozen spurious Porfiria comic books by various
authors and artists. Steele went off for a lunch break, and I
whiled away twenty minutes or so looking through the comics.
The vendor assured me these were the best ones he had, and
yet, like the fan fic stories, most of them were pretty amateur.
Even the most professional didn't have Dilley's genius.

More weight to the theory that the scrap the QB had been
clutching came from an authentic lost comic.

So Dilley's death was mysterious, and the scrap might be
an authentic piece of his work. Where did I go from here?

"I need a time machine," I muttered.

# Chapter 30

"What's wrong, Meg?" I heard Dad say. "Investigation not going well?"

"Not going at all," I said, glancing up to see Dad standing in front of the booth with a green parrot perched on his shoulder. "I'm leaving it to the cops. Are you helping round up the parrots?"

"Round them up?" Dad said. "Why? They're perfectly happy where they are."

Meaning that Dad was perfectly happy to have them around.

"How do you know?" I said aloud.

"Oh, you could tell right away," he said. "They'd exhibit signs of stress. Screaming and biting, and plucking out all their feathers. No, you can tell these parrots are perfectly happy."

Especially the one cooing amorously in his ear.

"Here, read some of these," he said. He began rummaging in his tote bag and extracting books with brightly colored parrots on the cover, and titles like *A Guide to Parrot Behavior* and *Living with Your African Grey*.

"Thanks, but I'm pretty busy," I said.

"Oh, right, with your investigation," Dad said, nodding as he retrieved his books. "I have something that may help with that."

He pulled Michael's tape recorder out of his pocket, held it up dramatically for a moment while looking around for eavesdroppers, and then pushed the PLAY button.

I heard the tape hiss for a few, long seconds, and then voices.

"—like this, then?" Dad's voice asked.

"Yes, that's it," Michael's voice replied. "Both buttons at the same time."

"Got it," the canned Dad said.

"Damn," said the live Dad. "I seem to have rewound it all the way. Oh, well; it's on here somewhere. And who knows, there may be other clues earlier in the tape that your greater knowledge of the case will let you recognize."

He fumbled with the tape recorder's VOLUME knob, somewhat hampered by the parrot's insistence on running its beak through what remained of his hair. He then proceeded to play twenty minutes of recorded parrot vocalizations.

If he'd made the tape as a testimonial for parrots' uncanny powers of mimicry, I'd have applauded his efforts. I heard parrots dinging like elevators, whooshing like vacuum cleaners, ringing like telephones, grinding like blenders, tinkling bits of classical music in the tinny tones used by cell phones, and, of course, flushing like toilets.

Unless, of course, Dad had taped real elevators, vacuum cleaners, blenders, and so on, to pull my leg. Always a possibility with Dad.

The parrots mimicked human voices brilliantly, though they were remarkably undiscriminating in what they chose to imitate. I heard a few phrases from our friend the Monty Python parrot. A lot of commercials, mostly the loud, repetitive, annoying kind I hated most. I was rather pleased to see that they appealed, quite literally, to bird brains. Dad had even caught a performance from two parrots that had learned the Porfiria theme song, although unfortunately, instead of singing it in unison, they interrupted each other and tried to drown each other out.

If I hadn't felt impatient to do something useful, I might have enjoyed the performance. Although I did enjoy the look on Alaric Steele's face when he returned to the booth to find us solemnly listening to a parrot sing a pizza commercial.

"Here it comes," Dad whispered shortly afterward.

"You've double-crossed me for the last time," came Maggie's voice, sounding ragged with emotion. "Prepare to die, you—whoops!"

Dad stopped the tape recorder after that and looked at me.

"Prepare to die, you—whoops?" I repeated.

"Suspicious, isn't it?" Dad said,

"The prepare to die part, yes," I said. "But whoops? Not that I have a lot of personal experience with the matter, but I really don't think many people say 'whoops' after coshing someone on the head with a blunt instrument."

"Could be evidence that it was an accident," Dad said. "If they were quarrelling and Miss Wynncliffe-Jones slipped and fell, for example. And hit her head on the wine bottle."

"Maybe," I said. "Still seems odd."

"You can hang onto it and study it for a while if you like," Dad said.

"Taking a break from sleuthing?"

"Not really," he said. "I may have found someone who has an in with the medical examiner, and then I'm supposed to get together with your friend the scriptwriter. So I'll be pretty tied up all afternoon—why don't you keep the tape recorder for now?"

"Thanks," I said, as he turned to leave.

Perhaps my voice betrayed my lack of enthusiasm for his ornithological investigations. Or perhaps I just sounded tired and discouraged.

"Is there anything else you need?" he asked, pausing and turning back to give me a look that was part doctor and part worried Dad.

"I need a time machine," I said, this time aloud. The parrot tape had distracted me briefly from my frustration at how little I knew. I couldn't go back thirty years and find out the real story about Ichabod Dilley's death. I couldn't even go back thirty hours and try to get the QB to tell me what she knew. I'd studied the original Porfiria comics, picked Cordelia's brain—I wanted another window to the past.

"Well, there are probably a few time machines around here," Dad said, "but I'm afraid I don't know where. You probably have a better idea than I do. Good luck!"

And with that he dashed off.

"Is he pulling your leg, or did he just not hear what you said?" Steele asked.

"With Dad, who knows?" I said.

Actually, I did, but I didn't really want to go into a long explanation. Dad always referred to Great-Aunt Zelda, who was now over a hundred, as the family time machine. Despite her age, she was as sharp-tongued and clear-witted as ever. And if you wanted to settle some question about the past, Great-Aunt Zelda was usually as reliable as any reference book, and a whole lot easier to consult.

So all I had to do was find someone who had been around Ichabod Dilley or the QB back in 1972. Or failing that, at least someone who had been around the QB enough that he might have heard her talk about old times.

Why couldn't she have had a faithful retainer? If we were

living in one of Nate's scripts, she would certainly have had one—perhaps a chain-smoking dragon lady who had looked after her wardrobe since they were both ingénues, and was the only person who dared to argue with her. And who, after initially seeming cynically unaffected by her employer's death, would eventually break down in tears and reveal the critical clue—whatever that was.

But she hadn't had a faithful retainer. She'd had Typhani. Latest, I suspected, of a long line of Typhanis. And maybe a few Geniphers.

There was always Nate. Not my idea of a faithful retainer, but at least, according to the costumer, he'd known the QB since they were much younger.

Of course, much younger didn't necessarily mean thirty years. But still—he'd been closer to her than anyone else I could think of.

And, I thought, glancing at the clock, he just might be in the green room, recuperating from his latest panel.

"I need to talk to Nate," I said, and barely waited for Steele's nod of acknowledgement before I raced away.

Nate was, indeed, on break, though I finally located him in the bar at the back of the supposedly closed restaurant. Not that he couldn't have drunk his cup of coffee in the green room. He probably wanted to be left alone. Ah, well.

"What's up?" I asked.

"I know the convention is important for fan relations," he said, "but my heart's just not in it right now."

Okay, maybe I was wrong about no one mourning for the QB. I nodded and tried to look sympathetic.

"I really need to be on the phone, trying to get a sense of what's happening back in California. Or back in my room, trying to come up with a coherent plan to save the show.

What a disaster! And after everything we went through to make this thing a success."

We. Okay, it wasn't exactly deep mourning, but perhaps I'd finally found the one person at the convention who sincerely wished the QB alive again.

"You'd known each other a long time, hadn't you?" I asked.

He nodded.

"More than thirty years," he said.

# Chapter 31

Yes! I thought, but I tried to stay calm and think of just the right thing to ask. If I wanted to be subtle, it was too soon to ask whether he'd been in love with her, or whether he knew anything about her buying the rights to Porfiria so soon before Ichabod Dilley's untimely and downright suspicious death.

"What was she like?" I asked instead.

"I don't know," he said. "What's anyone like when they're young? Ambitious, impatient. Beautiful, of course. You have to be, to get anywhere in this business. And tough. I mean, I know a lot of people call her a bitch and a dragon, but that's because they don't understand what she had to go through to get where she is. You have to be tough."

"And talented," I suggested.

"Yeah, well," he said, shrugging. "That's not as important as you think. Not that she was untalented. But it's not as if she ever pretended to be a great tragic actress or anything. Still, she could really have gone someplace, been much bigger if she'd only had the breaks."

Just then we heard Maggie's laugh, somewhere nearby. Nate smiled, involuntarily—the way most people seemed to when they heard her. Then he looked down at the table and sighed.

"Actually Maggie was the one who really should have gone someplace," he said.

"Why didn't she?" I asked.

"Who knows, with Hollywood?" he said. "She was good enough, and gorgeous enough, but maybe she didn't want it enough. Or wasn't mean enough. All I know is, I lost track of her for . . . I don't know. Fifteen years? Maybe twenty. Then I got an invitation to this fund-raiser she was running, and I went, just for old time's sake. And when I saw her, I thought, my God. She still had it. I thought it would be a great PR stunt, signing her for the show: old friends getting together to bring to life the long-neglected work of their dead buddy."

"Oh, they were friends of Ichabod Dilley? Maggie and the QB?"

"They all worked on the same movie," Nate said, shrugging. "I don't know about friends, but they probably met, one time or another. And if they didn't, what did it matter. It was just a PR stunt. Stupid idea."

"Only problem is that word 'long,' " I said. "As in 'long in the tooth.' "

"Yeah, stupid me for not realizing that," Nate said. "I was surprised when she hired Maggie anyway. And then, first week on the set, I realized why. Gave her the perfect excuse to make life miserable for someone she never liked. I was surprised Maggie stuck it out as long as she did."

"Stuck it out? I thought the QB fired Maggie."

"Yeah, she did, finally," Nate said. "Soon as she figured out how much the fans loved Maggie. Or maybe realized how much better Maggie looked on camera. You ask me, Maggie was probably relieved that the battle was over, and she could go home to her animals again."

"Her animals?" I said, feigning ignorance.

"Yeah, she runs this animal sanctuary up in the foothills outside L.A.," Nate said. "That's what she ended up doing when her career slowed down. Or maybe it was part of the reason it slowed down, that she started spending all this time rescuing abused animals. Not dog- and cat-type animals. Big animals. Orphaned lion cubs, neglected iguanas, abandoned boa constrictors."

"Do you think Maggie running a sanctuary had anything to do with the QB trying to buy a tiger?"

Nate shuddered.

"God, if I'd known she was serious about that!" he exclaimed. "Yeah, probably. She doesn't even like having to bother with a dog. I don't know what she'd have done with a tiger. But she's competitive. Maggie has tigers, she wants tigers."

He kept talking about her in present tense. Was that significant? Perhaps it meant that he hadn't really accepted her death. Didn't really believe it possible, and therefore couldn't possibly be her murderer.

Or maybe that was just what Nate wanted me to think.

"What did Maggie think about the idea of the QB owning a tiger?" I asked.

"I don't know," he said. "We never talked about it. Maybe she wouldn't—hell, that's a lie. We both know what Maggie would have thought about it, if she'd known. She'd have thought it was a crime, giving the QB custody of a helpless animal. Or even a not-so-helpless animal. She gave the convention organizers what for about the monkeys. And the parrots. Says it's cruel treatment, bringing them here."

We both glanced upward, involuntarily. Half a dozen monkeys lurked near the ceiling, intently watching the bar's human occupants. The staff had put the peanuts, pretzels, and other bar chum in jars with supposedly childproof safety lids, but the monkeys hadn't given up yet. The several illicit customers scattered throughout the room kept one hand over their plates while eating with the other. Several parrots perched near the widescreen TV, intently watching a baseball game and learning to sing the beer commercials.

"You ask me, the monkeys and parrots are having as much fun as anyone," I said.

"More than me, anyway," Nate said. "I just wish I knew whether I still had a job."

"When will you know?" I asked.

"No idea," Nate said. "After all, I'm only the writer."

I shook my head sympathetically, and then, as I'd expected, he shared what he'd found out.

"It's probably a good thing we've got the third season in the can," he said. "If we were in the middle of the season, with the meter running, they'd just shut us down for good. But this way, we'll have time to come up with a solution to the problem."

"Cast another actress," I suggested. "Soap operas do it all the time. There's no shortage of unemployed fifty-something actresses."

"Yes," he said. "But some fans always have trouble accepting the change. On the other hand, you can't just kill her off— she's the title character."

"What would you do if she went out temporarily?" I asked. "You coped when Walker broke his foot."

"We had Mephisto capture him and chain him to a dungeon wall," Nate said. "For a couple of weeks, we just showed him lolling around in a loincloth with his cast hidden in some straw. The fans loved it. But who would have a reason to kidnap Porfiria?"

"Just have her kidnapped," I said, shrugging. "Figure out who did it later."

"Ooh! Yes!" Nate exclaimed. "And everyone accuses everyone else of being responsible. A power struggle over who runs Amblyopia in her absence."

He reached into his inside jacket pocket, pulled out a pen and a mini legal pad, and began scribbling words, and making little drawings to illustrate the action—though I don't know why he bothered with the drawings. All he ever drew were stick figures, with or without indistinguishable objects stuck to the ends of their arms, so they all looked as if they were either shouting for help or brandishing dumbbells at each other. But it seemed to help him think.

"And then halfway through the season, we introduce a whole new group of villains!" he said, drawing another cluster of stick figures with such a heavy hand that he actually tore the paper, and then nodded as if in satisfaction at this concrete evidence of his new villains' dastardly nature.

"See, I knew you could do it," I said.

"We needed a new big nasty," he said. "Not monsters, this time; you have no idea what the prosthetics do to the budget. Something easy. Knights. All you need is tin foil. Knights with magic. Where's your father?"

"Dad? Why?"

I didn't think Dad's parrot project would increase Nate's confidence in his new technical advisor.

"I need a name for the knights. The Something Knights. Something with an M, I think. I should go and find him,"

"Mastoid Knights?" I suggested.

"Sounds obscene," Nate said, shaking his head. "What is a mastoid, anyway?"

"A bone," I said, reaching behind my ear to tap the bone in question.

"Still sounds obscene," Nate said.

"Metatarsal Knights?"

"Yes!" Nate said. "And in the big, two-part season finale, they all invade the Dungeons of the Metatarsal Knights!"

Just then Maggie sailed into the bar and beckoned to me to join her, so I left Nate covering sheet after sheet of his legal pad with illegible scribbles, muttering to himself as he did so.

We took a table at the back and to my surprise, the bartender appeared to take our order.

"Aren't you worried about the health department?" I asked.

"Guy hasn't been seen for hours," the bartender said, with a shrug. "We're thinking maybe he's knocked off for the weekend."

"He probably saw how mutinous the fans were and decided it was safer," Maggie said.

I fingered the mini tape recorder in my pocket. What would Maggie say if I played the tape and asked when she'd said the fateful words, "Prepare to die, you—whoops!" The appropriately subtle, nonchalant way to introduce the topic into conversation hadn't yet appeared.

"He looks like a kid with a new toy," Maggie said, indicating Nate.

"Working on some ideas to keep the show going without Porfiria," I said.

"God, wouldn't she hate that?" Maggie said. But instead of laughing, she shook her head. "Weird, isn't it? She fought tooth and nail for that silly show, first to get it on the air, and then to make it a success. And not twenty-four hours after her death they're having to write her out of the picture. It's almost sad."

I kept quiet, hoping she'd go on. She looked at me quizzically.

"Is that a stupid thing to say?" she asked. "That I feel sorry for someone that I hated?"

"Not really," I said. "Seems only natural after so much time. How long were you—did you know her?"

Maggie laughed.

"I've known her for thirty-two years," she said. "But that's not what you started out to ask, is it? You were about to ask how long we'd been friends."

I nodded.

"About the first ten minutes," she said, with another of her amazing laughs. And while I was congratulating myself at how well my time machine project was working, she sat back, held her glass in both hands, and stared down at it, shaking the ice a little now and then.

# Chapter 32

"We met on the set of this ghastly movie we both had bit parts in," Maggie said, smiling off into space. "Total crap. Blind girl runs away from the Midwest to San Francisco and falls in love with this psychedelic poster artist—who finally becomes a sculptor so she can understand his art. There was a subplot, something about her getting kidnapped by a biker gang, that I never quite understood. Then again, neither did the director, but he loved all the leather and chrome. Hollywood does Haight Ashbury."

"Trying too hard to be with it?" I suggested.

"Exactly," she said. "And failing, miserably. If they'd asked any of the cast, we'd have told them it was horribly dated. By 1971 the whole Summer of Love thing was deader than vaudeville. And the script was a travesty to begin with. Anyway, that's how we met, Tammy and I, working on that god-awful movie."

"Tammy?" I echoed.

"She was Tammy Jones when I met her," Maggie said. "Tamerlaine Wynncliffe-Jones came later, when she became a Serious Actress."

"What was she like back then?" I asked.

"I don't know," she said. "How much of what I say today about the Tammy of 1971 is true, and how much is colored by the bad things that happened between us later, and how much by the fact that she's dead, and we all get sentimental about dead people? Even dead enemies."

"Especially dead enemies," I said.

"Yeah," she said, laughing softly. "She was pretty, of course, but it was dimples and fresh skin pretty, not bone structure beautiful. You knew her face might not wear well—she probably knew it, too. I think that's why she was so . . . focused. She knew where she wanted to go and what she had to work with, and she could tell she had to get there fast, if she wanted to get there at all."

"No talent, then?"

"She had talent, yes; but not enough to match her ambition," Maggie said. "She had brains though, and not a lot of scruples. We both started off with bit parts, but she wanted more. Well, we both wanted more, but I wasn't unscrupulous enough to sleep with the scriptwriter to get it. Or maybe I'd already figured out exactly how little power the scriptwriter had. She learned fast, though; dumped the poor wordsmith for the director, and she got her extra lines—in one of the worst movies ever filmed, but you have to start somewhere."

"What was the movie?"

"God, what *was* the name of that stinker? Where'd Nate go, anyway? He'd remember, of course; but if I asked him he'd pretend he didn't. He doesn't like to be reminded of his early screenplays."

"Nate wrote it?" I exclaimed, glancing over at the table that Nate had apparently vacated. "He was the scriptwriter she . . . um . . ."

"You bet," she said, shaking her glass and smiling. "That's how they met, working on that movie. And probably how she met that comic book writer, too."

"Ichabod Dilley?"

"Yeah, that's the guy. He was an artist, actually. Nate dug a kid up somewhere to do the psychedelic paintings they used in the film."

So Nate had known Ichabod Dilley, too. Curious that he hadn't mentioned it just now.

"What was he like?" I asked.

"Dilley? I didn't really know him," she said, shrugging. "He was this total recluse who never came to the set, though perhaps Nate was just trying to be mysterious about his discovery. I think I only ever saw Dilley once: tall; skeletally thin; long, greasy brown hair. Had one of those unfortunate, mangy beards, the kind you see on a kid who's really too young to grow one but insists on trying anyway. And big, round wire-rimmed sunglasses, and an oversized pea coat. Unprepossessing."

"You didn't like him?" I said.

"I didn't *dis*like him," she said. "I didn't really know him. Tammy was the one who hung around with him. God knows why. From what little I'd seen, I couldn't figure out what she saw in him but, then, if Tammy thought she could use a guy to get something she needed . . ."

Maggie shrugged, and took a sip from her iced tea.

"I always thought the poor kid based those comics on her, if you really want to know," she said.

"The Porfiria comics?"

"Yeah," she said. "You ever read them? In the comics, Porfiria is pure Tammy. As she was then. No wonder she wanted so badly to play the part. It was perfect for her. Too bad the chance finally came about twenty-five years too late."

She sat back, clinking the ice in her drink, and smiling again. I waited, because I could tell the scene hadn't ended.

Maybe a melodramatic way of thinking, but I suspected that was how Maggie saw life: as a series of scenes that often hung together badly, like a movie made by an incompetent director from a wretched script. And there wasn't anything Maggie could do about that, but at least she could control her own performance. Make any scene in which she appeared as good as she knew how. I'd seen Michael trying to teach his acting students about pacing. I'd heard his lecture to the Drama 101 class on the structure of a well-made play. Even I could tell that this scene still needed a proper ending.

Maggie took a swallow, and then reached down into her tapestry bag, rummaged around for a bit, and came out with something.

"This was us," she said. "Taken on the set."

She handed over a plastic sleeve containing an 4×6 color photo that had obviously been around a while before someone decided it was worth protecting with the sleeve. In the shot, a group of about twenty beautiful young people smiled into the camera. They were wearing costumes from the early seventies. Okay, the photo was taken in 1971, but they were still costumes—Hollywood's idea of what flower children looked like. Flower children, and a couple of Hell's Angels who looked as young and innocent as the pseudohippies. All of them a lot cleaner than their real-life counterparts probably managed to be, and with hair so perfect you knew a stylist with a brush and a big can of hairspray lurked just out of the frame. The women, all sporting long, pre-Raphaelite hair, wore granny gowns, Indian-print dresses, fringed or beaded halter tops over artfully frayed jeans. The men's tresses were almost as long—some less obviously wigs than others—and most wore beards or mustaches and flowered shirts or tie-dyed t-shirts in rainbow colors.

I could see the younger Maggie, near the back of the group. The QB—Tammy, as she was then—near the center, draped artfully on the shoulder of one of the most attractive young men. All the men seemed to be standing closer to her than they had to. I could see why. She had a glow—that's the only way to describe her.

And off at one side, Nate, looking as if he'd walked onto the set from another movie, or maybe out of a bad high school yearbook picture. Tall, skinny, with thick glasses, wearing a badly fitting suit. Oddly enough, he looked less ridiculous than most of the men in the picture. Or at least less painfully dated. But he certainly didn't look as if he fit in, or expected to. The photographer had probably told them all to move closer together for the camera, and the men around Tammy had done so eagerly, and Nate had sidled perhaps an inch closer before the shutter immortalized him, standing awkwardly on the periphery, the perpetual outsider.

Which was usually how he looked today, even after thirty years. The badly fitting suit was visibly more expensive, but otherwise nothing much had changed. In the photo, he looked almost like a time traveler from the present. Had he been ahead of his time, or had he simply found, early on, a kind of anti-style that endured better than fashion? I recalled looking in my high school yearbook recently, and noticing, to my surprise, that from a distance of nearly two decades, the cool people didn't look nearly as cool anymore. The fashionable clothes and trendy hairstyles hadn't worn well. And all the rest of us, the little people who'd despaired of ever being that cool—we looked rather normal. Time, the great leveler.

I wondered if I'd recognize any of those beautiful young actors if I saw them today. Apart from Maggie and the QB, of course. Probably not. Thirty years can do a lot to a person.

Any one of them could be walking around, pretending to be nothing more than an aging Porfiria fan.

And Maggie was right. The QB looked like Porfiria. Not the aging Porfiria of the TV show, but the young, vibrant, earthy Porfiria of Ichabod Dilley's drawings.

"*Acid Dreams?*" Maggie said. "Acid something. *Acid Visions*; that was it. *Acid Visions*. God, what a stinker. I haven't seen it in ages. Not that I usually sit around watching my own movies, but I notice when they're on TV, and it's been years since I saw a trace of that one."

"Check the dealers' room," I said. "I'll bet anything one of the dealers has got a copy, even if it's only a bad quality bootleg tape."

"I said I hadn't seen it, not that I wanted to," she said, with a laugh. "But maybe I should go and buy up all the copies they have. Protect my reputation as a serious actress."

"You'd go broke buying up all the copies," I said.

"Yeah," she said, gulping the last of her iced tea. "If anyone gives me a hard time, I usually just tell them that I did my best, and it paid the rent that week. And besides—what the hell?"

A sudden shower of mixed nuts and pretzels rattled down on our heads, and we both looked up to see that a monkey perched above our table had learned how to open the child-proof lid of a snack jar.

"And on that note, I think I'll leave before the gathering primates descend," Maggie said, laughing as she tossed her head to shake the pretzels out of her mane. "Gotta run any-way; another panel."

She ran off, leaving more money on the table than neces-sary to cover her share of the tab. Since I could see monkeys traveling from the far corners of the bar to hover over our table, I decided she had the right idea. I added enough cash to the tip to make sure the bartender remembered us both fondly. As I stood up, the weight of the little tape recorder in my pocket reminded me that I still didn't know why Maggie was running around the convention telling people to prepare to die. And for that matter, now I had another question— why had she brought that particular photo to the convention? Was it only nostalgia? I sighed, brushed a few clinging peanuts out of my hair and reached the exit just as the first fight broke out among the swarming monkeys.

# Chapter 33

Once I stepped out into the lobby, I found myself wondering if I should even bother going back to the dealers' room. It was probably still deserted, since any fans not attending panels were still milling about the lobby and the hallway, trading rumors, and watching the press.

I went over, myself, to peer out the front windows of the hotel.

"God, there are more of them," I muttered.

"Yeah," said an Amazon security guard standing next to me. "And it's getting to be a real pain, keeping them out."

I glanced around the lobby. Yes, unless they had donned Porfirian disguise, the press were all outside, having grown tired of interviewing the desk clerks and photographing the wildlife. They hadn't gotten into the convention proper. My respect for the Amazon security guards increased exponentially.

"My lord wizard! Can you not dispel the rabble infesting my courtyard?" another Amazon trilled, in the high, affected voice fans usually used when mimicking the QB. The words sounded vaguely familiar, so I assumed they must be a quote from an episode I'd seen.

"They are the envoys of a wise and ancient people," a

nearby Michael clone intoned. "We must approach them with subtlety and discretion."

I recognized this as one of Michael's lines from a recent show. A line that, as usual, provoked gales of laughter, not because it was particularly funny in and of itself, but because on the show, after Michael said it to Walker in his most solemn voice, they had simultaneously whirled and punched the two envoys in the jaw. Fortunately the Michael clone omitted the fisticuffs from his rendition.

A thought struck me. I fished out the tape recorder, turned the sound down, queued up the scrap of dialogue in Maggie's voice, turned the volume back up, and stuck it out in the middle of the group of Amazon guards.

"Porfiria trivia quiz," I said. "Identify this."

I played them the snippet, the one where Maggie could be heard saying, "Prepare to die, you—whoops!"

"The Duchess, of course," one said. "Maggie West."

"Well, duh," another said. "But what episode?"

"Play it again, will you?" asked a third.

I backed up the tape and obliged.

"I've got it!" the second one said. "It's from the blooper tape. The Duchess threatening Porfiria in the 'Portents of Evil' episode, only this is the take where the Duke tried to draw his sword and hit himself in the chin with it."

"You're right!" the first guard said, shaking her head. "Damn, and I just saw the blooper tape again this morning."

"Great," I said. "Thanks. That one had us stumped."

I strolled on, leaving the guard who had answered looking very pleased with herself.

I should have asked Dad where he'd taped the parrot. Odds were it was in or around the fan lounge, where they'd been showing the blooper tape once an hour since Friday morning. Enough repetition for even the slowest of parrots.

As I made my way back down the hall, I passed the vine-draped door to Salome's room and noticed that someone had put a large CLOSED sign on it.

So if it was closed, why were there voices in there? One male and one female, and it wouldn't have seemed odd if the male voice belonged to Brad, the keeper, and the female to, say, Maggie. But the male voice was Walker's.

And the female voice was saying,

"Just leave me alone!"

I ducked under the vines—which required getting down on my hands and knees. Brad's camouflage efforts were definitely getting out of hand. The vines no longer merely obscured the opening, they practically blocked it. The door itself was slightly ajar, so I put my ear to the opening.

"Please," Walker said. "You've got to tell them!"

"I can't," a female voice said.

"If you don't, I won't have an alibi," Walker said. "And I think they're getting ready to arrest me."

Aha! Apparently Walker's luck was changing, and he had found his alibi.

Or had he only found someone he thought would be willing to lie for him?

"Do you know what my boyfriend will do to me if he finds out?"

Aha. Walker's luck was changing, all right, but not for the better.

"You don't have to tell your boyfriend," he said. "Just the police."

"He'll find out," she said. "The last time he got mad at me, he almost broke my nose, and that's nothing compared to what he'd do this time."

"Not if you—"

"I have to go!"

I backed far enough away from the door that I could pretend to be only just approaching as she flew out. Far enough, for that matter, to let me take a long hard look at her as she passed by.

Blond, pretty, on the skinny side, maybe early twenties but probably just barely legal—a lot like every other girl I'd ever seen at Walker's side. Even without the skimpy red harem girl costume, I could probably pick her out of a crowd. But just in case, I took a look at her badge. And a second look, just to make sure I'd read it correctly. Then I ducked under the vines and went into the room.

Salome opened one eye when I entered, then closed it again and apparently went back to sleep, as if to say I wasn't worth bothering with. Spike, still securely fastened to a post across the room, had curled up very carefully in exactly the same pose as Salome, though he was only pretending to sleep. Occasionally he would lift his head, look over at her, sigh, and put his head back down. I'd probably have found this adorable if I hadn't known him better. Walker was leaning against a wall, well away from both animals. He acknowledged my arrival with a half-wave and an unconvincing smile.

"Walker," I said, "I gather you have a problem."

"Yeah," he said. "The police are probably going to arrest me any minute now."

"And your only alibi is a teenaged tart with a fake ruby in her navel who's apparently registered for the convention as Concubine Aimee," I said.

"Holy—how did you know?" Walker asked.

"I was eavesdropping, of course," I said.

"Then you know how bad it is," he said. "She won't talk."

"Now that you know who she is, you could just tell the police," I suggested.

"I can't," he said.

"Now is not the time to get all chivalrous," I said.

"I'm not being chivalrous," he said. "I already threatened to tell, and she said if I did, she'd deny it."

"Walker, you can get her to tell the truth," I said. "All you have to do is—"

And then I paused. What were the odds that Walker could talk Concubine Aimee into anything? About the same as the odds he could get through a fight scene without hurting himself. Which was why Chris was his stunt double. At the moment, apparently, Walker needed a brain double.

"Let me talk to her," I finished.

"You really think you can talk her into it?"

I shrugged.

"Worth a try," I said. "Just lie low for a while."

I crawled out of the lair and reconnoitered. Concubine Aimee had disappeared, but that was okay. I didn't want to talk to her until I had a little more information about her, and I thought I knew where to look. I remembered seeing the Amazon security guards and the guest of honor escorts disappear into a room off the green room. I headed there.

Sure enough, when I walked into the room in question, I found two convention volunteers doing something with laptops.

When in doubt, pretend you know just what you're doing and have every right to do it, I told myself. It always worked for Mother.

"Hi," I said, going up to one of the computer users and flashing my badge, with its vendor ribbon. "I need to check an attendee out."

"Is there a problem of some kind?"

"Probably not, but I'd like to keep it that way," I said. "Can you look up someone by badge name and see if they're really registered?"

"Oh, God," the other computer volunteer groaned. "They're not faking the badges again, are they?"

"Not necessarily," I said. "It may just have been the light that made it look funny, but with all these reporters around, trying to sneak in——"

"What's the badge name?" the first volunteer asked.

"Concubine Aimee," I said, sidling around so I could look over her shoulder. "No, with a double 'ee'——that's right."

"Looks like she's legit," the woman said.

"Unless there are multiple Concubine Aimees running around," the other volunteer said. "One color copier and bingo! You've got clones."

"I know someone who probably took a check from this one," I said. "Let me see if the address and other stuff you have matches what's on the check she has in her cash box, and if there's a problem, I'll come back and let you know."

They liked that idea, so I copied down the relevant information on a While You Were Out slip, stuffed it in my pocket, and left before someone more security-conscious showed up.

Okay, it was convenient that they let me take down Aimee's personal information that easily, but not reassuring. Did they have information about Michael and me in the same computers, guarded by the same bozos?

I'd worry about that later. I set out to look for Aimee—whose real name was Amy Goldman. I also had a local address and a phone number.

But as I walked through the green room, I noticed Nate sitting in a corner. Quite apart from the fact that I wanted to tackle him on why he'd lied about knowing Ichabod Dilley, I wanted to know the reason for the singularly glum look on his face. Concubine Aimee could wait a few more minutes.

# Chapter 34

"How's it going?" I asked, slipping into the seat across from Nate.

Nate shook his head.

"What's wrong?" I asked.

"Walker missed a panel," he said in an ominous monotone.

Damn. Was this my fault? When I told him to lie low, I had only meant that he should avoid Concubine Aimee. I should have known that you needed to be a lot more specific with Walker.

"Why?" I said aloud. "Did he forget? Has someone gone to look for him? I might know where he is if there's still time to go get him."

"No, the panel started an hour and a half ago," Nate said. "And I know exactly where he was then—the police were interviewing him."

"Damn."

"They probably still are. They're closing in."

"Not necessarily," I said. "They've interviewed all of us."

"They wouldn't disrupt the convention this way if they weren't looking pretty seriously at him."

"I don't actually think making the convention run smoothly ranks very high on Detective Foley's priority list."

"God," Nate moaned. "Let's not talk about it. Let's talk about something else."

"Fine," I said. "Let's talk about Ichabod Dilley."

"What about him?"

"You never told me you knew him," I said.

"Didn't I? Well, you never really asked," Nate said. "I don't recall denying that I knew him."

I wanted to tell him that he'd implied it, but I suspected that would bog the conversation down into a long discussion of semantics, instead of letting me find out anything useful.

"How well did you know him?" I asked instead.

"How well did I know anyone in those days?" he said. "Especially from that side of my life. The private side."

"Private in what way?"

"Nothing . . . sinister, if that's what you mean," Nate said, looking alarmed. "Weekdays I was a hard-working, buttoned-down little writer. Very corporate. Nothing to alarm the studio execs. Weekends, I'd drive up to San Francisco and hang around Haight Ashbury. Go to concerts. Get stoned."

"I see," I said

"Don't laugh," he added, although I could have sworn I hadn't let any sign of amusement cross my face. "I wasn't always the staid, boring guy you probably think I am from seeing me on the job."

Actually, you were, I felt like saying. In fact, you used to be worse. I've seen the photo. Aloud, I decided to stick to vague platitudes.

"People change."

"Life changes them," Nate said. "Professional responsibilities."

Professional responsibilities like creating the Metatarsal Knights, I thought, but I nodded solemnly.

"So you met Ichabod Dilley while you were slumming in Haight Ashbury," I said.

"My script called for a psychedelic artist," he said. "You know—like a Grateful Dead poster. The studio hack kept bringing in things that looked like you'd smeared lime green paint on a Renoir. So I said I'd find someone."

"Dilley."

"I put him up in my own apartment the whole time he was working on those damned paintings," Nate said, with sudden heat. "The whole time he was supposed to be working on them. I found out later, he'd done the first Porfiria comic book—maybe the first several—while I was down on the set, making excuses for why the rest of the paintings weren't ready yet. And then, when he finally finished the damned things, I let him stay in case they decided at the last minute that they needed changes, or maybe another painting. When the movie was finally over, I thought I'd never get rid of him. Took weeks before I came home one day and found he'd disappeared. Taking half my wardrobe—the hipper half, of course—but I considered it cheap at the price."

He fell silent. Brooding over those long-lost bell-bottoms, I supposed.

"And then the thugs started showing up," he added.

"Thugs?"

"Guys claiming he owed them money. One of them actually beat me up when I said I had no idea where he'd gone. Which was true. I finally found a gallery that was showing a couple of Dilley's paintings, and started referring the thugs there, and eventually they stopped showing up."

"And then what happened?"

"What happened? Nothing. End of the story of Nate and Ichabod."

"You never saw him again?"

Nate shook his head.

"I figured he'd drifted back to San Francisco. Turns out he died, not long after that. Of course, I didn't hear he'd died until a couple of years later. The QB had me do a movie treatment based on the comics. Asked her why she didn't just have him do it, and she said he wasn't a screenwriter, and anyway he was dead."

And did Nate's helping the thugs find him have anything to do with Dilley's death? Probably not something he'd admit, even if he suspected it was true, so I didn't see any point in asking.

"So you did the movie treatment," I said.

He nodded.

"First of many," he said. "Every time fantasy was in, we'd do another damned treatment. When *Star Wars* came out in '77 we set it on another planet. In '82, when Schwarzenegger did Conan, we stuck in a barbarian warrior. *Princess Bride*'s a big hit a couple of years later, and we did a tongue-in-cheek version. Anne Rice gets hot, and we do one where Porfiria's an immortal vampire. I suggested an animated version once, but she never went for that."

"Sounds like the TV show's more authentic than the movie treatments."

He nodded.

"What would Ichabod Dilley think, if he were here?" I asked.

Nate didn't answer at first. Just when I was about to repeat the question, he spoke up.

"He wouldn't recognize it," he said, smiling and shaking his head. "Maybe when he realized it was supposed to be based on his stories, he'd have a big laugh at what life does to you when you're not looking. But then, Dilley's dead, and what the hell do I know. I've got a panel," he said, standing up abruptly. "I'll see you."

A little early to be heading out for a panel, I thought, but maybe he's still allowing plenty of time for getting lost in the hotel.

"Still asking questions?"

I glanced over to see that Francis had come in.

"Yeah, still trying to make sense of what happened," I said.

"The murder happened yesterday," Francis said. "Every time I see you, you're asking a lot of questions about things that happened twenty or thirty years ago. Do you really think all that has anything to do with the murder?"

"I have no idea," I said. "But it's rather intriguing, finding out about everyone's wild escapades in the seventies."

"Wild escapades?" Francis said. "What kind of wild escapades?"

He sounded alarmed. Why, I had no idea. It wasn't as if any of the aging boomers' youthful misdeeds could spill over and taint his current clients, who had been in grade school at the time.

"Apparently Nate inhaled," I said. "And Tammy Jones didn't play hard to get."

"Ah, well," he said. "Those were the times, weren't they?"

"I wouldn't know," I said. "I wasn't there. Is that what things were like, back then?"

"I'm sure I wouldn't know, either," Francis said. "I'm afraid if you want to hear exciting tales of rebellion and protest, I'm the wrong person to ask. I led a rather quiet life then."

And it hadn't gotten appreciably noisier since, I thought, with a sudden flash of sympathy. I wasn't sure I remembered ever hearing anything about his private life.

Then again, I wasn't sure I wanted to. If I were a better person, perhaps, I would think of some tactful, sympathetic way to draw Francis out on the subject of his quiet youth.

Later. When I had more time, I promised myself. I would sit down with Francis and have a long, friendly talk. Draw him out of his shell and get to know him better. Maybe while Maggie and Nate and the QB were off in Hollywood, Francis was still in college studying philosophy or poetry. I'd find out later. Right now, I needed to see what I could do about Walker's problem.

Finding one fan out of the thousand attending the convention wasn't easy, but I finally caught up with Concubine Aimee in the hallway.

Of course, she was ensconced in a nest of friends. Not the right environment for the kind of interrogation I had in mind. And she might be a little suspicious if I tried to lure her away.

Just then I felt a hand curl around my waist.

"Even the monkeys like you," Chris said.

"So this isn't a serious pass, just a case of monkey see; monkey do," I said, disentangling myself.

"I'm serious," Chris said, pointing up. "Look at them."

I glanced up. The perpetually solemn faces of half a dozen monkeys gazed down at me.

"Of course there are monkeys up there," I said. "There are monkeys everywhere."

"Yeah, but these are following you up and down the hallway," Chris said.

"It is possible, you know," said another voice.

I turned to see Brad, Salome's keeper, carrying two McDonald's bags.

"They often form attachments to individual humans," Brad went on. "Especially ones they perceive as dominant within their social group."

With that, he turned and strolled down the hall toward the entrance to Salome's lair, nearly invisible under its covering of vines.

"Very perceptive, these monkeys," Chris said, suppressing a grin, "and delightfully uninhibited."

He pointed to a pair of monkeys who appeared to be mating, oblivious to the chaos around them.

"You would notice that," I said. "I always thought that if you put an infinite number of monkeys in a room, they were supposed to rewrite Shakespeare. These monkeys are not performing up to expectations."

"Someone forgot the infinite number of typewriters," Chris said.

"Look, do me a favor, will you?" I asked.

"Will I earn your eternal gratitude?" he asked.

"I don't know about eternal," I said, "but you will make me grateful enough to significantly increase the odds that I show up for tonight's Blazing Sabers performance."

"Ask away, O Dominant One," Chris said.

"What are the odds that you can cut one fan out of the herd and lure her into the tiger's lair?" I asked.

"My kind of assignment," he said. "I assume you mean a particular one?"

"The blond over there," I said, trying to point discreetly, "standing in the middle of that group of decoratively if scantily attired young ladies."

"The one with the red rhinestone in her navel?"

"That's her."

"One blond groupie, coming up," Chris said. "Meet you in the lair."

"Just shove her in and wait outside."

# Chapter 35

While Chris went to hijack Amy, I walked down the hall, glancing upward from time to time. Was Chris right? Were some of the monkeys following me? It was hard to tell, because if you looked up in the hall, the whole ceiling appeared to be in vague motion, between the monkeys, the parrots, and the vines. Still, several monkeys did seem to be swinging purposefully along behind me.

Maybe we were just going in the same direction.

Several monkeys did pop into Salome's lair shortly after I finished crawling through the doorway.

"We're—"

"Closed, I know," I said. "If you're not going to let anyone see Salome, why not just take her home?"

"I'm trying to," Brad said. "I've been trying to reach Mrs. Willner all day."

"Why don't you try again?"

"I don't have a cell phone."

"Go use a pay phone," I said. "I'll guard the door until you get back."

Brad hesitated.

"You let my father do it," I pointed out. "Trust me, I'm at least as responsible as he is."

He nodded, and disappeared through the vine-covered opening.

Spike and Salome had already inspected and decided to ignore me. I untied Spike's leash and led him over to stand with me just inside the opening. He growled a little, but once he saw I wasn't taking him away from Salome, he calmed down.

A few minutes later, Concubine Aimee crawled out from under the vines, giggling.

"I don't see why we can't—" she was saying, as she emerged from the opening. She stopped, still on her hands and knees, when she saw me, but she didn't know quite how to react until she heard the door slam behind her.

"What's going on?" she said.

Her voice must have disturbed Spike's rapt contemplation of Salome. He whirled and snapped at her, growling. She backed away, hastily, still on her knees.

"You can stand up if you like," I said, tying Spike to a sturdy vine. "You'd be more comfortable."

"What's going on here?" she said, looking from me to Salome as if she wasn't sure which made her most nervous.

"Just a little friendly conversation," I said. "I overheard you talking to Walker Morris just now, and I'm—"

"If you think you can bully me into talking to the police, you're wrong," she said, sticking her chin out in a stubborn gesture.

"Nobody's trying to bully you," I said.

Not yet, anyway.

"You don't understand," she said.

"I understand perfectly," I said. "Walker only wants you to tell the police the truth. Which I gather is that you and he were together when the QB's murder took place. Is that true?"

She crossed her arms.

"Is it true that you and Walker can alibi each other?"

"I don't need an alibi," she said, startled.

"How do you know?" I said. "The police are still investigating."

She looked a little less smug, and crossed her arms a little tighter, which made her look more defensive than defiant.

"And that's why it's so important for you to talk to the police now—while they're still looking for the killer."

"My boyfriend would kill me."

"If you tell the police that, they'll try to keep it quiet. But what happens if you don't tell them and they arrest Walker?"

"He'll find another way to prove his innocence," she said.

"Maybe. But first he'll tell the police he was with you, and they'll interrogate you. And when you tell different stories, the police will start looking for evidence to see which of you lied. They'll ask everyone in the hotel if they saw the two of you together. They could even look for DNA evidence in whatever room you were in. And even if they don't find witnesses or DNA, the press will find out about it, and they'll put it all over the front page—the whole world will know they're looking. Including, of course, your boyfriend."

She looked a little stricken. I also noticed that she was holding her nametag so I couldn't see it. And she'd started to glance around as if looking for an escape. Evidently she still thought she could vanish into the crowd. Time to enlighten her.

"Imagine the headlines," I said. " 'Local Woman Denies Affair with TV Star. Loudoun County Police continue to investigate allegations that Ms. Amy Goldman of Fribble Lane, Alexandria, is actually the mystery woman named as Walker Morris's alibi in the—' "

"How do you know——" she began, and then her hands flew over her mouth.

"It was easy," I said. "And if you think it's easy for me, imagine what a snap it would be for the police."

I'd produced a change in attitude, but frozen panic wasn't necessarily an improvement over her previous stubbornness.

"Go and talk to the police," I said, as gently as I could. "Tell them why you were afraid to talk. They'll understand, and they'll try to protect your secret."

She nodded. She didn't look happy, but she looked resigned.

"You want me to go with you and make sure they understand how important it is to keep this quiet?"

She nodded with greater enthusiasm. I moved Spike back away from the door, and she followed me meekly through the opening.

I led her up to the rooms where the police were still encamped, intending to turn her over to the kindly sergeant. I wasn't sure whether it was a good thing or a bad thing that Detective Foley and his partner were there, too.

"Can I talk to you for a minute?" Foley said, when I'd explained, as briefly as possible, why we were there. Amy seemed to have lost her voice from fright and was losing the battle not to cry.

I followed Foley out into the hall while his partner and the sergeant fetched tissues and a Diet Pepsi for Amy.

"Thank you," Foley said. "I think. You're sure all you did was talk her into coming here?"

"I didn't talk her into lying, if that's what you mean," I said. "I have no idea if she's telling the truth—that's your problem."

"You think we're doing a bad job on this investigation?" Foley asked. "You think we need your help?"

"I have no idea—" I began.

"We may not be the NYPD, but we're not some hick outfit," he said. "If we don't have something in-house, we can call on the state or the FBI. Every forensic and investigative tool available to modern American law enforcement is at our disposal. We have a dozen trained professional police officers working full time on this case. You people come out here from Hollyweird with your—"

"Foley, I only brought you a witness," I said. "I happened to overhear her arguing with Walker, and I convinced her to come forward and tell the truth. If I hear anything else you can use, I'll come and tell you that, too. And for your information, I don't live in Hollywood. I came up for the weekend from Caerphilly, which in case you've never heard of it, makes Loudoun County look like Metropolis."

"Just don't bring me any more damned parrot surveillance tapes," Foley said, as he turned on his heel and strode back into the room.

Nice to know I hadn't single-handedly provoked his ire, I thought, as I headed for the stairs. More of a family project.

But something Foley had said stuck in my mind.

# Chapter 36

"Every forensic and investigative tool available to modern American law enforcement," I muttered.

"What's that?"

I looked up to see that Michael had emerged from the police suite.

"Damn, what did the police want with you again?" I asked, feeling a sudden flutter of anxiety.

"Questions about Walker," Michael said. "I gather I have you to thank for the decorative damsel whose arrival made them lose interest in me?"

"Yeah, Walker found his alibi, and I convinced her to talk to the police."

"Thank God," Michael said. "Of course, this means they'll go looking for another prime suspect."

"And looking in the wrong place, not to mention the wrong decade," I said.

"Wrong decade?"

"Okay, this is going to sound crazy, but here goes," I said. "Foley said something about them using every forensic and investigative tool available to modern American law enforcement. And yes, law enforcement has come a long way in the past thirty years. But even back in 1972, they didn't do too shabby a job on forensics, right?"

"At least in the big cities, where they had money to get the right equipment," Michael said, nodding.

"Yes, places like Los Angeles and San Francisco, where Ichabod Dilley hung out," I said. "But Ichabod Dilley didn't die in California, where the case would get decent police scrutiny. He died in a small Mexican town where the PI his family hired to investigate thought the authorities had been bribed to conceal something."

"Like what?"

"Suicide or murder—the story doesn't say which," I said, with a shrug. "And possible motivation for either; he owed a lot of money to the wrong people."

"Which is a lovely bit of Porfirian history, but how does it relate to the QB's murder?" Michael asked.

"One of the few people who knew Dilley back in those days has just been murdered," I said.

It sounded pretty weak when I said it aloud.

"Two murders, thirty years apart?" Michael said.

"And the second murder happened at a time when several of the people who knew Dilley happened to be around," I said. "Nate. Maggie. Francis, if he was stretching the truth a bit about when he'd represented the QB. Which wouldn't surprise me. If he knew something fishy had gone on back in 1972, wouldn't he try to hide the fact that he'd known her back then?"

"In a heartbeat," Michael said. "Right now, he's so freaked at having his clients turn into murder suspects that I suspect he'd try to hide his connection to me and Walker if he thought he could get away with it."

"Of course, they're all hiding things, or at least leaving out things, fairly crucial things," I said. "And if you call them on it, they shrug and confess, like children caught in a minor fib.

As if it didn't really matter. Or is that only another layer of deception?"

"What do you expect?" Michael said, looking suddenly tired. "It's a habit a lot of people pick up when they've been working too long in an industry that cares too much about youth. So you don't mention everything you've seen or done, or everyone you know, because sooner or later, someone will do the arithmetic and realize that you've been around a little too long. Hell, yesterday Walker asked me to stop mentioning how long ago we were in the soaps together. And it's not as if we're geezers or anything."

No, but the closer Michael got to forty, the less he liked big birthday celebrations. I wondered suddenly if some kind of male biological clock thing was behind his ever-increasing desire to discuss the M word, as we called it. I'd have to think about that.

Later. When I didn't have murder on my mind.

"Yeah, maybe that's an explanation for how Nate, Maggie, and Francis have been acting," I said. "But maybe one of them had something much more serious to hide than an inconveniently distant birth date."

"Such as?"

"I can think of two theories, actually. First, one of them killed Ichabod Dilley, and the QB knew about it, and was threatening to expose them."

"After thirty years?" Michael said.

"There's no statute of limitations on murder," I pointed out.

"Yeah, but why wait that long? Are you suggesting that the killer meekly endured the QB's blackmail all these years, only to lose his or her temper and bump her off this weekend?"

"Okay, maybe that's a little far-fetched, but what if the QB, after concealing her knowledge all these years, finally revealed it, only to have the killer strike her down?"

Michael nodded slowly.

"A little more plausible," he said. "I like the picture of the QB like a spider on her web, sitting on her secret for decades until just the right moment to use it. Yes, she'd play it that way. Only . . ."

"Only what?"

"Maybe a tad too melodramatic?"

"Yeah," I said, reluctantly. "A little too much like one of Nate's scripts, maybe. But I have another theory."

"I never doubted you would."

"What if the QB herself was the murderer?"

"Of Dilley, you mean?"

"Right," I said. The more I thought about it, the more I liked this theory. "I can imagine her killing someone who stood in her way. And maybe she didn't even have to do the deed herself—maybe all she had to do was set him up for the guys who were after him?"

"I'm not sure that counts as murder," Michael said.

"Legally, I suppose not, but morally, I think it does. So what if Ichabod Dilley didn't really sell her the rights to Porfiria? What if, instead of getting paid peanuts, he was the one who ended up paying—with his life?"

"And thirty years later, someone took revenge?"

"Someone who cared about Ichabod Dilley, and only found out what really happened to him recently—maybe even this weekend."

"Found out how?"

"The other Ichabod Dilley," I said. "If she'd killed the original, she'd have known her Dilley wasn't coming to the convention. And yet, with no picture in the program . . . maybe she thought it was some kind of trick, designed to expose her."

"A tall, gaunt scarecrow in bell-bottoms and a tie-dyed shroud, rising up out of the audience, like a boomer version of Banquo's ghost, pointing the accusing finger at her?"

"Not quite," I said. "Although you may want to suggest that to Nate if he does a script based on this weekend. But the idea that someone who had always suspected the QB of murder might make a deliberate effort to surprise and disconcert her and watch her reaction—very possible."

"Might be worth finding out whether the convention organizing committee thought of hunting down Ichabod Dilley all by themselves or whether they had help," Michael suggested.

"Good point. And even if no one deliberately engineered Ichabod Dilley's apparent return from the dead—even if it really was only a comedy of errors—it could have rattled her. Enough, perhaps, that she'd say or do something that gave her away as the murderer. And inspired someone to murder her."

"So if you like the scenario that someone killed the QB because he or she knew she killed Dilley—" Michael began.

"Or set him up to be killed," I said. "I like it a lot."

"That whittles the suspect field down enormously. Mainly Nate, Maggie, and Francis."

"Or some less-well-known person who knew Dilley," I suggested. "Or for that matter, Ichabod junior. We only have his word that he first learned of his uncle's existence here at the convention. What if his family has been obsessed for years with tracking down the person who murdered his uncle?"

"They could even have suspected the QB," Michael said, "but not had a way to prove it—until the convention invitation fell into young Ichabod's lap."

"Or until he engineered his invitation," I said. "I definitely need to talk to someone on the organizing committee. Find out just how the idea of hunting for Dilley came about."

"And I definitely need to get back downstairs," Michael said, looking at his watch. "I have a panel that should be starting almost immediately, assuming things are still running more or less on time, which I doubt."

"And I should make at least a token appearance at the booth," I said.

# Chapter 37

"Sorry," I said to Steele, as I slipped behind the table. "Please tell me you've been getting along just fine without me."

"I was until he showed up," Steele said, jerking his thumb toward where Walker was standing at my end of the booth, fiddling with things and trying to pretend not to have noticed my arrival. "And I could continue getting along fine if you'd take him somewhere and patch him up."

"Patch him up?" I echoed. "What happened?"

"Hey, Meg, how's it going?" Walker said, waving one hand at me in a casual greeting that would have looked a lot more natural if he hadn't had a wad of bloody paper napkins wrapped around his fingers.

"Playing with the merchandise," Steele said, rather contemptuously. "Actors."

"You keep some of this stuff sharpened," Walker said, his tone more hurt than accusing.

"Yeah, some of the customers want it that way," I said. "Come on; I think I know where to find a first aid kit. Alaric, see if someone can find my father in case Walker needs more patching up than I know how to do. I'll be in the convention office; it's off the green room."

"Right," Steele said and began scanning the ceiling. Apparently he'd noticed Dad's parrot project.

"Meg," Walker said, as he followed me through the room. "Did you get her to—"

"Not here," I muttered, and he got the message and shut up until we reached the convention organizers' room.

They did, indeed, have a first aid kit. I'd have let the two volunteers do the honors of patching him up, but Walker's presence seemed to reduce one to paralysis and the other to silly giggles, so I took charge of the bandaging. He'd sliced open three fingers on his left hand and gouged the base of his right thumb rather badly.

"Ow," he said, as I took the napkins off. "Not so rough."

"The thumb looks pretty ghastly," I said. "It might be a good idea to go to the emergency room in case it needs stitches."

"No, no," he said, curling his hand back protectively. "I really hate hospitals."

Probably because he spent so much time in them, I thought.

"So how did it go?" he stage-whispered.

"She's with the police now," I said.

"Yeah, but what is she telling them?"

"I think I managed to convince her that she'd get in less trouble telling the truth to the police herself than having you tell the newspapers."

"Wow!" Walker exclaimed. "You're incredible! I can't believe you actually—Meg? Is something wrong?"

I realized that I'd been staring at him.

"Sorry," I said. "I just realized something."

"Something about the murder?"

I shook my head, and went back to washing his cuts. I'd suddenly realized why I'd been spending so much energy worrying about Walker. He reminded me, uncannily, of my kid brother who, though far from stupid, seemed content to cruise through life on looks and charm, letting other people take care of him. Sometimes I got tired of being one of the other people, but he was my brother.

Walker was just a friend. More Michael's friend than mine. And yet here I was, cleaning up after him.

Evidently I'd made less progress than I thought in conquering my tendency to take care of the world.

Just then, fortunately for Walker, Dad arrived, and they both forgot all about me. Dad had partially retired from practicing medicine, which meant that he only saw patients with interesting diseases or injuries. His joy at having a nice gory injury to treat was matched only by Walker's hypochondriac delight at having a doctor fussing over him.

I stayed long enough to ask the two volunteers if they knew who had arranged Ichabod Dilley's appearance.

"Todd chaired the program committee," one of them said.

"Great," I said. "Where is he?"

"Home," the volunteer said.

"He's not here?" I asked. I probably sounded critical. Well, I felt critical. "Doesn't someone have to keep the program lurching along? Rearranging it when necessary due to deaths, interrogations, and arrests?"

"Well, not Todd," the volunteer said, as if I ought to know better. "He doesn't cope well with change. We gave him a Valium and sent him home. Sandra's doing all that."

Sandra, it turned out, was the diminutive Amazon who'd been acting as a combination emcee, stage manager, and babysitter for the events taking place in the ballroom, where she was currently running the trivia contest.

So I'd have to wait to interrogate her until the contest ended. By now, any resemblance between what was happening around the hotel and what was printed in the program would be purely coincidental. Still, it gave me a guideline. The trivia contest was supposed to last from three to four. Sometime between four and seven, it would end, and I could interrogate Sandra. And perhaps later the sedated and calmer Todd.

"Will Todd be back?" I asked.

"He said he'd come in for the costume contest," the first volunteer said.

"He'd better," the other volunteer muttered. "If he flakes out like last year . . ."

"We managed last year," the first volunteer said.

"We didn't have all these animals last year," the second volunteer muttered.

"Oh, is Todd in charge of the animals?" I asked.

The two looked at each other.

"I suppose so," the first said.

"He's the one who found them," the second volunteer said. "Which means he's the only one who knows what we're supposed to do with them when the convention is over."

"And I suppose he's the one who managed to get permits to have them here in the first place," I said.

"Permits?" the first volunteer said.

"Oh, great, you mean he should have gotten permits?" the second volunteer said.

"You know Todd," the first one said. "Easier to beg forgiveness later than get permission beforehand. Sandra can take care of any problems, like she did last year."

"Yeah, and I bet by the time we're finished, last year's fire and water damage will look cheap," the second volunteer said.

I decided I'd rather not know what had happened at last year's convention.

"Rounding up the monkeys and parrots seems to be going rather slowly," I said instead.

"Someone kept letting them go again," the first volunteer said.

"You should have had someone guarding them," I said.

"We did, of course," the volunteer said. "It was the guards who were letting them go."

"We've got better guards now," the other said.

"Well, different guards, anyway," the first muttered.

"We're going to have to change our name again to get a hotel for next year," the second volunteer said.

"Three years in a row?" the first said. "We're running out of names."

On that note, I decided to return to the dealers' room. The more I learned about the inner workings of the convention, the more anxious I felt.

"What is this crap, anyway?" Steele said, when I slipped behind the table. "Part of your sleuthing?"

He'd gotten into the stash of fan fic and spurious Porfiria comics I'd stuck under the table.

"Just some stuff I found," I said. "I was thinking of pulling Michael's leg with some of it. He gets so embarrassed by all the action figures and fan fic."

"You might want to check it out first," he said. "Some of this stuff is pretty . . . raw."

He was holding one of the fake comics by one corner, as if it were a loathsome object. Which it was, actually; I recalled that particular comic as an unpleasantly lewd parody without even the saving grace of any humor.

"Good idea," I said.

I noticed that the receipt from the booth where I'd bought the spurious comics had fallen out of the stack and lay on the floor. I faked dropping my pen and managed to snag the receipt and stuff it in my skirt pocket while Steele was still shaking his head over the offensive comic. Silly, but I hated to admit paying good money for the stuff.

But before long, neither of us had time to worry about the fan fic. Either Harry's efforts as an improvised sandwich man had helped or the convention-goers had gotten tired of watching the police and the press. More of them started coming into the dealers' room, and for a while I had enough to do to keep me from fretting.

Steele and I each made a few more sales. Actually, I made more than a few sales, about half of them of Steele's merchandise. Without discussing it, we'd fallen into a comfortable pattern. Steele kept an eye on the stock, packed and unpacked, cleaned and polished things, filled out sales forms, wrapped purchases, and generally took care of all the mundane and routine work, while I charmed swords and daggers into the hands of customers. Even without counting the savings on the booth rental, we were doing much better as a team than either of us would have solo.

Steele kept giving me approving glances, and I decided it was lucky I hadn't worked with him like this a few years ago, before I met Michael. Under the right—or wrong—circumstances, I'd have assumed that because we worked together so well, we were meant for each other. I might have found his brusqueness with customers strangely appealing. After all, he obviously didn't dislike me. He found me useful. You could even say he needed me. Once, that, combined with my innate compulsion to take care of people and his attractiveness, would have spelled trouble. The kind of trouble that's hard to avoid because even when you spot it a mile off, part of you still wants to walk right in.

Thank God I'd learned better. Or maybe just thank God for Michael.

"Meg?"

I looked up to see Typhani standing in front of the booth.

"A messenger just dropped this off for you at the front desk," she said, holding up a nine- by twelve-inch Kinko's envelope. "I said I'd deliver it."

Finally!

"Thanks," I said, trying not to look too eager as I took the envelope out of her hand.

I grabbed a dagger from the table display and slit the envelope open. I peeked in, and was glad I hadn't just fished the pictures out in plain view. Apparently Dad had reached Kevin to ask for blowups of my photos of the QB's body. They were on the top of the stack, and I didn't exactly want anyone seeing those.

Anyone included Typhani, who seemed to be hovering.

"Yes?" I said.

"It's okay?" she said. "The desk clerk can describe the guy who dropped it off if you like."

"No, thanks," I said. "I mean, unless you think there's something I ought to know about the guy who dropped it off."

"Well, you know, if it's some kind of hate mail . . ."

"No," I said. "Kinko's and I are on reasonably friendly terms these days. Did Miss Wynncliffe-Jones get her hate mail in envelopes like this?"

"Yeah, some of them," she said, nodding. "Well, not in Kinko's envelopes. They came in the mail. But in envelopes like that."

"Big, flat envelopes with cardboard inside to keep the contents from bending?"

She nodded.

"The first time she yelled at me for throwing away the envelope," she said, shaking her head. "I mean, how stupid can you get? Like whoever sent it would put a return address!"

I nodded. Typhani seemed to find that satisfactory and went off after fluttering her fingertips at me, the way a child would wave bye-bye.

So whoever sent the QB's hate mail was taking some pains to make sure the contents arrived in good condition.

Not hate mail at all. Hate comics; I'd bet anything. And the shred of paper she'd been holding had probably been part of one of them.

I sat back a little—far enough that I could still keep an eye on the booth, but where passing customers couldn't see what I was holding—and pulled out the photos.

# Chapter 38

Kevin and the Kinko's staff had done a nice job. I stuffed the 8×10 blowups of the QB's body back into the envelope to save for Dad and concentrated on the two shots of the comic strip.

I'd done a good job, too. Or maybe I should give credit to Kevin again, for picking out such a good digital camera. Every line of the drawing was as sharp and crisp as if I had the original in front of me. Looking at it brought back something else: the drawing had been done on nubby-textured paper, off-white with colored flecks in it. I could see the flecks as clear as anything, and the faint shadows from the nubs.

Some kind of specialty drawing stock. All the artists I knew were particular to the point of superstition about their tools. They'd go to the ends of the earth to track down their favorite brands of pens, pencils, and drawing paper. Not that I didn't understand. I felt the same way about my metal-working tools. So the paper was probably a useful clue for the police, who had the resources to identify it, track down where it was sold, perhaps even discover which suspects had bought it.

All it told me was that this wasn't from a published comic. They generally used plain white paper, and much cheaper paper at that.

So I was looking at either an original, unpublished cartoon by Dilley, or a very plausible imitation.

And if I had to bet on it, I'd say the real thing. A real Dilley. I couldn't prove it. Couldn't even explain how I knew. But just as I didn't need to look for a maker's mark to see whether I'd done a piece of ironwork or whether it belonged to one of my blacksmith friends, I could tell Dilley had drawn this, and not some skilled imitator.

And then again . . . it felt different. In the published comics, the artist seemed to like Porfiria, despite her flaws. There was a strange innocence to her promiscuity, and a certain glow to her features.

But this Porfiria looked different. A faint piggish look to the eyes. A slight suggestion of blowsiness. And was that an ink blob, or had the artist drawn a large, dark speck stuck between her front teeth?

It still looked a lot like the QB. To me, even more like her than the published comics. Of course, maybe I wasn't the best judge, since I thoroughly disliked the QB.

Maybe that was it. In the published comics, Porfiria was Tammy Jones, and Ichabod Dilley clearly worshipped her. But in this sketch, though apparently no later, she had become Tamerlaine Wynncliffe-Jones, and he'd learned to hate her. What had she done to turn him against her? And did it have anything to do with her death?

Or for that matter, with his?

"Found something interesting?"

I started, and clutched the photo closer to my chest as I glanced up to see Steele looking at me with curiosity.

"No, just looking at some possible new PR stills for Michael," I said. That seemed the most plausible explanation for why I'd been so absorbed in studying something from an envelope clearly marked "Photos—do not bend!"

Then again, maybe it was time to enlist another brain and another set of eyes. I longed to talk things over with Michael, but he was off dutifully schmoozing with his fans. Maybe I should stop being so cagy and bounce my ideas off someone. Failing Michael, Steele would do as well as anyone. Better than most in fact. Someone who wasn't part of the TV show crowd might have a more balanced perspective on the whole thing.

I glanced back at the photos, and this time I noticed something else. When I'd studied the pictures in the camera, the image was so small that I could barely decipher the words of Porfiria's dialogue. In the blowup, I could see that I'd misread it. She wasn't saying "Bring in the Vagan ambassador." It was "Bring in the Viagran ambassador."

Viagra hadn't been invented in 1972. I didn't know precisely when it came on the market, but surely no earlier than the 90s. Probably the late 90s.

Which meant that no matter how sure I was that Ichabod Dilley had drawn it, that just wasn't possible.

Or was it?

"He's alive," I said.

"What's that?" Steele said.

I slipped the photos back into the envelope and then shoved that into my haversack. Then I took a deep breath. Time to see how this sounds when I say it aloud.

"This is going to sound crazy," I said.

He lifted an eyebrow and glanced briefly at the troupe of dancing trolls performing at the other end of the room, as if to suggest that my definition of crazy needed updating.

"What if Ichabod Dilley is alive?"

"The comic book guy?"

"Yes. When I found the body—I also found something that—well, it doesn't make sense unless Dilley's alive," I said, figuring that I was at least technically keeping my promise not to talk about the scrap of paper. "What if he just disappeared? Went into hiding—after all, he had a good reason to."

"What reason?" Steele asked.

"He owed money to some very impatient people," I said. "So he changed his name, disappeared, and left his friends and family to settle with the loan sharks. Maybe he kept tabs on the QB through the years, or maybe he didn't care. But then the TV show came out, and he saw her getting rich from his creation, and he came back to confront her."

"Sounds weak to me," Steele said, frowning. "The show's been running a couple of years. Why wait till now?"

"I don't know," I said. "Maybe he's been working up to it. Typhani said the QB had been getting hate mail. Of course, Typhani's only been with her for six weeks, but maybe he's been sending her hate mail for years, and this convention was the first chance he'd had to strike."

"Hasn't she done conventions before?" Steele asked.

"Yes, but not a lot on the East Coast," I said. "Or—wait! Maybe he saw an announcement about Ichabod Dilley appearing at the convention, knew it wasn't him, and finally lost it. He would have no way of knowing that the convention organizers, not the QB, had recruited the wrong Dilley. And if he thought her responsible, he might have thought that not only had she stolen his work and made a travesty of it, but now she was stealing his very identity."

I savored the idea.

"You watch a lot of TV, don't you?" Steele asked.

"Come on," I said. "Work with me, Steele."

Bouncing ideas off Michael was much more satisfactory, I

thought. Michael bounced them right back. So call this a dress rehearsal for bouncing things off Michael at dinner.

"Okay. You think Ichabod Dilley was here, at the convention," Steele said. In a voice that clearly showed he was humoring me.

"Is here. In disguise," I said. "And the only thing we knew about him is his approximate age. Only a few of the backstage crowd are in the right age group, but we only need one. For that matter, he doesn't have to be part of the backstage crowd. He could be any of the fans. A killer, hiding himself in a crowd of a thousand innocent fans."

"You going to interrogate them all?" Steele asked, glancing around at the passing convention goers.

"Most of them are too young," I said. "Most of them are in their teens or twenties. Probably only about five percent of them are even close to the right age."

"Yeah, but there's another five percent wearing costumes that don't let you see how old they are," Steele said, pointing to two passing figures in space suits.

He was right. Some of the costumes obscured faces and hands so completely that their wearers could be any age.

"But they're still a minority," I said, after a minute. "Maybe another five percent, for a total of a tenth of the crowd. But then take out the roughly half who are women, because I'm pretty sure Dilley's still a guy. Back down to five percent."

"Of course, five percent of a thousand means fifty people," Dilley said.

"And that's where the police come in," I said. "There's no way I can find and investigate fifty people. But for the police, it's a piece of cake. Especially since they do have one witness to narrow down the suspect list, or even pick Dilley out of the crowd."

"Witness?" Steele said. "Who?"

"Nate," I said. "They knew each other—Dilley stayed with him for several months, when they worked on a film together."

"Long time ago," Steele said, shaking his head. "People change. Wait till your high school class has its twentieth reunion and you'll see."

"That's true," I said, wondering briefly if Steele realized how close I was to that twentieth reunion. "And Nate didn't exactly give a good description. Maggie did ten times better, and she claims she only saw him once or twice."

"Women usually are better at that stuff anyway," Steele said.

"Or maybe there's another reason," I said. "Maybe Nate doesn't want Ichabod Dilley found. Maybe Nate *is* Ichabod Dilley."

"Nate?" Steele echoed.

"Okay, not necessarily the real Ichabod Dilley, the kid who left Kansas for the bright lights of San Francisco and then supposedly died tragically young," I said. "But back around 1972, writing and drawing underground comics and painting psychedelic posters probably weren't the kind of things an ambitious young screenwriter wanted on his resume. So maybe he knew Dilley and used him as a front for his counterculture projects."

Steele shook his head, but he was listening.

"And that would explain how Ichabod Dilley could change from his high school's most-likely-to-succeed golden boy to the awkward, taciturn character Maggie describes," I said. "It wasn't drugs. He would try to say as little as possible because he'd need to avoid giving away the fact that he hadn't painted the paintings or created the comics."

"Or maybe when Dilley showed up, it was really your friend Nate, in disguise," Steele said.

"That's the spirit," I said. "And you know, that's not a bad idea. It fits with what little physical description I've heard of Dilley—he and Nate were both tall and painfully thin, with brown hair. And I saw Nate in a photo from around that time—even in the 1970s, Nate kept his hair short and his face clean-shaven. So what better disguise than to put on a wig and a fake beard when he wanted to pretend to be Dilley? When you add the trench coat and the dark glasses, it positively shouts disguise. I wonder if Dilley the nephew could get any pictures of his uncle. Maybe the real Ichabod was short and round like him."

Steele shrugged.

"Anyway," I continued. "The Porfiria comics ended, not because their creator was dead, but because the front man was. Nate could no longer publish them under Dilley's name. And if his screenwriting career was starting to take off by then, maybe he was just as glad to end the comic series."

"Still doesn't explain why he would kill the QB, as you call her, this weekend," Steele said.

"I haven't quite figured that out yet," I admitted. "Dilley disappeared not long after they all worked together on that movie. Maybe Nate killed him, or set him up to be killed by his enemies, and the QB found out this weekend, and he killed her to keep her from fingering him. Or maybe she knew all along, and was blackmailing him—that could explain why he's stood by her so loyally all these years. Until this weekend, when he snapped. Who knows? If I can just get the police to consider the idea that the creator of the comic books is alive, they can probably figure out the rest."

"Still sounds pretty far-fetched to me," he said. "Of course if you—damn!"

"What's wrong?"

"I need to make a call before five," he said. "Preferably from someplace quieter. Can you watch the booth for maybe fifteen minutes?"

"I owe you a lot more than fifteen minutes," I said.

"Thanks," he said. "You can tell me the rest of your theory when I get back."

I wasn't sure there was much more to my theory, I thought, as he strode away. In fact, I'd already found a flaw. Nate didn't know about Ichabod Dilley naming his characters out of a medical dictionary.

Or pretended not to know. After all, even if Nate hadn't figured out the naming scheme over the years, odds were someone would have done so, and that Nate would have heard about it. In fact, his claiming not to know was downright suspicious.

And his stick figures, which I'd always seen as evidence of Nate's complete lack of drawing ability—were they deliberately bad?

Yes, I liked my theory. It explained everything, from the scrap of comic to her last words.

I could see it. Nate protesting something she was doing to the show. Telling her she couldn't do that to his comics, or his characters, or his words—it didn't matter which. And both Nate and the parrot heard her reply: "I can do anything. I *own* them; I can—"

And that was where he cracked. And killed the QB.

Suddenly, I was impatient for Steele to return. I had to tell this to the cops. And the sooner the better.

# Chapter 39

I was looking around for Steele, or someone else to watch the booth, when I felt someone tugging at my elbow.

"Excuse me?"

I turned to see the pudgy figure of the producer who'd been talking to Steele about doing the armor and weapons for his movie.

"Alaric's stepped away for a few minutes," I said. "Can I—"

"Yes, I know," the man said, looking around furtively. "That's why I came over. I've been discussing a project with Mr. Steele—"

"I noticed," I said. Maybe it was rude, cutting him short like that, but quite apart from the fact that I didn't see what I had to do with his deal with Steele, I saw Detective Foley and his partner step into the dealers' room.

"I'd be interested in your perspective on the project," the man said

"My perspective?" I said.

"Frankly, we're looking for something a little less expensive," the man said. "Perhaps if you could look these numbers over. Give us your thoughts."

He held out a piece of paper. Something Steele had given him as part of their discussions, I surmised. I could see rough sketches of a helmet and an ornate sword hilt. And numbers.

Impressively large numbers, but then he wanted quite a lot of custom iron work.

My perspective? He wanted a lower bid. Someone to do the work more cheaply, or maybe just competition to help him push Steele's price down.

"I don't think——" I began.

"Just look it over," the man said. "Here's my card; I already picked up yours yesterday. I'd like to talk to you."

With that, he disappeared into the crowd.

What a little weasel! Was this how TV producers really worked? Not the top drawer ones, I'd bet. I slipped the card and the paper into my pocket. When Steele got back, I'd warn him what the producer was up to.

In the meantime, the cops had gone from one end of the dealers' room to the other, looking around. Looking for someone in particular, or just looking?

It didn't matter. They were about to leave the room, and I wanted to talk to them. I glanced around and spotted a familiar face.

"Dad!" I said, running out into the aisle and catching his sleeve. "Can you watch my booth for a few minutes?"

"Well," he said, "is it important?" I could see that he had his eye on a bright green parrot fluttering overhead.

"It could be," I said, in the mysterious and conspiratorial tone I knew would catch his interest. "It could be what cracks the case. I'll come and tell you as soon as I see what the police say."

"Right!" he said, and scrambled behind the counter.

I followed the police into the wide hallway outside the dealers' room.

Detective Foley and his partner were talking to several uniformed officers when I reached them.

"When I give the word," I heard Foley say, and then he turned to me, frowning. "What can I do for you?"

"This may sound crazy," I began.

"Why not?" he said. "Everything else today has."

But he listened while I explained my theory. Listened intently, but I wasn't sure whether he found my theory fascinating and plausible or just had trouble following it.

I confess, at the last minute, I waffled, and didn't indict Nate as definitively as I'd originally intended. After all, if I was wrong, Michael still had to work with him. Probably a mistake. It weakened my argument, so all you had left was an impassioned but confusing plea that Foley look a lot more deeply into Ichabod Dilley's death, his relationship with the other members of the cast of *Acid Vision*, and the real identity of every fifty-something person in the hotel.

"That's very interesting," Detective Foley, said, glancing at his silent partner.

"You don't believe me," I said. He could probably tell from my voice that I wasn't pleased.

"Oh, actually we believe you," he said. "We'll be talking to Ms. West and others to develop the information you've given us. It dovetails very nicely with our theory of the case."

"Your theory?" I said.

The other detective gave him a baleful look, as if to suggest that he was talking a little too much to a civilian, but Detective Foley was on a roll.

"Yes," he said, tucking his thumbs in his pants pockets and rocking back on his heels. "We happen to agree with your basic assumption. We think Ichabod Dilley is very much alive. And we can't find any trace of our mild-mannered suspect over there before around 1970."

He was pointing across the lobby, to where Nate was standing, talking to Francis and Walker.

My brain reeled. Okay, I had pointed the finger at Nate. But maybe I wanted to be wrong. I liked Nate, and I certainly hadn't expected the police to confirm my suspicions quite this readily. As I watched, Walker clapped Nate on the shoulder and strolled off.

"If you're finished showing off, maybe we can arrest the guy now?" Foley's partner suggested.

Foley nodded, and the two of them headed across the lobby with a firm, purposeful air.

Nate and Francis looked up. Nate looked alarmed. Of course, so did Francis, but that was his normal expression.

Detective Foley reached into his inside jacket pocket for something. His badge, maybe.

Nate and Francis could see it, too. Nate looked anxious.

Francis turned and ran.

Francis? Wait a minute. I thought they were after Nate— but he just stood there with a puzzled look on his face. Francis was the one running away.

The detectives followed. Because he was the one they were after, or just because he was running?

No matter. They followed him. So did I. At a safe distance. My Renaissance wench costume slowed me down, but then I didn't want to overtake the police, just see what happened when they caught Francis.

Glancing up, I saw a growing number of monkeys, always curious about new human antics, swinging along above us, chattering eagerly. The half-dozen parrots currently infesting the hallway merely squawked as the monkeys shoved them aside.

The crowd grew thinner, and I could see that Francis's flight was destined to end shortly. The detectives were gaining on him, and the path ahead was blocked by an unexpected obstacle. Apparently Brad, Salome's keeper, had gotten permission to pack up and bring her home. Under his direction, several nervous bellhops were pulling her cage along the hall toward the open double doors leading to the parking lot.

Francis crashed into the cage. Salome roared and began flinging herself from side to side. The bellhops fled, knocking Brad down on their way.

Francis looked startled for a moment, and then he reached out and jerked aside the latch holding the cage door closed.

"Stand back or I'll turn her loose!" he yelled.

People started leaving. Fast.

"Power to the people!" Francis shrieked. "Free the Pasadena Pair!"

Just then, Salome hit the cage door, which popped open, sending her sprawling ten feet out into the middle of the hallway floor.

She lay there for a few moments, as if stunned—or perhaps feeling the same sense of acute embarrassment domestic housecats suffer when they do something clumsy.

I flattened myself against a wall, convinced that I'd be trampled by the panic-stricken mob. But I had to hand it to this crowd. For a panic-stricken mob, they did an astonishingly efficient job of emptying the hallway. By the time Salome shook her head and bounded to her feet with a roar, only a dozen people remained.

I decided it was stupid to be one of them and began backing slowly down the hall, feeling behind me for a doorway.

Salome lashed her tail and looked around.

I saw Brad, the keeper, slipping out through a doorway.

I felt a doorframe behind me. I backed up, hard, pushing the door open. I could see tile floor. I was in a bathroom. Okay. I kept on backing, staring at the door, until I hit something hard, and grabbed onto it. I kept expecting Salome to burst in. As seconds passed and nothing happened, I could feel my heart slow and my brain start working again.

I glanced back and decided to let go of the urinal.

# Chapter 40

"Hello?" I said, not too loudly. "Anyone in here?"

No answer, just the usual hollow bathroom echo.

And I didn't hear any roars outside, or any screams of terror or anguish.

But I didn't hear any reassuring sounds of the convention resuming, either.

Great. I was trapped in the men's room.

At least if I'd found an exit door, I could mill around outside with the rest of the evacuees. Find out if the police had caught Francis, or if his diversionary tactic had worked and, more important, find out when they'd caught Salome. As it was, I could either stick my head out and risk having it bitten off or lurk around here until someone came in and found me crouching among the urinals. I'd be a long time living that down.

Also a long time getting over the ick factor of fondling a urinal. I washed my hands, twice, and then realized the bathroom was out of paper towels.

Typical of this dump, I thought, drying my hands on my skirt.

Something crackled in my pocket.

I reached in and found the folded piece of paper. My fingertips rasped over the rough, pebbly texture. I pulled it out and stared at it. Off-white with little flecks of color.

"I know who killed her," I said, half-aloud. I'd been wrong. And the cops were wrong. And I knew how to prove it. Provided the killer didn't do away with the evidence before I could get it to the police.

I opened the bathroom door a crack and peered out. Nothing. No Salome. No people, either, which probably meant she was still on the loose.

The only sane thing to do was to stay in the bathroom.

Of course, sanity has never been my strong point.

I slipped out into the hall. Still nothing. I crept quietly across the hall, and then along the opposite wall, until I got to the small side door that led into the dealers' room. I opened it as quietly as I could.

Of course, all this silent creeping might prove useless. Maybe tigers relied more on smell than hearing. If I'd known I'd be trying to elude one, I could have looked it up before coming to the convention.

I glanced into the dealers' room. No sign of Salome.

Of course there were things she could hide behind. Just a few, but still.

I heard a faint noise in the hall. Monkeys, chattering softly.

Chattering at what?

I slipped inside quickly and closed the door. I'd have felt better if some idiot hadn't left a door at the other end of the room hanging wide open.

I half-ran over to the booth and grabbed a sword—one of the ones I'd sharpened because, crazy as it had always seemed to me, some customers wanted them that way.

Not so crazy now. I felt suddenly, though quite irrationally, safer. Stupid; what could I really do with a sword if Salome came at me? But I didn't put it down, even though it hampered me a bit when I searched the booth.

Alaric Steele's side of the booth.

I might be risking my neck for nothing. He might have already gotten rid of the sketchpad, the one containing the off-white paper with the colored flecks. Of course, I still had the sheet of paper in my pocket, the paper on which Steele had done his estimates for the producer on making armor and swords for his TV show. Neat, legible letters and numbers—his printing had an almost calligraphic elegance. Several very deft sketches—I wished I could draw designs for potential customers that well. It looked quite good on that sheet of pebbly, color-flecked drawing paper. More like fine art than a craftsman's sketch. But he could always claim he'd found the paper somewhere. It would be so much more satisfactory to find . . .

The pad. He'd hidden it among the packing materials, sandwiched in between several sheets of cardboard at the bottom of a box filled with Styrofoam peanuts.

Inside, I found pages of the same rough-toothed paper, covered with sketches. I hadn't seen him sketching at the booth, but suddenly I could see him sitting alone in his room, drawing. Just him and the sketch pad.

He was good. Hell, he'd been good thirty years ago. He was brilliant now. His figures, always strong, were cleaner, simpler—now but just as subtle and lifelike, as if he'd learned to achieve the same results with fewer lines.

The first few pages contained small sketches of various people at the convention. You could tell at a glance how he felt about each subject. He mocked the costumed fans, but gently, as if their antics amused him. He wasn't quite so kind to the bearded professor or Walker. I was relieved that he hadn't drawn Michael.

He liked Maggie. He didn't idealize her, didn't remove any lines or gray hairs, and yet the sketch of her had a warmth and vibrancy that made you smile just to look at it. It wasn't unlike the glow Porfiria had in those early comics. Yeah, he liked Maggie.

He liked me, too. The sketches of me didn't quite have Maggie's warmth, but they did have their own kind of heat. I didn't think my Renaissance wench costume was quite as low cut as he'd drawn it, and I knew perfectly well he'd exaggerated my figure. Nice to know I retain my appeal to the criminal element.

But the QB—he'd sketched her, more than anyone, and the pictures radiated a cold hatred that made me hesitate to touch the page. And they made her look startlingly ugly and repulsive. The more startling because they didn't seem distorted. More like photo-realism, and yet through some subtle alchemy, he'd made the seemingly straightforward lines and curves reveal not only the outer shell but the cruel soul inside. I found myself staring into the eyes of one sketch and thinking that Medusa must have looked just like this, to turn her viewers into stone. I certainly stood staring down at the page for far too long.

A monkey chattered overhead, and I snapped out of it.

"I need to get out of here," I muttered.

But which way? Back the way I'd come, or out the other side of the dealers' room?

I should have paid more attention to which way Salome was going. Or, for that matter, where Steele went when he left the dealers' room a few minutes before Francis turned Salome loose.

"Lady killer or tiger?" I muttered, looking back and forth between the two escape routes. Though for all I knew, if I chose the wrong path, they'd both be lying in wait.

Maybe I could sneak out the back way while they were fighting over who got to finish me off.

"Chill," I told myself. Odds were Steele was outside, with the rest, waiting to hear that Salome had been recaptured. The last time we'd talked, I'd been busy explaining why I suspected Nate. He had no way of knowing that his producer friend had just handed me the clue that gave him away.

"Just move," I muttered. I decided that if I were Salome, I'd steer for the lobby, so I headed toward the opposite side of the dealers' room, where the back exit would take me near the ballroom and the green room. It would have taken Salome longer to reach those.

Though between the time I'd spent cowering in the men's room and the time it had taken me to search the booth, she could have strolled halfway downtown.

I walked as quickly and quietly as possible to the other end of the room and peered out the open door. Quiet out there.

Possibly too quiet? Would the parrots and monkeys shut up if they knew Salome was nearby?

No way to tell. I peered around the doorway, carefully. Nothing. I slipped out and headed toward the ballroom door. My plan, to the extent I had a plan, was to slip into the ballroom and then out again through the back door Michael and I had used the night before. Odds were few people at the convention knew that route, and Salome would have trouble with the door handles.

Halfway down the hall, I heard a noise. From the ballroom.

Or was it my imagination?

I crept into the ballroom. Definitely a real noise, and coming from a utility closet. Which was locked, from the outside. Perhaps someone had taken refuge in the closet, as I had in the bathroom, and been locked in.

I opened the door and found the bound, gagged figure of the man from the health department.

"Ah, so that's where you went," I said.

He wriggled frantically, and made a lot of loud umphing noises that didn't really need translation.

"Yes, I can untie you if you like," I said, "but it really might be better to wait until they catch the tiger, and besides—"

Just then, I felt the point of a sword at my back.

# Chapter 41

I react quickly in moments of crisis. Not always usefully, but quickly. This time, I managed to whirl and meet Steele's sword with mine, slamming the closet door along the way.

Which would have made me feel better if the smile on Steele's face didn't suggest that he wanted me to fight back, and if I hadn't realized, a second too late, that slamming the door might be a bad idea. Now Steele didn't have to worry about a possible eyewitness if he slit my throat.

"I'd like my sketchpad back," he said, with a token thrust of his sword by way of emphasis.

I shook my head. I tried to think of something suitably cutting to say, but the brain wasn't cooperating, so I settled for parrying and returning to my best on-guard pose.

"Yeah, you're one tough dame," he said, with a sneer. "But I never bothered with that pretty, choreographed stage combat you and Chris like. I learned to use this thing as a weapon."

"I should have known the name was too good to be true," I said. "A blacksmith named Steele."

"Well, I got to choose," he said.

"I think Ichabod Dilley suits you better, though," I said. "Mind if I call you Ichabod?"

"Yes, I mind," he said, taking a step forward—not quite a lunge, but enough to make me scramble back a few steps as

I parried. "Alaric Steele is my legal name now. Ichabod Dilley is that little twerp in the cheap suit."

"Your call," I said.

"Give me the damned sketchbook," he said.

"Just for the sake of argument, what if I do give you the sketchbook?" I asked. "You're going to say, 'Gee, thanks,' sheathe the sword, and go away quietly?"

"No, but I'll make it quick and painless," he said.

"Like I've been meaning to tell you all weekend, you're a lousy salesman," I said.

"But a damn fine swordsman," he said, lunging forward, and for a few terrifying moments, I parried frantically and backed up as fast as I could, Steele following, until we reached the open area in front of the stage. Then Steele's attack eased off and we went back to circling each other warily.

The blacksmith part of my brain noted with disapproval that both our blades had gotten rather nicked in that last flurry of thrusts and parries. Another part, probably inherited from Dad, observed that it was certainly a lot harder to avoid being hit when you're fighting someone who really wants to kill you, wasn't it? And didn't the snick of the blades sound just like in the movies? I'd have told both parts to shut up, except that they seemed to be drowning out, for now, the part that kept yelling at me to drop the sword and curl up in a little ball. Not a good plan.

Do something to distract him, I thought.

"So," I said, backing away a little more. "While you're trying to kill me—I say trying, because of course I plan to stop you if I can—satisfy my curiosity, will you?"

"You want to know if I killed her?" he said, stepping forward and gently brushing his blade against mine. "Well . . . if you really want to know . . . *YES!*"

As he shouted, he lunged, aiming for my throat. I parried easily and backed away again.

"Lucky you," he sneered.

Lucky, my eye. Powerful lunge, well executed . . . but telegraphed. I'd known the answer to his question, of course, and I'd suspected he would lunge when he said it.

I managed to back up the stairs onto the stage, which was damned hard in long skirts. I resented the fact that Steele got to see where he was going when he bounded up the stairs after me.

Of course, if I'd known I'd be dueling a crazed killer, I'd have worn something more suitable than a low cut, full-skirted wench costume.

"Of course you killed her," I said. "You must have gotten a good laugh, sitting there listening to me telling you all the reasons why Nate had to be the killer. But I was wondering why."

"Why?" he snapped. "Isn't it obvious?"

And again, he'd lunge on the words he wanted to emphasize. I was starting to like his fighting style. Predictable. Although I wished the monkeys overhead would stop chattering. They distracted me, and he didn't even seem to notice.

"I mean, was it really just about the show and a bunch of comic books?"

"A bunch of comic books? Are you trying to tick me off?"

Actually I was. Make someone lose his temper and you have an advantage over him, my martial arts teacher always used to say. Of course, he wasn't necessarily thinking of people waving yard-long sharpened broadswords.

Steele stopped for a moment, pulled his sword back, and took a breath.

"It was mine," he said, "and she made a travesty of it."

"You did sell her the rights, you know," I said, as gently as I could.

"It wasn't supposed to be a real sale," he said. "I had these guys after me, trying to collect money I couldn't possibly pay, and I had to disappear."

"I figured your disappearance had something to do with the debt collectors," I said. "Just out of curiosity, how did you get so far in debt? Your nephew thinks drugs."

"Drugs," he said, with a bitter laugh. "You can tell who raised him. Just what my brother would say."

"So if it wasn't drugs—"

"I paid for printing the last four issues of the comic," he said.

He was getting caught up in what he was saying. Maybe if I kept him talking, he'd put down the sword, or at least give me a chance to knock it out of his hands.

"The publisher claimed he had cash-flow problems, so I borrowed the money," he continued. "And then he disappeared, leaving me with all the bills. He never even printed the last issue."

"The thirteenth issue," I murmured.

"Exactly," he said. "Tammy and I figured if we could get a bigger publisher to pick up the comics, I'd have more than enough to pay back the loan sharks. Or better yet, a movie deal. And once we had all that money, I could pay off my debts and resurface. But for the time being, I had to disappear, so I pretended to sell her the rights so she'd have legal authority to cut a deal."

"And you didn't have a backup plan in case she couldn't cut the deal?"

He shook his head.

"I know it sounds stupid, but I never imagined it wouldn't happen."

"So you changed your name, faked your death under the old name, and waited for her to sell the comics and rescue you."

"And she never did a damned thing," he said. "The bitch!"

Predictably, he lunged on the last word, sending me scuttling backward again while overhead the monkeys shrieked and leaped about. Glad someone was enjoying the show. I wasn't; this time he kept coming, testing my defenses again and again while I backed away, step by step. So much for distracting him.

"You never asked what happened?" I said.

"She never took my calls or answered my letters," he said. "Didn't want to admit she'd stopped trying."

"Or maybe she didn't want to admit she'd failed," I said. "From what Nate says, she put a lot of work into it, over the years, but selling an idea for a movie or a TV series isn't easy."

"And when she sold it, look what happened. Crap. And you know what really ticked me off?"

I shook my head, and got ready, because I knew he'd strike when he snarled out whatever he was about to say.

"The credits!" he roared, and even though I was expecting it, I almost didn't manage to parry. "She stole my creation, after thirty years she finally did something with it, and then she didn't—even—mention—me—in the credits!"

He nicked me, once, during that mad flurry of thrusts, and I could feel a trickle of blood running down my arm. Maybe more than a trickle; I didn't dare take the time to look too closely. I'd backed up, nearly to the edge of the stage. I was panting a little—as much from stress as exertion. Steele wasn't. He was still feinting and slowly advancing. He didn't really look all that winded. Just my luck to tangle with the one fifty-something at the whole convention in better shape than me.

"Maybe she thought you were dead?" I suggested, sliding to the side as I parried and parried again. His style was getting better, dammit. Fewer dramatic lunges and more constant pressure.

"She knew I wasn't dead," he said. "She helped me fake it."

"That was in 1972," I said. "You could have died for real in the thirty years since."

"And that makes it all right to pretend I never existed?"

"Maybe she thought you wouldn't want to be credited as Ichabod Dilley!" I suggested, "And it would spoil the whole purpose of the phony death if she credited Alaric Steele."

"Hardly matters now," he said. "She's dead. And it's her fault I had to give up my art all these years."

"Give it up?" I asked. "You mean completely?"

"Going from one lousy job to another," he said.

"Until you took up blacksmithing," I suggested.

He shrugged.

"Gives me independence, I'll say that much for it," he said.

Maybe it was the insult to my chosen profession, but I parried his next several feints a lot more easily.

"Why didn't you do another comic, when you saw Tammy wasn't going to sell Porfiria?" I suggested. "Make your own deal."

"Didn't dare," he said. "I had people after me, remember? What if they recognized my style?"

"I think you're overestimating the aesthetic sensibilities of your loan sharks," I said. "Not to mention their staying power—why would they keep chasing you after your brother paid your debts?"

"Well, I didn't know that until yesterday," he said. "That's another thing she did to me . . . she had my address, and never passed along any messages from my brother. If I'd known he paid them off, I could have come out of hiding then."

"So you were mad that you gave up your art all these years for nothing."

Probably the wrong thing to say—he snarled and lunged again.

"You're wasting my time," he said. "I want my sketchbook—"

"Over there, by the door," I said, jerking my chin in the right direction. "I dropped it when you surprised me."

"And that little scrap of paper—"

I was running out of space to retreat.

"And then—"

Bad luck. This time, when he lunged, I tripped over a power cable and went sprawling. He loomed over me, sword in hand, and the smile on his face wasn't the least bit reassuring.

"And then I'm going to make sure you can't tell anyone. Sorry you—"

Help arrived. One of the monkeys dropped onto Steele's head, shrieking, clawing, and biting. He grabbed at the monkey with both hands, nearly skewering me with the sword when he dropped it. Half a dozen other monkeys were swinging about overhead, shrieking and chattering as if working up their nerve to join the attack. It only took a few seconds for Steele to throw the monkey off, but when he turned around again to look for his sword, he found himself staring at the business end.

"You won't use that, you know," he said, with a menacing smile.

"Really? Try me," I said.

"It's a lot harder to kill than most people think," he said.

"I'll just have to try, won't I?" I said. "Inflicting grievous bodily harm is also fine. I'm not going to stand here and let you kill me."

I could see him tensing his muscles for a spring, and I didn't even know myself whether I'd have the nerve to impale him when he did. I never found out. Just as he was about to move, I heard a noise overhead.

A low, rumbling growl.

We both froze.

I could see that Steele was darting his eyes up, above my head, to the left, to the right. Since he kept flicking his eyes in different directions, he obviously wasn't seeing anything. I was doing the same thing, only I finally did spot something.

An African Grey parrot.

As I watched, the parrot opened its mouth again, produced a surprisingly low, rumbling growl, and then preened its feathers, looking very pleased with itself.

And rightly so. Now that I knew it was a parrot, I thought I could tell that the growl was a little less deep and resonant than Salome's. Then again, maybe I only thought that because I was looking at the parrot. If you expected—perhaps dreaded—hearing a tiger, maybe it sounded just fine. I hoped so, anyway.

I leveled my gaze on Steele.

"Supposedly tigers have very bad eyesight," I said, very quietly. "They attack on motion. Maybe if we both keep very, very still."

The parrot conveniently practiced its growl again. I imitated Steele's menacing smile.

Steele stayed very, very still.

Now what? We couldn't stand here forever, me holding the sword pointed at Steele's throat. Sooner or later, my arm would get tired. Or the parrot would switch from menacing growls to knock-knock jokes and give the game away. Or the real Salome would turn up.

Just when I was about to turn and make a run for it, I saw Steele begin to move. I stepped out of the line of his attack and was aiming a thrust at his midsection when I realized he wasn't lunging at me—he was falling. I barely avoided skewering him as he flopped face first to the floor, with a small projectile protruding from his left buttock. A dart.

"Got him!" came a voice.

A woman in some kind of uniform appeared over the edge of the stage.

"Roger," came a voice from the back of the ballroom. "You stay there; we've got a location on the tiger."

"You can put the . . . weapon down now, ma'am," the woman said. "He'll be out for a while. We calibrated the dosage in the tranquilizer dart to knock out a two hundred pound tiger for an hour. I figure he's in about the same weight range."

I dropped the sword.

She wasn't the cops, I noticed. The patch on her sleeves said "Loudoun County Animal Control."

"I'm just glad you tranquilized him instead of me," I said. "After all, I was the one holding the sword."

"Yeah, but we saw what he was up to before that," came another voice. "We caught most of it."

Detective Foley.

"Caught most of it?" I said. "You mean you were watching somewhere and just let him chase me all over the room trying to cut my throat?"

"Relax, d'Artagnan," he said, chuckling. "I meant we caught it all on camera."

He pointed to the balcony. Yes, the cameras were there, pointed at the stage. I supposed that the little blinking red lights meant they were running.

"A whole bunch of people locked themselves in the Rivendell Room when the cat got loose," Foley said. "They were watching the whole thing, and when they realized it wasn't a skit, one of them called 911 on a cell phone and got patched through to us outside. Luckily the animal control truck had just pulled up; I felt a whole lot better coming in with them and their tranquilizer darts than I would have with just our guns."

I glanced up at the balcony again and saw Foley's partner appear.

"Of course, the sound quality's probably pretty poor, but they can enhance that in the lab for the trial," Foley said. "You want to say anything to your fans before we shut the cameras off and seize the tapes?"

"Shut the damned cameras off, Foley," I said, sitting down on the stage. "What I have to say I don't want on tape."

"Yeah," Foley said, nodding. "You can probably turn them off now, unless—"

"Freeze, Steele!"

We all whirled at the sound, and saw that Michael had burst out onto the ballroom stage from the door leading to the kitchens. He looked around at the half-dozen police officers aiming guns at him, glanced down at Steele's unconscious body, and then his shoulders slumped, and he lowered the fire extinguisher he was holding.

"I thought I told you to stay out in the parking lot and let us take care of the situation," Foley said, holstering his weapon and nodding to his troops to do the same.

"I would have, except your idea of taking care of the situation was to sit around watching while that lunatic killed Meg," Michael said.

"Oh, Meg's not as easy to kill as all that," Dad said, following Michael onto the stage. "Though I would like to take a look at that cut."

He was, of course, toting his small traveling doctor's bag.

"Can you take a look at this guy while you're at it?" the animal control officer asked, indicating Steele.

"How much longer will he be out, anyway?" Foley asked, glancing down at Steele.

"Beats me," the officer said, shrugging. "We've never used the tranquilizer darts on a human before."

"What kind of tranquilizer?" Dad asked.

While they fussed over Steele, Michael put down the fire extinguisher, walked over, and put his arms around me.

"Do you know how I felt when they told me what was happening?" he said.

"Hold that thought a second," I said. "Foley! Are those damned cameras off yet?"

# Chapter 42

By the time Michael and I finished celebrating my survival, Dad had pronounced that the tranquilizer dart wasn't going to kill Steele. Foley won his argument with the newly arrived ambulance crew who wanted to whisk Steele away to the hospital, Foley's partner gave up trying to evict Walker, who managed to sneak in with the medics, and a uniformed officer had rescued the irate health department man from the closet.

"Now, let's see that cut," Dad said. "Yes, I think a butterfly bandage and a bit of gauze should take care of it."

"Should we be staying here?" I asked. "Have they caught Salome yet?"

"Safely sedated, and they'll take her back to her cage as soon as they rig a stretcher," Foley said. "Although considering how much prime rib she ate in the restaurant, she'd probably just have curled up to digest anyway. So how long have you known that your business partner was actually Ichabod Dilley? Am I going to have to arrest you for obstruction of justice?"

"He's not my business partner—we were just splitting a booth for the weekend," I protested. "I didn't know he was the killer until after Francis set the tiger loose, and then it was too late to tell you."

While Dad continued to do necessary but uncomfortable things to the cut on my arm, and Michael went off with his cell phone to call Mother and reassure her that I would live, I explained how the scrap of paper the producer had given me led me to Steele.

"At least we were right about Dilley still being alive," Foley said, filing away the now-battered paper in an evidence bag, "even if we all had the wrong suspects."

"Okay, so Nate's innocent, and Francis isn't Ichabod Dilley," I said. "Do we have any idea who Francis is? And why seeing the police sent him scampering off like someone who just got top billing on *America's Most Wanted?*"

"Oh, yes," Michael said. "He broke down in the parking lot and confessed everything. He's a student radical who's been on the run since 1970 when he and an accomplice burned all the files at the local draft board. The accomplice was arrested while disposing of the empty kerosene cans—that's the other half of the Pasadena Pair he was shouting about. But Francis escaped and was never heard from again. Until today."

"Wow," Walker said. "So are they turning him over to the FBI?"

"Wouldn't there be a statute of limitations on that?" I asked, glancing at Foley. "I mean, unless they killed someone, surely the FBI wouldn't be all that interested after thirty years."

"The FBI wasn't all that interested after thirty days," Foley said. "We did make a little progress on the case while you were swashing and buckling on stage here. Not only did the Pasadena Pair not kill anyone, apparently they didn't even burn any draft board files."

"That's Francis all over," Walker said, nodding. "Give him a can of kerosene and he still can't light a fire."

"Oh, he and his accomplices lit a fire, all right," Foley said, suppressing a smile. "They just got the wrong office. Instead of the draft board they got the animal control office for a nearby town called La Cañada. Torched the dog license files."

"That's definitely Francis's style," Michael said, with a sigh.

"Apparently your friend just assumed he was a hunted man," Foley went on. "Went off and created a new identity for himself. Been living a few miles from La Cañada for twenty years now and never bothered to look up his accomplice or check the newspaper records or anything."

"That's Francis," Michael and Walker said, in unison.

"There's just one thing," I said. "If this all took place in La Cañada, how come they called themselves the Pasadena Pair?"

"Well, what were we supposed to call ourselves?" Francis said. "The La Cañada Two? Oh, that's really catchy."

Apparently he'd entered the ballroom while Detective Foley was talking.

"Besides, if we called ourselves the La Cañada anything, the newspapers wouldn't print the tilde, and everyone would think we were some kind of radical Quebec separatist group. So," he added, turning to Foley, "am I free to go?"

"As far as Loudoun County and the FBI are concerned," Foley said.

"So Francis isn't in trouble after all?" I asked, hoping I didn't sound too disappointed.

"That's California's problem, not mine," Foley said, shrugging.

"I imagine there will be repercussions," Francis said, lifting his chin and straightening his back. He strode over to where Michael and Walker stood.

"Kids," he said. "I hate to do this. I've enjoyed working with both of you. But it's not fair to you. I don't want my notoriety to rub off on you, and I don't want to take the chance that my legal troubles could distract me from handling your careers properly. I think it would probably be best for all concerned if you sought representation elsewhere."

They all shook hands solemnly, and Francis strode off, head high, eyes fixed on the horizon.

"What do you think?" Walker said.

"Humphrey Bogart, last scene from *Casablanca*," Michael said. " 'Where I'm going, you can't follow. What I've got to do, you can't be any part of.' "

"Nah, Ronald Coleman," I said. "As Sidney Carton. 'Tis a far, far better thing I do—' "

"I meant, do you think he's pulling our leg?" Walker asked.

"Sounded serious to me," Foley said. "Crazy as a bedbug, but serious."

"Who cares?" Michael said. "We don't have to fire him; he fired himself in front of witnesses."

"True," Walker said. "Cool. I've got to go make some phone calls."

He ambled off, looking very pleased with life.

"Don't you need to make some phone calls, too?" I asked Michael.

He shook his head.

"I already made my phone calls," he said. "My old agent is getting bored just running the restaurant. She jumped at the chance to take me on again and get back in the business."

"That's great!" I said. The one time I'd met her, I'd liked Michael's former agent—now, thank goodness, once again his agent. "And does she think she can solve your contract problem or—oh no!"

People were still on edge. Everyone whirled at my exclamation, and the cops kept their hands near their weapons. But I was the only one who ran out into the hall where the uniformed animal control officers were hauling the sedated Salome along on an improvised tiger-sized stretcher.

"Careful," one of the officers warned. "We don't know how deep she's under and—what are you doing?"

They probably weren't used to seeing tigers that often, and they certainly weren't prepared for the sight of a civilian sticking her hand into the tiger's mouth and removing something trailing from Salome's teeth like abandoned dental floss. Although this something was considerably more substantial than dental floss.

"Isn't that Spike's leash?" Michael asked, coming up beside me.

"She's eaten Spike," I muttered.

# Chapter 43

I stared down at the leash. The last foot of it, the part that should have been attached to Spike's harness, was missing. A wave of guilt washed over me. I hadn't even stopped to worry about Spike after Salome's escape.

"We've got to do something," I said. Sounding rather fierce, I suppose. The nearest officers stepped between me and Salome as if to protect the sleeping tiger.

In spite of my best efforts, neither Dad nor the animal control staff seemed to understand the importance of performing an emergency Spikectomy on Salome. I followed the stretcher out into the parking lot, fuming.

"There's nothing you can do," Michael said. "There's no way he could survive being . . . um . . . whatever. I'll break the news to my mom."

"I'm sure he didn't suffer," Dad said, patting my shoulder.

"Michael! There you are!"

Chris Blair was running over to see us. Michael turned to greet him, but I continued watching as the animal control officers dragged Salome back into her cage. Maybe when they had her safely in the cage, they'd stop watching her so closely, and I could do something. If I stuck my arm down her throat, would she cough up Spike? Or was she more likely to wake up and eat my arm for dessert?

"Is that okay with you, Meg?"

"Is what okay?" I asked, turning reluctantly to see what Chris wanted. Didn't anyone else care about poor Spike?

"Can you rehearse the combat demonstration with Michael now?"

"Now? With Michael?" I said, my eyes still drawn to Salome's cage.

"Yeah, he's good enough with a sword to take my place."

"What happened to you?"

I emerged from my obsession with rescuing Spike long enough to notice that Chris was sporting a large bandage on his right hand.

"Didn't you hear a word I was saying? That evil little mutt of yours tried to take my hand off when——"

"Evil little mutt!" I exclaimed. "How can you call him that, after what happened to the poor little thing?"

"What do you mean, after what happened to him?" Chris said. "You mean the fact that I single-handedly rescued him from the tiger or the fact that he's sitting in Maggie's van right now, stuffing himself with ground sirloin?"

"Salome didn't eat him?"

"He's fine," Chris said. "I, on the other hand, was rather badly bitten, and probably won't be able to work for a couple of weeks, which means tonight's show is off unless someone can take my place. Which Michael has agreed to do, provided we can get in some rehearsal time."

"No problem," I said. "Just tell me when and where. You can't imagine how grateful I am."

"I have a very good imagination," Chris said, waggling his eyebrows. "Any chance you'd be grateful enough to——"

"To rehearse your stage combat demonstration, yes," Michael interrupted. "Half an hour from now in the Shangri-La Room."

Chris laughed, and strode off to find Harry.

"So Spike is safe," Michael said. "Shall I assume, from the touching concern you just showed for his welfare, that I can tell my mom we'll be happy to adopt Spike, now that she's found out she's allergic?"

"No, but just because I don't want to adopt him doesn't mean I don't care about his welfare. Here, Dad," I said, handing my father the truncated leash. "Go stick this back in Salome's teeth. Just in case she has charmed any fans into thinking tigers make nifty house pets."

"Good thinking," Dad said, and trotted over to Salome's cage.

"Dad, I was kidding," I began, but he was already out of earshot. "Of course, I can't believe I just blew the chance to weasel out of doing another stage performance," I said, turning to Michael.

"What? You'd rather act with Chris than with me?"

"I'd rather not act at all, thank you," I said. "I get stage fright."

"You'll get over it."

"I don't plan to do enough acting to get over it," I said.

"Not even to solve my contract problems? While your dad was bandaging your arm, I got another call from my agent. Also your agent, if you're interested."

"Why would I need an agent?"

"Apparently all this weekend's publicity has convinced the network to renew. And our agent thinks once they see the footage of your sword fight, they'll probably want to arrange a guest appearance on the show."

"Me?" I squeaked. "On the show?"

"Only if they agree to meet all our contract demands," Michael said. "Which will include a schedule that doesn't interfere with my teaching responsibilities."

"Is that possible?"

"Dead easy," said a voice at my elbow. I turned to see Nate, looking up owlishly from the yellow legal pad on which he was scribbling words and whole chorus lines of stick figures. "I can probably have scripts for the whole season done by the end of next week without the QB's interference, and odds are we can get signoff pretty quickly and come up with an efficient shooting schedule. Is your Dad around? I need some names."

"Over there," I said, pointing to where Dad was standing with the business end of his stethoscope pressed against Salome's tawny flank. Mother was circulating through the crowd with the jar in which Brad had been collecting donations for Salome's upkeep, and from the looks of it she would soon need a second jar.

"Walker's staying with the show," Michael said, as Nate wandered off in search of Dad. "With the QB gone, they need as many of the old cast as possible. And Maggie's coming back—Nate's still figuring out how. She'll insist on a tight shooting schedule. She doesn't want to spend any more time than necessary away from her animals."

I spotted Maggie nearby, talking to Brad.

"And we have a very good benefit program," I heard her say.

"Maggie's hiring Brad?" I murmured to Michael.

"To keep Salome happy," Michael said. "Or didn't you hear—Maggie's buying Salome. Oh, and apparently she's convinced the animal control folks to do something about the monkeys and parrots."

He pointed to where the head of the Amazon security guard and the hotel's acting manager were talking, apparently simultaneously, to one of the animal control officers. The officer was writing something in a notebook. A citation, I suspected, as he tore off a page and handed it to the Amazon, who looked at it and stopped talking.

I moved a little closer so I could hear.

"And as for you," the officer said, turning to the hotel manager, "you should have called us Friday, as soon as you knew you had a problem."

"Go ahead," the manager said. "Fine me, throw me in jail— I don't care. Just get those things out of my lobby, will you?"

"We're working on it," the officer said, and began writing again.

"I want you to arrest them!" someone shouted nearby.

We turned to see the man from the health department talking to a uniformed officer.

"I understand, sir," the officer said. "But unless you can give us a better description—there must be fifty people here wearing space suits and carrying ray guns."

"You haven't heard the last of this!" the health department man shouted, storming off into the crowd.

"Where's Foley?" someone said behind me.

I turned to answer, and then realized that a passing cop was speaking into his radio.

"Roger," he said. "Tell Foley we secured the suspect's car. Had all his stuff in it—looks like he was about to make a run for it."

"Well, that answers another of my questions," I said, as the cop strolled out of earshot.

"And what was that?" Michael asked.

"How Steele knew to come after me in the hotel when

everyone else had evacuated," I said. "I bet he wasn't coming after me at all—he was coming to pick up his stuff from the booth."

"I'm sure Foley's happy you prevented his escape," Michael said.

"Yes, I'm sure everyone's happy," I said.

"Almost everyone," Michael said, pointing back toward the hotel entrance. The police were bringing Alaric Steele outside, and a police cruiser, lights flashing, was slowly making its way through the crowd surrounding the hotel's front door.

"There goes Ichabod Dilley," Michael said.

"No," I said. "There goes Alaric Steele. It turns out Ichabod Dilley died a long time ago after all."

I moved a little closer, so I could see his face, but the public mask was back on. Steele might look down on actors, but he had a little talent in that direction himself. He moved a little slowly—probably still groggy from the tranquilizer dart—but he stood with his head high, his back straight, and an expression of noble, resigned suffering on his face. He towered over the two uniformed officers on either side, looking like a patient Gulliver among the Lilliputians—couldn't Loudoun County find any reasonably large officers to escort him?

Ichabod Dilley the younger hovered behind his uncle—trying to be helpful, apparently, or at least feeling he ought to show a little family solidarity. Though from the way he shrank when Steele glanced his way, I suspected his loyalty hadn't met with the grateful response he probably expected. Steele merely pretended to ignore him.

As I watched, I felt a brief pang. Of what I wasn't quite sure. Regret, perhaps, that someone so talented had so foolishly wasted his life. Or maybe self-doubt—I'd gotten to like Steele, thought I knew him, only to have him completely fool me and turn out to be a crazy killer. And I felt anger, definitely. Lots of anger.

I sighed.

"Feeling sorry for him?" Michael asked.

"No, just mad at myself for not seeing through the louse sooner," I said.

"He put on a good act," Michael said. "I'm just hoping they don't broadcast his trial on *Court TV*. If they do, he'll get proposals and propositions from dozens of impressionable women who can't see past the handsome exterior to the warped mind inside."

"Well, maybe the videotape will help," I suggested.

"What, the part where he's doing his Cyrano de Bergerac number up and down the stage in boots and that linen shirt with the long, flowing sleeves women seem to like so much?" Michael said. I glanced up to see that he was staring at Steele with a rather fierce frown on his face.

"Well, no; but maybe they caught a shot of him with the tranquilizer dart in his rump," I said. "Or maybe—what's that?"

That was the sound of glass shattering, as a luggage cart burst through one of the plate glass windows to the left of the hotel entrance. In the wake of the luggage cart, a throng of monkeys and parrots spilled out of the newly created opening and scattered. The parrots mostly fluttered toward the bushes while the monkeys scrambled to the roof.

To my delight, one of the monkeys raced over to Steele and tried to use him as a ladder. Steele brushed it away with his cuffed hands and then tried to kick the poor thing. He missed, and landed a solid kick on his nephew's shin instead. But the crowd saw where he'd aimed the blow, and the police had to hurry Steele into the waiting police car when the crowd began pelting him with pine cones and empty soda cans.

"That was most satisfactory," Michael pronounced, as we watched the car carrying Steele drive off.

"Yes," I said, though I was looking at last night's hapless newlyweds, apparently reunited and strolling hand in hand through the crowd. She now wore an Amazon guard outfit, and he looked quite dashing in a replica of the costume Walker wore on the show.

Back at the hotel entrance, the animal control officers had found ladders and were leading parties of Amazon guards and bellhops up onto the roof, in pursuit of the monkeys. You could tell already that the monkeys really liked this new game.

Parrot retrieval was proving less difficult, largely because most of the birds seemed to have grown fond of Dad, and would emerge from the bushes when he coaxed them. Although the process would probably take a lot less time if someone could persuade Dad to concentrate on capturing the birds. Then again, perhaps after a few hours, even Dad would grow tired of strolling around with a gaudy parrot on each shoulder, posing for the photographers, and muttering "Avast!" and "Shiver me timbers!"

"At this rate," Michael said, "I think it highly unlikely that much will be happening for the next hour or two."

"You call that nothing?" I asked, pointing to the chaos in front of the hotel.

"Nothing official," he said. "Nothing that's listed on the convention program. In short, nothing that urgently requires our presence. Under the circumstances, what do you say we—"

"There you are!" Maggie said, coming up between us and grabbing one of us with each arm. "You're not just going to stand around wasting time, are you?"

"Actually—" I began.

"Come on then," she said, dragging us back toward the hotel. "We need to catch those poor creatures for once and for all before they hurt themselves. It could take all night. And I'm not taking no for an answer; we need all the help we can get!"